The F

R.D. RONALD

The Elephant Tree

Matador
5 Weir Road
Kibworth Beauchamp
Leicester LE8 0lQ, UK
Tel: (+44) 116 279 2299
Email: books@troubador.co.uk
Web: www.troubador.co.uk/matador

ISBN 978-1848764-569

A Cataloguing-in-Publication (CIP) catalogue record for this book
is available from the British Library.

Typeset in 11pt Sabon by Troubador Publishing Ltd, Leicester, UK
Printed in the UK by TJ International, Padstow, Cornwall

Matador is an imprint of Troubador Publishing Ltd

Acknowledgements

Thanks for encouragement and critique at vital times during the writing of *The Elephant Tree* go to the following: Debbie Marsh, Robert Brand, George Elliott and Gemma Davison.

Also for acts of kindness and dedication at a very difficult time, I'd like to thank: Rose Mullins, Robyn Bancroft, Betty and Alan Thornton, Sarah and David Bullerwell, David Anderson and again George Elliott.

Chapter 1

The call came in at 01:48 on Saturday morning as Detective Mark Fallon was catching up on his paperwork at the station. A shooting at Aura nightclub, one of the more luxurious establishments in Garden Heights.

Fallon's partner Alan Bryson pulled their green Volvo up behind some squad cars already outside the club. Officers on the scene were taking statements. A few clubbers had been detained for questioning; others hung around hoping something interesting would happen.

Fallon stepped over empty beer bottles and discarded Chinese food cartons that lay on the pavement. An empty pizza box lid opened and closed like the mouth of a mute in the cold night breeze.

'Wait out here Alan,' Fallon said. 'Talk to this lot, get some impressions.'

The Aura manager was hovering in the entrance.

'Nick Baker,' he said, giving Fallon a tremulous handshake.

Baker wore a sharp-fitting fashionable suit, or it would have been if he was ten years younger and a few inches narrower in the waist. Fallon guessed he was forty-five. He looked distressed, probably because the victim was his brother.

'How is he doing?' Detective Fallon asked.

'Fred, he's stable, thanks for asking. The Doctors say he was lucky, no arteries or organs were hit in the attack, just tissue damage and blood loss.'

'Do you have any reason to suspect your brother was targeted?' he asked, and flipped open his notebook.

'No, not at all,' the manager replied, perhaps a little too quickly, Fallon thought. His eyes darted around the room as he spoke, never settling on anything for more than a second before they took flight again. 'Surely it was just a random act of aggression.'

'A random act of aggression outside the club, perhaps. Maybe a fist-fight inside. But a shooting in a prestigious venue like this one would appear to be anything other than random, Mr Baker. Especially considering the security measures you have in place,' Fallon said, and tapped the metal detector archway they stood beside at the club's entrance. 'I'm presuming everyone has to walk through here when they come in, no exceptions?'

'Yes, I mean no – no exceptions,' the manager confirmed.

Fallon nodded and paused as if in thought, but really just watched Baker as he grew more and more uncomfortable under what had been pretty soft questioning. 'Is there anything else you would like to tell me at this time?'

'No, I'd really just like to go see Fred.'

'OK,' Fallon said, handing him his card. 'Go check on your brother, Mr Baker, I'm gonna have a look around.'

Nick Baker nodded and took the detective's card. 'Any other questions you can ask my assistant, Stephanie Hutton.'

Fallon surveyed the subtle placement of security cameras as he walked along the corridor and through the double glass doors into the main room of the now eerily quiet but brightly lit nightclub. An attractive brunette in a masculine grey business suit walked confidently up to him.

'Hi, are you from the police?'

Fallon flashed his credentials.

'Detective Mark Fallon.'

'Stephanie Hutton, Mr Baker's PA. He's very upset.' She

was below average height but stood square shouldered looking him directly in the eye.

'I have a lot to deal with right now, but if you have any questions...'

'OK how about you show me the exact spot of the attack.'

Stephanie led him to a curved chrome staircase. Bright red blood drops marked the polished floor like scattered berries. 'We have a staircase on either side of the main doors that lead to the balcony and two other rooms above. The right hand staircase is covered by one of the main cameras above the bar over there,' she said, pointing.

'Do you mean this area here isn't monitored by any of the other cameras?'

'As far as I know it's the only black-spot in the club.'

'Who else other than yourself and the manager would know this?'

'The security staff would know, they had hands on input regarding placement after our last refit a few months back.'

Fallon had taken out his notebook and pen when Stephanie was talking and eagerly wrote down the information. Stephanie had stopped talking by the time he finished and Fallon looked at her to see if there was anything else she could offer. The confident gaze she had initially confronted him with had been replaced by one more guarded and wary. She still looked him in the eye, but it now seemed forced and uncomfortable.

'Who is in charge of security at the club, Miss Hutton?'

'That would be Paul McBlane.'

'Right, of course he is,' Fallon said, writing down the name; the same name that had cropped up more and more frequently in recent months. McBlane had been a small time gangster years ago, but these days turned his talents to running a security firm that seemed to be associated with most of the city's prestigious venues, a lot of which had found themselves on the receiving end of a spate of vicious attacks targeting patrons, staff and owners. Not all of the incidents that Fallon had investigated had occurred at the bars and clubs, but McBlane's involvement in the industry definitely appeared to be the common denominator.

'Is there anything else you can tell me that might help with the investigation, Stephanie?' Fallon asked, softening his voice and holding her gaze.

She instinctively looked away, but then forced herself to again look him in the eye. 'There's nothing I can think of right now.' Her voice was flat and expressionless. Fallon sensed there was something she was holding back but left it alone. Pressing her further now might make her clam up even more.

'OK Stephanie,' he said, handing out another card. 'Thanks for your help. I'm sure we'll speak again soon.' That was a given. If she hadn't contacted him within a couple of days Fallon would go and see her, and next time he would press a lot harder.

Back outside and Bryson was finishing up talking to a mountainous tuxedo-clad doorman.

'You done for now?' Fallon asked his partner.

'Yeah got accounts from the on duty door-staff and tapes from all the cameras are already on their way to the station.

* * *

Scott was the last person to leave the office. At 18:44 on a Saturday evening that wasn't particularly unusual. He clicked to send his last design through to the main office computer, went to the bathroom and ran his head under the tap before wringing out his shoulder-length brown hair and tying it back in a pony tail. He wiped his face and stared at his reflection in the mirror for a few seconds, stretching out the skin where dark circles ringed beneath his eyes. The mirror didn't reflect the image of a reasonably fit twenty-four-year-old. Scott grabbed his jacket, left the office and locked up after himself.

His phone had been set to silent, but undoubtedly would have a host of texts and voicemails from Neil wondering where the hell he was already. 'A Friday night is a terrible thing to waste, Scott, but a Saturday night is unforgiveable,' was the last text he saw from Neil as he flicked through the phone. He fastened up his coat as he walked down the deserted stairwell and deleted the messages.

The city centre was still crawling with Christmas shoppers looking to add to their already burgeoning piles of gifts. To Scott they were like ants at a picnic, teeming from store to store trailing oversized carrier bags and infants behind them as they went. Scott felt alien in this environment; pulling up his hood he hurried through the crowds, dodging pushchairs, lit cigarettes and charity collection tins.

Jam was a dimly lit bar situated underground in the heart of Garden Heights. Giving a cursory nod to the doormen as he walked in, Scott went down the flight of stairs. The rumble of music grew louder as he descended and the harsh glare from the streetlights outside was replaced by a soft glow of wall lamps, with spotlights illuminating the optics behind the bar. Saturday night was well underway and the bar was already full.

Scott lit a cigarette and looked around the room for his friend. Neil was sitting on a stool at the far end of the room, unsurprisingly chatting to an attractive barmaid. His unkempt dirty blonde hair hung down loosely and spilled just over his broad shoulders. His trademark crooked smile and reasonably well maintained physique ensured that Neil was pretty popular with the ladies, and judging by the coy smile he prised from the barmaid as Scott walked up, looked like he was again onto a winner.

'Hey dude, sorry I'm late,' Scott said, propping up the bar next to Neil.

'I'm used to it by now, don't worry. This is Emma,' he said, nodding at the blonde.

'It's Gemma,' she corrected.

'Hey Gemma,' Scott said without much interest, and turned back towards Neil.

'Did you bring everything?' Neil asked him after Gemma moved away to serve a customer.

Scott patted one of the bulky pockets in his faded green cargo pants. 'I fetched the whole lot to work this morning in case there wasn't time to make the trip back home.'

'Fuck, Jack would blow up if he knew you'd taken all that into the office. You know how pissed he is that you even do this shit anyway.'

'Yeah well, working for your brother can be a royal pain in the ass at times but he's hardly likely to fire me. Besides he wasn't in the office today at all, so it wasn't a problem.'

Neil ordered drinks for him and Scott after Gemma returned. Scott scanned the interior for familiar faces, made a mental note of who he saw and their locations as he casually withdrew a handful of small plastic baggies from his pocket without glancing downwards, and placed them in Neil's open palm beneath the bar.

'There been many requests so far?'

'Yep. Pretty much what you'd expect for a Saturday. I guess this lot have already finished their Christmas shopping,' Neil said, grinning. 'By the way you look like shit.'

'Thanks a lot,' Scott said, and self-consciously ran a hand over his stress-taut forehead.

All the tables in Jam were themed to various rock bands. Under the thick glass surfaces were CDs, posters and other memorabilia depicting the featured artists. At quieter times people would flock around the table of their favourite performers, making locating them a much simpler job for Scott and Neil. You know their favourite band, you know where they'd be sitting. At this time on a weekend though, people just got served and squeezed into a space wherever they could find one.

Neil moved off into the crowd, casually wandering through the smoke, loud music and laughter. He stopped off for a minute or two at a time to exchange words and more with various members of the Saturday night faithful, who were looking for more than just happy hour at the bar. Scott sat down on the freshly vacated stool and began stashing his remaining bags into custom-made inner pockets of his army surplus cargo pants. Thanks to current fashion trends, virtually everyone else in the bars and clubs they frequented wore them too. His movements were slow but efficient, unseen in the crowd.

All of the drugs had been prepared the day before: ecstasy, speed, cocaine and cannabis all sorted according to price and weight and sealed up tight inside the plastic bags. Stitching their own pockets into the pants had been Scott's idea a couple of years back. It made the stop and search policy of the clubs a lot more difficult for the doormen involved. Usually they'd only receive a cursory pat down to make sure no obvious weapons of any kind were being brought inside, but any enthusiasm from doormen to delve into pockets as well would turn up nothing but cigarettes, keys, a cell phone and wallet.

Scott watched Neil work his way around the room with a practised efficiency they had both developed over time, as he sipped on his beer and finished his cigarette. Within ten minutes Neil was back, all deals supplied and time to move on to the next bar.

They walked back up the stairs and outside into the cold December evening where a light drizzle had begun to fall. Scott pulled up the hood on his jacket, squinting against the intrusive glare from the streetlights and instinctively moved to walk in the shadow beside the rows of closed and shuttered shops. Neil talked enthusiastically about what the night may have in store for them, how much they'd make and which girl he might end up with. Scott was used to the process and just nodded and grunted his agreement at what seemed like relevant moments while keeping pace in the direction of bar number two.

'I ran into Ferret earlier,' Neil said. 'He reckons he's got a good contact for a load of ecstasy tablets way cheaper than we're paying for them now.'

'You know my position on that, man.'

'Yeah, unless you know the source then we don't switch. But seriously man with the saving we'd make on these you could pack in working for Jack and have a little more freedom.'

'You remember what happened to Paige last year. I'm not having us in that position with some poor fucker. No.'

'Paige was unlucky I admit. But that's all it was. She got a contaminated pill but it wasn't one of ours.'

'Which is exactly why we stick with the supply line we have now. These shipments of ultra cheap drugs that hit the market every now and then, who knows what the fuck is in them. I don't want someone's death on my conscience just to make a little more cash.'

'That could have happened to anyone though. People know the risks when they take stuff, isn't like we don't do our fair share as well. Sometimes bad shit happens but that's the same with any recreation.'

Scott knew that Neil tended to get wound up on this subject sometimes so he just kept walking and figured Neil would get bored with his rant eventually.

'Horse riding. More people die doing that every year than from taking X, but if someone falls off a horse and breaks their neck they don't go blaming the guy who supplies the hay.'

Scott nodded and lit a pre-rolled joint he'd had stashed away with the other bags of drugs, and took a few hits.

'And what about all the crap they put into food these days? Who knows what all that shit will do to us in years to come. And mobile phones? Portable radiation generators that we have glued to our heads for much of the day. Seriously Scott you worry about stuff way too much,' Neil said, and took the joint Scott held out to him.

Neil did have a point though. Since Scott's uncle Bob had killed himself six years ago, the mortgage and other bills for his cottage in the country had initially fallen into the lap of Jack, Scott's older brother by four years. Jack was nineteen then and as there were no other living relatives he had been awarded custody of Scott. That was how the situation stayed for a while, but as soon as Jack managed to set up his own company he moved out to live in the city, leaving Scott on his own most of the time. He'd given Scott a little training and an unofficial position at his company but the wages allowed Scott to do little more than just get by. Scott didn't care though, he liked the seclusion offered by country life and he'd managed to find his own way of supplementing his income.

Scott did have ambitions above and beyond the situation he was in, but his thoughts often returned to Paige. She had been friendly and pretty, but just another face in the crowd until after she died. He had been at the party that night and had spoken to her briefly a few hours before her death. They'd joked a little, just light-hearted stuff but she'd been happy. Scott had left the party a little after that and didn't hear of her death until a few days later. Neil was right, the pill she'd taken hadn't come from them, but it could have, and since then she'd become almost a talismanic figure to him. Scott hadn't taken anything himself for a few weeks after, and hadn't gone back to dealing for a few months, but once people found he wasn't selling they just went and bought elsewhere.

Scott appreciated the futility of the situation. People were ultimately going to do what they would do. But despite this he had grown a social conscience because of Paige's death. He snorted a short laugh at the notion, the morally aware drug dealer.

'You seen Twinkle tonight?' Scott asked.

'Not yet but he'll be out. Not being out last night was a miracle, but two nights in a row? No chance,' Neil replied with a laugh.

That was true enough. Twinkle was generally out somewhere every night. Even when the clubs were closing he was always looking for somewhere to go on to afterwards. Scott could understand that. Some people couldn't be by themselves for too long. Solitude led to retrospective thinking, and if the past is what you are trying to get away from, then constant distractions in the present were needed.

Twinkle was an ageing drug dealer that they'd known for years as a regular around their most frequented drinking establishments. He'd taken a shine to Neil early on, which allowed them to get good prices on the speed and ecstasy they'd take whilst clubbing. Quickly becoming regulars themselves, they'd started buying a little more each time and made a little cash selling them on inside the clubs.

The Highlander was their next stop. Among others a lot of bikers hung out there, especially at the weekend. The function room upstairs played a variety of rock and metal so the clientele were a pretty mixed bunch. It was a lot brighter than the last bar. The landlord was conscious of the drug dealing and taking that went on, so he kept the place relatively well lit to stop it being too blatant, forcing all deals to take place under the many thick oak tables scattered around both upstairs and down.

They switched roles this time, Scott surveying the place for customers while Neil went to buy their drinks.

When Scott had finished he made his way back down and through the crowd by the bar, glancing around the room to see where Neil had ended up. He spotted him at a table near the back of the room beside the pool table, and made his way over.

The air was thick with smoke, and empty glasses and bottles were piled up on tables and ledges all around them. Neil, playing around with his phone, looked up and saw Scott returning, took his feet off the stool he had been saving and pointed to a bottle of Budweiser on the table.

'Listen Scott, I kind of need a bit of a favour,' Neil said, leaning in towards Scott and resting his elbows on his knees. 'This Emma bird, the one from Jam.'

'Apparently it's Gemma,' Scott chipped in.

'Yeah whatever. Well I kind of told her that we were having a party back at yours and there'd be loads of people going,' Neil said.

'What did you do that for?'

'She wasn't up for clubbing tonight and I kind of wanted to spend some time with her. It's still early though, we can round up a bunch of people and get shot of everything back at your place instead. What do you think?'

'Alright man, but this is your project. You invite everyone and make sure you don't go vanish with whatever she's called before your pockets are empty.'

'Thanks Scott, I owe you one,' Neil said, happily tapping away at his phone again. 'Looks like there's someone we can invite straight away.'

Scott followed Neil's gaze and saw Twinkle and another guy he recognised but didn't know the name of, walking into the bar.

'Alright Twinkle, you heading to Blitz later?' Scott asked, when they came across.

Twinkle was probably around fifty, Scott reckoned, although depending on the severity of his current drinking and drug taking binge he could appear ten or fifteen years older. He was below average height with a mass of dark curls flecked with grey that spilled down his head, usually obscuring much of his deeply lined face. Years of substance abuse had left his frame very thin and frail looking. If the onset of wrinkles in middle age were referred to as laughter lines then to look at him, Scott thought, Twinkle's life must have been hilarious. He had sharp eyes that often seemed to visually contradict the lack of intelligence that could be derived from listening to him talk. There might not be a lot to respect in Twinkle, but Scott liked him. He just didn't want to end up like him.

'Maybe yeah, just got some stuff to do first,' he said to Scott before turning to his associate. 'Dom, why don't you and Neil go have a game of pool.'

Neil curiously looked up from his phone but went along with what he'd suggested, allowing Twinkle to sit in his vacated seat, leaving him and Scott alone at the table. Twinkle looked at him with squinted eyes and a pained expression, as if operating under the weight of a heavy hangover.

'You look a bit rough mate, big night last night?' Scott asked innocently, but for a moment felt Twinkle's gaze sharpen.

'Was up drinking, pretty late yeah,' Twinkle said evenly, composing himself.

'Thought after you weren't out last night that maybe you'd been picked up by the cops for something.'

Twinkle took a swig of the beer Neil had left on the table before looking at Scott again and answering, 'nah, I'm not holding anything, mate, so nothing they could get me for.'

'It isn't like you to come out with empty pockets Twink. You got other stuff going on?'

Again Twinkle took a long drink from the bottle and for a few seconds seemed to carefully select his words before answering. 'There's gonna be a chance to make some good cash coming up, Scott. The kind that need someone who has their head on right, not some daft fucker.' The look Scott got from Twinkle told him this was no longer just a conversation. He had the feeling of being weighed up, like he had accidentally walked into a job interview for a position he didn't want to fill.

'To be honest, maybe it would be better if I didn't hear anymore,' Scott said, backtracking while he felt he still could.

'I know you've got ambitions above shit like this,' Twinkle

said, waving the beer casually around the room. 'I've heard you trying to get Neil to step up for bigger deals in the past. Fair enough, I won't say anything else now, but if you decide you want to hear more, come find me and we'll talk then.' He finished with a smile that suggested he knew what Scott's response would be, before adding 'just don't take too long.'

Twinkle finished Neil's beer, fetched his friend from the pool table and they both left.

'What was that about?' Neil asked as he sat back down, but Scott just shrugged. 'I don't know what Twinkle is up to but he wants to watch mixing with people like that.'

'Who was the other dude then?' Scott asked.

'Dominic Parish. You heard of him?'

'The name sounds familiar, who is he?'

'Supposed to have been a decent boxer in the day, middleweight I think. He got mixed up in some shit after he retired from boxing and did some time inside. Now he's pretty tight with Paul McBlane and that crowd. What I heard was that he could have avoided jail pretty easy, but kept quiet and maybe did McBlane a favour.'

'Twinkle always was looking to move up in the world, maybe this is his chance,' Scott said, and swallowed the last from his bottle. It was true that Twinkle had always been looking to swim with the big fish. He craved the notoriety that life as a gangster would provide; the same notoriety that Scott had worked so hard to stay away from.

'The only moving up in the world he'll do is if he gets the top bunk during a ten year stretch,' Neil said, and they both laughed.

'I'll get two more,' Scott said, and went to the bar.

Twinkle was a close associate in a circle that both Scott and Neil preferred to keep small. A bigger network would mean better prices and better selection when it came to their buying power, but it also meant bigger risk. Twinkle might want to turn heads when he walked into a room, see people whispering as he went by, *'Do you know who that is?'* but that was the last thing Scott wanted. Any progression Twinkle might hope to make through the ranks made Scott nervous and he didn't like it.

He saw that Angela was serving and edged around to her section. She wore a pair of faded jeans that had worn so thin in a couple of places on the thighs that areas of pale skin were visible beneath. Her current hair colour of choice was a deep red and was held back loosely in a pony-tail, with just a hint of her natural blonde roots beginning to show through. She was smiling a polite rebuttal to the slurred flirtation of a customer, but when she caught sight of Scott her smile became more natural and touched her eyes. She handed some change to the guy and turned to Scott as he eased through to the front.

'Hey Scott, what you having?'

A neon sign advertising Heineken buzzed steadily behind Angela, so Scott ordered two of those. He reached into his pocket to extract a note while watching Angela saunter over to the bottle fridge. All the other guys at the bar watched her too. She opened the fridge and crouched to pick the bottles from the bottom shelf. Scott noted the thinly veiled looks of disappointment from some of the spectators that she hadn't bent over to get them, leaving them with a colourful memory to take home that night. Angela was a beautiful woman, anyone could see that, but she wasn't the type to gratuitously flaunt it just to make more money in tips.

She exchanged the uncapped bottles with Scott as he handed her a ten. He held her gaze for a second before she went to make change, and grinned at the glint he saw in her eye. She knew the power she held over these guys, but for her this was just a job, and none of them would ever get more from her than a cold beer and a warm smile.

'You staying out clubbing after you finish work?' he asked her as she gave him his change.

'I got a message off Steph earlier saying she had an unexpected night off. She's coming in here at some point and we'll probably head to Blitz after my shift. I haven't seen her in ages so it'll be nice to catch up again. You gonna be in there?'

'Nah, Neil has arranged a last minute party back at mine so we're gonna head there instead.'

'Very nice, and am I on the guest list then?' Angela asked, grinning.

'Sure, VIP all the way. I'll inform the staff,' Scott said and pushed back through the crowd towards their table.

The air thrummed and reverberated with the music from the room above the bar now, drowning out most of the jukebox volume downstairs. He dropped the two bottles onto the table and sat back down. Scott licked his finger and casually dabbed it into a wrap of speed in his pocket he had carefully unfolded. Taking his now white-coated finger back out, he covered his mouth as if stifling a cough and quickly sucked off the bitter powder. His attention drifted around the room, taking in only snatches of everything as he drank his beer. A group of four Chinese men gathered around the fruit machine behind him, talking quickly in their native tongue. The familiar sing-song notes playing out as the reels spun and dropped into place were punctuated by bursts of laughter from the Chinese like machine-gun fire. Neil continued his texted flirtation with the barmaid from Jam and Scott felt his own phone vibrate, glanced down and saw it was a message from Angela. He looked up and saw her give him a little wave from behind the bar.

'Meet me outside here when I finish my shift, I'll tell Steph we're going back to the party instead.'

Chapter 2

The first time Scott met Angela was under very different circumstances, where the last thing on his mind was finding someone he could grow to feel so close to. He was going to meet a contact that he and Neil had been introduced to in a bar by Twinkle. The guy's name apparently was Putty, and for years he'd been a regular supplier to Twinkle, able to get cannabis deals at a reasonable price, even at times when other suppliers were suffering from a drought. Twinkle told them after Putty left that he always did business at his own place, a bit strange as most preferred to stay off home soil in case the deal went south and everybody had to scatter. Twinkle had also warned them that before discussions took place many joints would be passed around to create *the right mood,* and that this guy could smoke till it came out of his ears without any problem at all. Hearing this, Scott decided that it would be best if he went alone. Neil would likely get carried away by it all and end up agreeing to a terrible rate that they'd be unable to back out of later.

Following the directions he'd been given by Putty, Scott made his way through the run-down estate in the western quarter of Garden Heights. Around a third of the houses had been boarded up and graffiti grew over everything like ivy on an old country cottage. Scott was aware the locals would be suspicious of new faces as they never got any sightseers. If you were there, you were there for a reason, and not knowing what it was could make some of them nervous. Scott avoided any prolonged eye contact and kept to the route he'd been given, ignoring the direct stares from two oil-smeared guys who were either dismantling or reassembling an old Ford, pieces scattered across the road like flotsam on a beach. The three-storey flats came into view at the end of the road, and Scott walked to the far entrance of the middle block. He'd heard that all of the flats and some rows of houses were due to be demolished in the next few years in the name of redevelopment. The whole area reeked of decay and looked to have been given up on by the local council, who were just waiting for the bulldozers to move in and give them a blank canvas to start over.

When Neil had asked at their initial meeting over a few drinks why he was called Putty, he had grinned and replied that it was because he used to have a little motorbike years ago that went put-put-put. Twinkle had further informed them, after Putty's departure, that it was actually because where women were concerned, he wasn't particular in the slightest, and had been known to put his cock into pretty much anything.

Scott pushed open the heavy steel door and went into the stairwell. Enveloping him along with the gloom was the smell of stale smoke and urine. He climbed to the middle floor and checked door numbers until he found the one he'd been given, although even without the number it would have been impossible to miss. The other doors on the landing were all painted wood, whereas this one appeared to have been reinforced with a thick steel plate. He banged on it and after a moment a muffled voice asked who was there. He gave his name, heard the rasp of a large bolt being withdrawn and the door swung inward allowing him inside.

The interior was dark and pungent but otherwise nondescript. Small chinks of light snuck through gaps in closed curtains in the dimly lit corridor. He was led into the living room. Most of the light was supplied by a large screen plasma TV that was currently hooked up to a games console. Three tracksuit-clad males in their late teens or early twenties were sat on an old couch against the right-hand wall. They were holding controllers and jostling for superiority on a racing game that Scott didn't recognise. The air was thick with the scent of cannabis resin. The smell made Scott think of black coffee and old cupboards. He greeted them briefly, before turning to Putty who sat pride of place in front of the giant TV. He was reclining in a big black vinyl chair, an ashtray perched on one arm and a tall glass of Coke on the other.

Putty looked reasonably in shape for someone who, Scott had been told, would only get out of his chair, or throne as Twinkle had called it, in the face of a dire emergency. He looked to be mid to late forties, with thinning slicked back brown hair, and a face that looked as if something was missing, as if he'd recently shaved off a lifelong moustache.

The other chair was now occupied by the heavy set black guy with close cropped hair and a goatee beard who had let him in at the front door. Putty took one last slow drag from a joint, leaned towards the black man and said *Keep*, although it was in more of a grunt so as not to let any smoke out of his lungs. Scott didn't know if this was an indication that the joint was now his, or if Keep was actually his name. Putty slowly eased back into the chair and turned towards Scott, exhaling a thick stream of smoke.

'Greetings Scott, welcome to my humble home,' he said with a grin that reminded Scott of the cat in Alice in Wonderland. The man Putty had identified as Keep stood up and went to the couch, taking the joint with him. One of its current occupants moved to sit on the floor without taking his eyes from the screen, and Keep sat in the spot he'd vacated. Putty motioned to the now empty chair and Scott sat down. Leaning forward Putty picked up the tray covered with joint making paraphernalia and began to roll up. 'You like to have a bit of a smoke then Scott?'

'Yeah I'm partial, but usually just in the evenings. Slows me down a bit much during the day, you know?'

'I like the pace,' Putty replied, 'like those darkies in the adverts for the Caribbean or wherever 'we likes to taake it eeaaasssyyyy' he said in a badly imitated West Indian accent and cackled. Scott glanced over at the room's only black occupant but the remark elicited nothing but a casual grin. Brief sniggers from the other three showed that they were at least half conscious of the conversation, and that such comments were not out of the ordinary.

Scott figured he had his bearings here, pretty much as Twinkle had indicated. Putty would keep smoking and delaying talking about the deals Scott was here to discuss. Putty obviously figured that either peer pressure or passive smoke inhalation from the lack of ventilation would have Scott pretty much wiped before long and then talk would turn to business. The guy was obviously just a low level dealer and this was his domain, but according to Twinkle he did have useful connections, so Scott planned to just wait it out and get the best price he could. He could see Putty was an old hand at this kind of situation. A set-up like this tended to be a young man's game so either he was bad at plying his trade and therefore unable to move up into middle management, or he was good at what he did but with no ambition and happy to stay a big fish in a very small pond. Scott watched as Keep passed what was left of the joint he had to the guy who had given up his seat. Putty nudged Scott's arm with his elbow, holding out the joint he had just lit. Scott took it with a smile and a nod, which obviously pleased the host, his smile turning feline again. As Scott took his first drag there was a knock on the front door. Keep stood up and went to check it as Putty reached down to retrieve the tray and again began rolling another.

A moment later Keep returned, followed by a pretty young woman that Scott at first assumed must be here to score a deal.

She looked to be about 21 with the figure of someone who either regularly works out or is naturally blessed with an athletic frame. She wore a tight white t-shirt with a baby blue cardigan over the top, washed out green army fatigues and Nike trainers. Her hair was long and mostly blonde with a few blue streaks running through it, but looked brittle like it had been bleached too many times. She said 'hi' in no particular direction as she entered the room, walked over and kissed Putty on the cheek. As she bent down, Scott noticed that she wore little if any make-up and no jewellery other than a small silver hoop in her right ear. Her presence in the room was also the only thing that had distracted the three gamers' attention from the screen since Scott had entered, although a steady gaze from Putty refocused them back onto their racing. She walked out into the kitchen.

Maybe Scott hadn't given Putty enough credit, he thought. This girl was way above the level of any part-time pussy he'd been led to believe Putty would have snagged. From her entrance and carefree attitude around the place, she was obviously afforded a certain level of respect too. He continued smoking the joint and listened as sounds from the kitchen echoed along the hallway. Running water – the kettle being filled and then switched on – drawers opening and closing – then the fridge – a clink of crockery. The only noise in the living room now was from the TV, and the slight rustle of the latest joint Putty was intently focused on applying the finishing touches to.

Scott took another drag from the joint, enjoying the unexpected twist in his afternoon. He relaxed back into the chair and slowly let out a stream of blue smoke in the manner he'd seen Putty do following his arrival. The young woman came back out of the kitchen, walked up to him and plucked the joint from between his fingers.

'Thank you kindly,' she said, and flashed Scott the same grin that he'd already seen twice on the face of his host.

'My pleasure,' he replied with a laugh, now realising what the relationship between her and Putty must be.

She walked back into the kitchen with the joint, as the bubbling kettle reached its peak and clicked off. Putty finished his careful rolling procedure and lit up, took two quick drags without exhaling in between and handed it straight to Scott.

'You staying for long?' Putty yelled, without looking away from the TV.

'Why, aren't you glad to see me?' came the reply from the kitchen.

'Of course, it's just we're talking business in here.'

'OK Mr. Chairman of the board, I'll check with your secretary next time before I drop in,' she said, walking back into the room.

'Alright Princess, always great to see you but duty calls.'

'OK, I'll call back in later on.'

'That would be great, Keep will walk you to the bus stop.'

'No, I'd like him to do it,' she said looking at Scott.

'It can be rough out there, sweetheart. I'd feel better if Keep did it. No offence Scott.'

'I still want him to.'

'I don't mind, I can come back right after and we can get this tied up,' Scott said, getting up out of the chair. Putty looked nonplussed but waved his hand as if to indicate he was fine with that, not taking his eyes from the TV.

Angela winked at Scott and walked to the door.

'What was that about then?' he asked, as they went down the acrid stairwell.

'I just like to wind the old man up. He's pretty overprotective sometimes so I just like to remind him who's in charge every once in a while,' she said, grinning, and pulled open the doorway out of the flats.

'I don't even know your name,' Scott said, following her back out into daylight. 'I take it you weren't christened Princess or Sweetheart, but I'm taking nothing for granted what with Putty and Keep in there.'

She laughed and formally held out her hand for him to shake. 'My name is Angela, pleased to meet you.'

'Hi Angela, I guess you already know I'm Scott,' he said, feeling slightly embarrassed, and shook her hand.

She released his hand after firmly shaking it twice, then linked her arm through his and continued to walk.

'Yeah I knew who you were before I saw you in there.'

'You did?' Scott said, a little surprised. He was sure if he'd seen Angela before he would have remembered.

'I've seen you out around town a few times. My mate bought some speed off your friend with the blonde hair. He had no change so you took some cash out of your wallet and gave it to her. I remember 'cause you had that photo in there. It looked old so I guessed it was from when you were a kid. I thought it was cute,' she said, and shrugged.

Scott pulled out his wallet and flipped it open. 'It's me and my brother at a fairground years ago,' he said, showing her the dog-eared picture. 'Sorry, I don't remember you.'

The picture showed Scott wearing a sour expression, his brother with an arm wrapped around his shoulder, beaming at the camera. They both wore bright blue matching rain hats and grey coats that each looked a size too large.

'I can be pretty shy sometimes,' she said, but he found that difficult to believe. 'You're the little one, right?' She pointed to the picture.

'Yeah with the sulky face. The other kid with the cheesy grin is my big brother.'

'You may look sulky there but you seem nice now.'

'Thanks, although you kind of sound like that wasn't what you'd have expected.'

'No, I wouldn't say that. Just most of the guys dad deals with tend to be pretty mean types. Not with me of course, just their general attitude towards life, I suppose.'

'So I don't fit the bill?' Scott asked, putting away his wallet.

'I don't know yet,' she said, looking at Scott appraisingly, like an old woman eyeing a chipped vase in an antiques shop. 'I haven't made up my mind on you. Anyway, here's my bus coming so I have to go.'

Angela ran a few steps before she turned back towards him.

'You want to have a drink tomorrow night at Jam?' she said, seemingly as an afterthought.

'Yeah, sure,' he answered without thinking.

'Right, see you at eight then,' she said, then ran the last twenty yards and jumped onto the bus as it wheezed to a halt at the stop.

Scott watched as she took a seat and waited until the bus had vanished around the corner before walking back to Putty's flat.

Keep was waiting at the door as Scott came back up the stairs. He nodded at Scott, waited until he went inside and then pulled the door closed, remaining outside in the corridor.

In the living room Scott saw the curtains had been opened slightly to let more light into the room. The three youths who'd previously been playing on the games console were gone now as well, leaving Putty alone in his chair watching horse racing on the TV.

'You want a drink of anything Scott?' he asked, as Scott returned to the seat he'd occupied before leaving.

'No thanks, to be honest time's getting on. What do you say we sort out an arrangement and then I'll take off?'

Putty nodded, took a piece of folded white paper from under the ashtray on the arm of his chair and put it down on the table in front of Scott.

'You seem like a decent lad, and Twinkle vouches for you as well so I'm happy to be able to work with you. However some things fall outside of a working relationship, but can still muddy the waters.'

Putty's previous pomp and bravado had now been replaced by a level of decorum that he wouldn't have imagined possible from their meeting twenty minutes earlier.

'Open it,' Putty said, and nodded towards the folded paper he'd placed on the table.

Scott obliged. On the paper were incremental prices for weights of cannabis. Prices Scott wouldn't have even have hoped to achieve when he'd left the house that morning.

'So long as our business is conducted in an orderly fashion without any complications, I'll be happy to abide by what's on the there. You happy with that Scott?'

'Yeah,' Scott said, 'I'm happy.'

'So we have an understanding?'

'Yes,' Scott nodded, 'we do.'

Chapter 3

At closing time the rain had stopped but the temperature outside had dropped below freezing. Scott, Neil and Gemma met Angela outside the Highlander but Stephanie hadn't showed. The neon lights of the bar fronts opposite were mirrored on the wet streets, as if they walked along the edge of a lake on the way to where Neil had parked the car.

'Watch out for patches of ice on the way back,' Scott warned. 'We don't want to crash when we have all these drugs on us.'

Neil waved away his concerns and took a drag on the joint Angela had fished out of her handbag. Unsurprisingly his driving was a little erratic, and Scott had to remind him a few more times to slow down and pay more attention.

It was still freezing in the car so Scott reached forward to turn up the heating, which resulted in a blast of cold air through the vents.

'Takes a while to warm up before the heating will work', Neil said, and turned it back off again.

His eleven year old Hyundai still performed admirably considering the starship mileage it had accumulated, but these days some sacrifices had to be made from the old girl, one of which was apparently interior warmth.

Before long the brightly lit main streets of the suburbs were behind them and the poorly maintained, sparsely lit country roads made the journey back feel a little perilous. Especially,

Scott felt, as Neil was spending more time looking at Gemma and Angela as he chatted with them in the rear-view mirror than looking at the road.

Scott glanced out of the side window. It was pitch black now that they'd passed the city limits. Neil failed to spot a pot hole in time and the car bounced and lurched toward the grass verge. He glanced quickly at Scott but neither said anything. Neil lowered his speed anyway.

Arriving back at the house Scott quickly realised that the invites had gone a little further than he'd anticipated. Within minutes about a half dozen taxis had pulled up and started emptying out and there were probably more on the way. Nothing he could do about it now though. Scott opened the door and led the way through to the living room, indicating towards the chairs and sofa for people to make themselves at home. Boris, his uncle's soot black cocker spaniel seemed a little perturbed by the number of new faces invading his space, but Angela soon eased his anxiety with plenty of ear scratching and belly rubs. Scott didn't have too much in the way of alcohol to offer around, but Neil said he'd told people not to turn up empty handed. As the guests filed through the front door most were laden down with bags full of various types of liquor.

'We stopped off at a 24-hour place on the way,' Putty said, grinning as he and a few friends carried in full bags and Keep struggled in after them with a big box. 'We were out anyway and Angela told us of your little soirée, hope you don't mind us crashing.'

Back in the living room, Scott turned on the stereo and plugged in his iPod. Larrs, one of Putty's friends who had bleached blonde hair spiked up into tufts and an accent that sounded Scandinavian, immediately showed an interest and came over to act as digital deejay.

Angela slid an arm around Scott's waist and handed him a

beer she'd taken from the growing mountain in the kitchen. 'Not a bad turn-out for such short notice.'

'Yeah but when a drug dealer throws a party, you tend to not get many no shows,' he replied with a sly smile. 'Come on let's go find somewhere to sit.'

Angela picked up a CD case and ashtray from the coffee table and followed Scott. Four reasonably well dressed people that Scott didn't recognise were just vacating a spot in the hallway so they quickly sat down and claimed it before anyone else could. Putty saw them as he walked back out from the kitchen with an armload of bottles.

'Saves getting back up every few minutes,' Putty explained as he eased down onto the floor beside them.

Angela put the ashtray in between them, and the CD case in front of her which she used to chop out three substantial lines from a wrap she'd taken out of her pocket, placed her credit card back into her purse, and took out a twenty. Rolling in into a tight tube she snorted the first line and passed the case and rolled note to Scott.

'You're getting pretty professional at all this Scott. Anyone would think dealing was a career choice for you and not just a short term thing,' Angela said, sounding playful; yet when Scott looked up at her he could see a shadow of concern in her eyes.

Scott took his line and placed the CD case in front of Putty.

'It's been a few years now,' Scott said with a shrug and breathed out slowly through his mouth. 'I suppose whatever you do, you either just get older or you get better.'

'And this is what you want to get better at?'

He hadn't wanted to think about his future any more that night, and discussing it all with Angela hadn't been something he'd considered until then.

Putty lit a joint and took a few hits until the tip glowed orange before passing it over to Scott. He exhaled a column of blue smoke that pooled around their feet.

'This was only ever gonna be a short term thing. I just need to get enough money together for a fresh start. All the time growing up uncle Bob was always going on about his Buddhism stuff, and how one day he would go and live out in the Far East, go touring through the countries which gave birth to all that philosophical stuff he loved.'

'So you want to go out there and do it instead now cause he can't?' Angela asked.

'No I don't give a shit about all that, but I do want to get away though. The point is, he had his dream, his light at the end of the tunnel, and now he's dead and it's gone. From what Jack and my uncle have said, it was always the same with Mum and Dad too. That they were never happy, Dad worked such long hours, Mum was always miserable. It just seems like everyone either gives up on their dreams and accepts mediocrity, or they wait so long to do what it is they want to do that they can't even remember why they wanted it in the first place.'

Angela smiled but slowly shook her head and looked a little puzzled. 'So what is it that you want Scott? What's your dream that you can't wait any longer for?'

'You know that my family originally emigrated here from overseas, right?'

Angela nodded so he continued.

'I want to go back. There's nothing left for me over here now, both my parents and my uncle are dead, and it's hardly like me and Jack are or have ever been close.'

'So that's why you're dealing now, to save up enough to begin a new life where your parents came from?' Putty said.

'Is that so surprising?' Scott asked.

'It's a pretty drastic step,' Angela said, 'what about your friends here? Don't you think you're underestimating what they mean to you with you not really having any family?'

Scott took another hit from the joint and passed it on. Angela's words were no big revelation; he'd thought this stuff through himself a thousand times. But her empathetic look made them seem a lot more poignant. 'Maybe you're right Angela, but this has been my dream for a long time now and if I don't at least try then I'll be living the rest of my life with the *what if* always in the back of my mind.'

'What about the *what ifs* if you get caught and end up in jail for years? What if you hadn't got caught, just lived your life here and made the best of the situation you have?'

'You've done pretty well for yourself, Scotty,' Putty said. 'Business looks to be good, I know you're buying plenty of weed off me and these folks in here tonight seem to be doing a lot more than just smoking. This cottage must be worth a decent amount anyway. If you wanted to go so much can't you just sell it and use that money to start over?'

Scott shook his head. 'Bob left us with a huge mortgage on this place after he died, and the insurance wouldn't pay out with it being suicide. Jack paid the interest while he was here and now I can barely cover it myself.'

'Doesn't seem to make much sense wanting to throw it all away to go back to a country you've never even been to, to start with?' Putty said, and reached down for the CD case with his line of cocaine on it. Part of it had become dislodged a little, giving the straight, white line the appearance of an exclamation mark. He snorted it, punctuating his sentence aptly, Scott thought. Putty breathed out and sniffed, wiping his nose on a forefinger. Unconsciously Scott mimicked the movement himself.

'How much do you reckon you need to have to get your cabin and whatever else out there for your Grizzly Adams existence?'

'A lot.'

Putty chuckled. 'You think you'll hit the kind of bankroll you need doing this?'

'I know I won't, that's why I need a change,' Scott said.

'I may have a project for you in the new year Scotty,' Putty said, making sure no-one else in the hallway was close enough to hear their conversation.

'That seems to be something I'm hearing a lot these days,' Scott replied, eyes narrowing slightly as he levelled a cynical gaze at Putty.

'Some propositions are better than others though,' Angela added, straightening up from the CD case, three new lines laid out, like snow drifts beside freshly shovelled paths. She handed him the case and note for Scott to select his line first. Angela continued to look at him for a moment before she spoke. 'To be honest, Scott, it doesn't seem like you know what you want.'

Scott finished the last of his beer in a long slow swallow, feeling the cool liquid calm his thoughts. 'I know you said that because you care, but let's just drop it and enjoy the rest of the night.'

'OK,' she said with a little shake of her head. 'Just promise you'll talk to me before you go and do anything rash.'

They each did their line of coke and sat back drinking for a while, just listening to the background noise of the party. Angela moved up beside Scott with her back against the wall. Her arm felt soft and warm against his. Some voices from the living room argued over song selection. A couple crept guiltily out of a bedroom and snuck into the kitchen. The crash of a broken glass came from somewhere, followed by a muffled apology. Scott felt the warm flow of the cocaine and alcohol coursing through his veins. His heart rate had accelerated, seeming to keep pace with the music booming out from his stereo; he closed his eyes and relaxed into it.

'Gonna make another ATM run', Neil bellowed.

Scott opened his eyes and saw Neil surrounded by a cluster of partygoers in the hallway, apparently with cash cards burning holes in their pockets.

'OK man, keep your speed down though, don't get pulled

over,' he said to Neil, and then to the waiting passengers, 'take your coats, it'll be colder in his car than it is outside.'

Neil gave a falsetto laugh and clutched his stomach before ushering the group out to the car.

Neil's girlfriend, Gemma or Emma, Scott had drunk too much to come close to remembering now, hovered around the hallway for a moment undecidedly after Neil and the group left, before finally going back into the living room.

'More happy customers then,' Putty said, watching her go. 'I'm gonna go find that lot and see what time they want to head off later. You coming back with us Angela, or you just gonna hang out here?'

'I'm gonna stay a while longer, I'll just get a cab myself, don't worry.'

Putty nodded and stood up, a little unevenly at first. 'I'm getting a bit old for this staying up all night partying shit I think.' He said, and steadied himself against the wall for a moment before following Gemma into the living room.

'You in any hurry to get to sleep?' Angela asked.

'You're joking, after all the speed and coke tonight, I may black out at some point, but I won't be drifting off to sleep anytime soon.'

'What about some fresh air then, you fancy taking a walk?' she asked.

'Sure, why not.'

'We've got no more beer,' she said looking down disappointedly at the empty bottles littered around them, 'I'll see what's left in the kitchen.' Angela stood up in a single fluid motion and stepping over assorted bodies along the hallway, made her way gracefully towards the kitchen.

'Ok,' Scott said, standing with less conviction than Angela, 'I'll meet you at the back door. It'll be cold out, I'll go and fetch some warm clothes.'

He pulled two thick hooded sweatshirts out of the

wardrobe, a scarf, a woollen hat and two zip-up jackets. Outside Angela knelt down next to an uncorked bottle of red wine with her arms wrapped around herself, talking to Boris. The atmosphere of the party had mellowed a little now, groups of people still mingled, but the overall mood was more sedate.

'Here,' Scott said, offering up the selection of garments for her to choose from. Watching Angela pick through the clothes as if she were searching for a bargain in a thrift shop made him laugh.

'What's funny?' she asked, grinning, as she pulled on the blue woollen hat and a grey sweatshirt with a faded ice hockey logo on the front.

'Nothing,' he said pulling on the other hooded top and fastening the jacket over it, 'just you.'

Angela took a swallow from the wine and passed the bottle to Scott, as she pulled on the other jacket. 'OK where we going then?' she asked excitedly, her eyes glittering with reflected moonlight as she stood in the doorway.

'Go on Boris, hyyaaahh,' Scott said, making a shooing motion to the dog. 'We just follow him.'

Taking his cue, the spaniel was already a hundred yards away by the time they began to follow. Angela linked his arm and leaned in close, pulling up the hood on her sweatshirt. It was a cold night but there was no frost. The full moon reflected patches of silver light, through the sparse cloud cover, which they used to traverse the uneven ground.

'It's really pretty out tonight,' Angela said and looked up. 'The moon seems even bigger than usual.'

'It's known as the Cold Moon, the last full moon of the year.'

'You're full of shit,' Angela laughed, 'anyone can say it's called a cold moon when we're in bloody December, what's the next one then if you're so smart?'

'The next, after our new year is called the Wolf Moon,' he

said, faking a smug grin, and watched Angela trying to read his expression in the partial light to see if he was attempting to fool her.

She took a slow breath in and out of the cold night air. 'Well I don't care what they call it, I think it's beautiful.' Angela clutched his arm tighter. 'You're lucky to live out here, it's really nice.'

Boris had circled back around and was exploring not too far ahead of them now. They reached the only part of the boundary fence that still remained, a small section with a stile to the South that they climbed over, navigating their way through the tufts of dead scrub grass and into the woods. Long slivers of moonlight fell between the naked branches; the close proximity of the surrounding trees made their being together seem more intimate, almost secretive.

'How come you never asked me out on a date, Scott?'

Scott's mind had become entwined in a fluid spiral of thoughts and feelings, which he swam back out from at the sound of her question. 'That's a bit out of the blue, isn't it?'

'I don't think so. We get on really well and I sometimes catch looks from you that I've had from other guys at work, usually just before they ask me out, but you never have.'

'I kind of made a promise.'

'I knew it,' she said, with an unfamiliar stern expression, 'this is gonna be my dad's doing, isn't it?'

'It's understandable really, when you think about it.'

'Great, so it is then.'

Scott wasn't too concerned with breaking confidences right now. The alcohol and cocaine had made his whole body feel warm in sharp contrast to the cold night air. 'He just wants more for you than to fall in love with a drug dealer. The uncertainty and danger of that kind of lifestyle, he doesn't want you to end up with someone like me.'

'Or him.'

'Yeah I suppose, or him.'

As Scott stooped a little to pass under a branch from a nearby oak, Angela reached up, held his face between her hands and kissed him. It was slow and soft and for a few seconds the rest of the world seemed to melt away. She opened her mouth slightly and he felt her tongue run gently across his lips. Angela slowly withdrew. Scott opened his eyes and she looked deep into them, reading him, searching for his reaction. He felt naked and vulnerable under her gaze, but he didn't care.

'You taste like strawberries,' he said once his senses began to unravel.

It took a second for what he'd said to register, but then she laughed. 'That'll be the wine you can taste,' she said grinning, and held the bottle up for him to see before taking another drink. Boris had stopped a little way ahead and looked back at them expectantly. Scott motioned with his hand to keep going and the dog continued off on his circular patterns of exploration.

'Well I certainly didn't see it coming,' Scott said with a laugh he hoped didn't sound nervous. His mind was fuzzy from the cocktail of drugs and alcohol and struggled to comprehend what meaning, if any, it might hold.

'Kind of an impulse thing, I think,' she said.

A shaft of moonlight illuminated a row of sentinel silver birch in a phosphorescent glow, appearing almost ethereal in the relative surrounding gloom. Boris had stopped again, his silhouette a stark black juxtaposition against the background of the illuminated branches.

'Now, that looks kind of trippy,' Angela said, 'have you been here before?'

'Yeah it was a regular stop when uncle Bob would take me and Jack on walks when we were kids. It's just become habit since then when I'm out walking the dog, he pretty much always makes his way here.'

'Like a migration,' Angela said with a laugh. 'Or a pilgrimage.'

'Yeah or just an old dog who's stuck in his ways. Here check this out,' Scott said and led her past the cover of the silver birch.

'Bob first showed me and my brother this when we were kids,' he said, pointing towards a strange looking tree ahead. It was a large oak. All of the branches had long since been cut off leaving only thick stumps protruding from the enormous trunk.

'We used to stay over on weekend sleepovers, before we came to live here permanently after our parents' death. Bob told us the tree must be special 'cause no leaves or any other signs of life ever grew from it, yet year after year it showed no sign of degrading or rotting away. He'd point out other trees in the woods that had been struck by lightning or died from disease; over time the bark would drop away and the trunks would soften, the roots rot and usually end up being blown over in a storm. He reckoned since he'd first seen the tree at around the time we were born, the branches had already been removed, so it had been standing in its present condition for at least as long as we'd been breathing.'

'It does look rather strange,' Angela said, as she studied the old oak.

'Well that would have been enough to single it out from the other trees in the woods, but its most redeeming feature, in Bob's eyes, was this,' Scott said, and pointed to bring Angela's attention to particularly odd growth surrounding the formation of a branch roughly a third of the way up the trunk.

'Oh wow, it looks just like an elephant,' Angela said, studying the protrusion from the trunk. 'But not a happy one.'

'From there yeah, but when you move around here,' Scott said, and slid an arm around Angela's waist.

'So your uncle came here and prayed or whatever at the shrine of the pissed off elephant?' Angela asked, giggling.

'Shh, just watch,' he said, and led her slowly around to the other side of the tree.

The growth, when looked upon from the West, clearly gave the appearance of an elephant's head. The contours of the face, an eye, the large ear and even its trunk that ended abruptly where the branch had been sawn off, were intricately defined in the old wood. When slowly moving from this vantage point around to the other side of the tree and looking from the East, the face would begin to change. The elephant's features would appear to melt and run into one another before re-gathering form and appearing as human. This still creeped Scott out even now, but as a child it had scared him outright; yet despite this he still felt intrinsically drawn to the spot. Both dimensions of the face when looked upon could appear to convey great emotion to Scott, although depending on his mood, and maybe the lighting at the time, the emotions were subject to change. Illusions of childhood were often displaced with the reason of a rational adult mind, but standing in the same spot he would have been in when first introduced to the tree by his uncle all those years ago, Scott repeated the procedure with Angela, of first focusing on the elephant face before slowly walking around the circumference of the tree. Again he watched the face morph from that of elephant into man. To him the elephant face appeared calm, almost serene, but as it reshaped into human, it looked troubled or even afraid.

For Angela the way silvery light reflected down cast the eye socket and mouth in deep shadow, they appeared as vacant black chasms, the mouth twisted in a frozen expression like pain or anguish.

Scott nudged her and she moved around the tree. 'Keep looking at it,' he told her.

'No fucking way', Angela said, moving back to where she had first stood, to repeat the process. 'Now it looks like a man's face, laughing hysterically. Shit, that has to be the drugs.'

'Uncle Bob always seemed to think there was some mystical significance to this tree, although he could be pretty weird sometimes,' Scott confessed.

'Weird can be a misinterpretation of an enlightened mind,' Angela said, and grinned again. Scott couldn't tell if she was serious or pulling his leg.

Scott stepped back from the oak and sat on a nearby fallen tree trunk. 'I'm sure they haven't dampened the effect at all, but no it's pretty much always like this. Well not always, the expression, or what we kinda perceive to be the expression, seems to change each time you come back. That's what I think my uncle used to find so alluring, he was into all the Buddhism stuff and elephants are a big deal to them, apparently.'

Angela seemed transfixed by the metamorphosis from elephant to man, and continued slowly side-stepping from left to right and then back again. 'So what was so special about elephants?'

'Strength, according to my uncle. Physical and mental strength. He would come here alone sometimes and just sit for hours. I don't know if he hoped he'd absorb some of it himself, just by being here. I know he used to come when he had difficult decisions to make, though.'

Scott glanced at his watch but didn't register what it said. The notion of time had become as absurd as the quietly glowing trees around them.

Chapter 4

Angela hadn't expected to see anyone new when she'd arrived at her dad's place that afternoon. The usual interchangeable faces of local up-and-coming thugs or the more recognisable characters she had come to know from growing up around the scene through childhood. When she'd noticed Scott sitting in the chair, the light fluttering she'd felt in her chest had taken her by surprise.

Angela knew she seemed a pretty cool character where men were concerned, but the confidence she put forth wasn't born out of experience. Far from it. In fact the only serious relationship she'd ever had was with Anthony Baxter, a short and rather awkward boy back in high school. They had been a couple for over a year before they slept together, and stayed in the relationship for another year afterwards. Angela's fingers moved unconsciously to the silver hoop in her right ear; a reminder as if she needed one of her only sexual partner. He had bought her it as a gift the day after they'd first had sex.

She had first become aware of Scott while out clubbing with her friend Stephanie around a year ago. Angela hadn't known exactly what the attraction was to begin with. Sure, he was good looking, but she knew that she could have her pick from any number of good looking guys. It wasn't the dangerous drug dealer image either. Having grown up surrounded by those types, she found it more of a bore than a turn on, but still she couldn't deny that she was drawn to Scott.

Stephanie had picked up on her interest after a while and despite endless encouragement Angela still had refused to go up and introduce herself. Stephanie's initial attempt at introductions were a little wide of the mark as she'd ended up going home with Scott's friend Neil after buying some speed from them, leaving Angela to get a taxi home alone. That hadn't lasted though, Neil never called her back and Steph gave up, having been given a couple of brush-offs after bumping into him again around the bars.

Maybe it was fear of rejection that had put Angela off from pursuing Scott. Anthony's advances had captured her attentions ahead of a group of more popular boys back in school, and the handful of first dates she'd bothered to turn up for since then had always come about from her alcohol weakened defences being lowered enough that she'd eventually say yes to a come-on in a bar or club. Whatever trepidation she had previously felt though, she'd managed to cast aside when she saw Scott in her dad's flat that afternoon. She'd masked her nervousness well and now was going out on a date with him, well for a drink or two which pretty much seemed like a date.

She arrived at Jam just after seven-thirty the next night. An uneasy restlessness had descended upon her during the afternoon and despite trying to engross herself in other activities it had refused to lift. Best to just get there early and have a drink to calm her nerves, she thought. Maybe a guy at the bar would hit on her while she waited. Turning away offers of a drink might bring back some sense of control and make her feel less uneasy and skittish.

Angela took a seat at the bar and ordered a Bacardi and coke with a slice of lemon and lit a cigarette while waiting for the barman to pour it. She paid for her drink, flicked her cigarette against an ashtray and surveyed the bar. There was no sign of Scott yet but it was still early. Angela glanced around to see if any unattached males would try and make eye contact because she was sitting alone at the bar, but everyone seemed preoccupied and she went unnoticed. Angela took her time sipping the drink, but before she realised it she was ordering her third and the clock above the bar read twenty past eight. Still there was no sign of Scott. She replayed their conversation in her head, looking for any possible misunderstanding, but it seemed pretty straightforward. They hadn't exchanged numbers so there was no way to find out if Scott had just been delayed.

By the time she'd finished her fourth drink, Angela decided Scott wasn't coming. She had a burning feeling in the pit of her stomach but didn't know if it was from the rum she'd drunk or the disappointment and shame of being stood up.

Angela smiled at the barman as she got up to leave and he smiled back, somewhat sympathetically she thought. As she climbed the stairs on the way out, Angela's earlier nervousness combined with the alcohol formed a cocktail of determination that the night wouldn't be a complete loss. She'd gone shopping especially for the low cut blue and white speckled dress she had on that clung tightly to her in all the right places. Right now she needed some attention from the opposite sex to boost her failing self-esteem.

She walked for a while through the city streets without any particular destination in mind. Groups of men and women, couples, mingling, drifting in and out of bars. Angela kept walking.

After wandering for around twenty minutes she stopped outside a bar called Steam. Unlike the more popular venues that she'd passed by on the way, there was no queue outside here. She stepped into the gloomy interior. A familiar dance track was being played by a deejay stationed at the bottom end of the bar, but judging by the clientele dotted around the place, it was more of a distraction than entertainment to them. Angela stepped up to the bar and ordered vodka and lemonade. Outdated neon strip lighting illuminated behind the bar.

Elsewhere that may have been an attempt to create a retro feel, but judging from the rest of the fixtures and fittings, it had probably been there since being fashionable years before.

Angela leaned back against the bar with the cold glass of vodka in her hand and took a sip. A man in a pink polo shirt fixed her with an eager stare, detached himself from his group of friends and walked over.

'I buy you a drink?' he asked her, grinning. He leant in too close, the concentration of alcohol on his breath smelt almost combustible.

Angela kept staring ahead and pointed at her glass indicating that she already had one. The man took this as a sign that she wanted another and flagged down a barman.

'There you go,' he said proudly displaying the drink he had bought, and when eventually she made no move to take it from him, put it down on the bar beside her. 'Cheers.'

'Are you waiting for someone?' he asked, confidence unscathed despite her lack of interest so far.

'No,' she said, turning to look at him for the first time. She had often used her unwavering stare as a weapon to disarm even the most confident of advances in the past, but this guy was too drunk to be deterred and didn't back down an inch. The whole thing now seemed like a really bad idea, she began to wish after Scott hadn't shown up she had just gone straight home.

Angela looked around the bar again in vain for someone who might save her from this dull, intoxicated conversation but the social groups around the room were already formed and she could see no opening. The current song playing faded out as another mixed in but the deejay messed up the transition and one of the records skipped causing a few heads to turn in his direction.

Despite her predicament Angela found herself giggling and pushed past pink polo shirt and made her way toward the deejay box at the bottom of the bar.

'Sounds like your night is going about as well as mine,' she said, smiling at the deejay as she approached.

'I'm just filling in for someone,' he said. 'not used to the equipment.' His attention switched back onto the mixing deck, but his eyes surfaced again a few seconds later to take a more detailed look at her. Angela nodded to spare his blushes and took a sip from her glass.

'Aren't you a little well dressed to be in here?' he asked, after a few minutes had passed and she still stood watching him.

'I was just passing and thought I'd stop in for a drink before I head home. It's my first time here. You aren't the regular deejay then?'

He shook his head, one ear pressed against an oversized pair of headphones.

'Favour for a friend,' he added.

The crisp white shirt and well tailored black pants told Angela that she wasn't the only one who was overdressed for the particular venue, and perhaps inclined her to believe his story.

'So you're off home after your drink then?' he asked, once the next track had begun to play.

Angela watched him for a few seconds and then shrugged. 'I guess, depends if I get a better offer.'

'I have a club gig to do a little later but I'd be happy to go for a drink with you before that.'

She nodded, her earlier lack of confidence now forgotten and memories of being stood up began to fade.

'By the way,' he said holding out a hand, 'I'm Jack.'

Angela slept with Jack on that first night. He was charming and she'd been drinking but that was a situation she'd been in many times before and never gone home with the guy. She'd waited around while he finished his shift, sipping on a further two complementary drinks he'd had brought across to her from the bar before they went on to his next gig at a nearby club.

She enjoyed the VIP treatment she'd received there, no queues, no paying for drinks, everyone was polite and courteous to her. He didn't seem to notice the extremes the staff went to so Angela assumed it must be part of his everyday life.

She hung out beside the deejay booth nursing more free drinks while he performed the set, watching the steady flow of attractive women who would saunter over to talk to him. They'd lean suggestively over the rail, and a few times a scrap of paper with presumably a phone number on would flutter down and land beside the equipment before they left. Jack talked politely with them without being flirtatious, but his indifference to their advances seemed only to fuel their attraction. His more intimate attention was saved for Angela, and she was impressed.

They left the club after closing time when the crowds outside had mostly dispersed. Angela hugged her arms around herself against the chill night air. Jack took off his jacket and draped it over her shoulders. Around the corner was parked his blue BMW, she noticed the shade exactly matched the blue in her dress as she slid down into the cool leather seat. He drove for a while without talking much and she never asked their destination. She'd already decided how the night was going to end.

* * *

The next morning Scott woke up and felt like his tongue had been velcroed to the roof of his mouth and he had porcupine quills embedded inside his skull.

Squinting against the harsh morning glare coming through the bedroom window, he realised that at some point last night the curtain rail had been pulled off the wall, which was now the reason for the inappropriately bright bedroom.

His thoughts ran like a chased rabbit as he tried to piece

together the fragments of memory from the previous night. Firstly, he was clothed so that was probably good. Gingerly turning over he recognised Angela's shoes on the other pillow, and presumed it was her feet still inside of them. So she'd stayed over but was also clothed, which was a relief. Apart from the promise he'd made to her dad, Scott felt that with all the other complications he had in his life right now, a serious relationship would only end badly, even if it was with Angela.

Shaking her gently by the ankle resulted in a groan from the bottom of the bed, followed by a clunk as an empty wine bottle rolled out from under the quilt and fell to the floor.

Scott eased out of the bed avoiding another empty wine bottle, an overflowing ashtray and a generous scattering of empty beer cans. The ground seemed to lurch toward and then away from him as he tried to maintain balance; like standing in a small boat on uneven waters. Angela's face poked out from underneath the quilt, and he could see his unease of footing was at least providing a source of amusement for her.

'Coffee,' Scott mumbled as he tentatively made his way towards the kitchen, the rustling of bedclothes behind him indicating that Angela had probably decided to follow.

The mess in the bedroom had apparently just been a warm-up act for the carnival of disarray that lay within the confines of the kitchen. Every surface and the majority of the floor were decorated by empty bottles and cans of various sizes and colours. Pieces of broken glass also adorned the scene like sprinkles on cake. Scott guessed they must be from drinking glasses after checking to make sure all the windows were intact. The room was freezing as the back door stood wide open. Scott wondered if the three visible sleeping occupants in the room had caught pneumonia during the night.

Stepping over the debris as best he could, Scott made his way to the kettle and filled it up at the tap. Hearing the clatter of dispersed cans on the bench, Boris came trotting back in from outside, seemingly quite happy at the new open door policy allowing him the freedom to come and go at will. Seeing the dog and broken glass in close proximity, Angela quickly began to scoop up all she could find into an empty cardboard box that had previously been used to carry in some of last night's liquor supply.

He took a bottle of aspirin out of the cupboard next to the kettle and fetched that and the two coffees to the bench outside and shook out a couple of tablets for each of them.

'Here,' he said, handing a cup and aspirin to Angela as she sat down. 'It's strong and sweet.'

Angela put the cup on the floor, flipped open her mobile phone and turned it back on to check messages, as she took a drag from a freshly lit cigarette held between shaky fingers.

'Three missed calls from Steph late last night. I texted to tell her about the party when she didn't show up at work, I wonder why she didn't just come by.

Scott shook his head and lit a cigarette.

'I'll call her back later, once I'm more together.'

'I'm gonna go see Twinkle today. Find out what he was talking about.'

'Really? Is that such a good idea, Scott?'

'I'll just hear him out, that's all.'

By midday the rest of the stragglers had left and Scott had cleared away the remaining party litter from around the house. Angela had showered, and then left in the last car load into the city driven by Neil, who was still sullen after discovering Gemma had left with someone else by the time he'd made the trip back from the ATM last night. Angela had a shift that afternoon, although Scott didn't know how the hell she'd manage that after the night they'd had.

They hadn't counted up their profits, but the thick roll Neil had handed to him before leaving indicated that it would be good. Breakages had been minimal, mostly glasses and cups, nothing expensive. Not that Scott had much in the way of valuables anyway, but he was glad the windows and especially the TV had made it through the night without incident and his uncle's various ornaments seemed to have been left unscathed as well.

Turning his phone back on there was a message from Jack: 'Hey Scott, we haven't caught up for a while. If you're in town today then call in and see me, we need to talk.'

Scott deleted the message. It was pretty rare to hear from Jack, so he wondered if there was anything wrong. He could drop by the bar and see Angela as well he supposed, Jack's apartment was only a ten minute walk from there, and then there was Twinkle as well. He hadn't known he was going to go and meet him until he heard himself say it to Angela. Apparently his subconscious had been mulling over the dilemma while he had gotten wasted. Three coffees and a sobering shower later, he hadn't changed his mind so he grabbed his iPod and phone and headed out for the bus.

Avoiding the busiest shopping streets, Scott made his way to his brother's apartment block. The sky had begun to cloud over and looked like it would rain soon, which only seemed to fuel the afternoon shopping frenzy. Jack's penthouse was in an exclusive block positioned in the heart of Garden Heights. He'd moved there just before Scott turned eighteen, although the year before the brothers had rarely run into each other despite still living under the same roof.

Jack had always been a driven personality but seemed to throw himself even more completely into his work following their uncle's death. No matter how busy he always seemed to find time to take on new ventures. Scott was glad that his brother was doing well and he enjoyed his own company, so didn't much mind the long hours spent alone at the house.

Jack's career in the design business had begun when Scott was still at school. He got a job working for a moderately sized company designing posters and flyers for various outlets mainly in the entertainment business. Being a stickler for attention to detail, Jack would often follow up his design jobs by going to visit the various venues where his work was on display to see the impact it had on creating new custom. This earned a level of respect from the bar and club managers. Realising the commitment Jack had for his work they would start to request him specifically when placing new orders. Moving in these circles and making friends, Jack started to learn the business from the inside. During an infrequent conversation with his brother, he had voiced his desire to own a string of bars and clubs himself one day. With a small amount of money he'd managed to save up Jack formed his own company, Zebra design, and took a number of clients with him. He already deejayed at club nights around the city and a while after began to host regular weekend spots on local radio. His different enterprises went hand in hand and furthered the popularity of each other, enabling Jack to buy the penthouse shortly after. Scott had been taught the ropes of designing some of the more basic artwork from his brother and had earned a modest but steady income from Zebra design ever since.

He recognised the concierge on duty as Eddie. Eddie was mid-thirties, had short brown hair, was close shaven to the point that it looked to irritate his skin and wore the standard blue uniform and cap. They'd chatted a couple of times previously when Scott had visited. Eddie let him go straight up while he buzzed ahead to announce his imminent arrival. Scott crossed the polished marble floor of the foyer in the direction of the bank of lifts. He moved his hand over the sensor to summon one just as the doors to his left sprang open. As he turned to enter, a young woman in a sharp grey suit, carrying an attaché case, stepped off and walked past him before Scott recognised that it was Stephanie.

'Hey Steph, small world,' he called after her. 'Are you here on business or pleasure?'

Stephanie stopped and turned to face him.

'Hello Scott,' she said, with a minor reshaping of her lips that could perhaps be interpreted as a smile. 'Either there's only room for business these days or the two have become one and the same. Sometimes it's hard to remember.'

'Angela was expecting to see you out last night.'

'I had hoped to get away but then there was someone I had to see unexpectedly,' she said, and briefly looked genuinely sorry.

'I didn't realise you knew Jack.'

'I've been personal assistant to the manager at Aura's for the last few months, so our paths have crossed, yes.'

'You look a lot different to Angela's friend with the braided hair I used to see out clubbing at Blitz years back,' he said grinning.

'Yes, well the braids don't really go with the suit,' she said stiffly. 'Nice to see you again Scott, but I have to be going.' He watched as she cut across the foyer towards the revolving door, the tock-tock-tock from her departing heels echoing around the marble foyer like the inside a giant clock. Eddie seemed to recognise her and tipped his cap as she passed by, making Scott wonder if she was a regular visitor to the building.

Slightly surprised by her presence, but more so by her sharp attitude in their exchange, he turned back and entered the lift. Scott pressed for the top floor and made the smooth ascent in silence, trying not to look directly at the polished chrome in the elevator that reflected the high intensity lighting as brightly as the inside of a jewellers window. His eyes still felt overly sensitive following the previous night of excessive consumption.

The lift doors opened out onto a wide carpeted hallway that seemed to glow from recessed lighting hidden away in the ceiling. Taking in a deep breath of the alpine scented, warmly conditioned air, Scott walked around to the door of his brother's penthouse apartment; one of eight on the uppermost floor of the Walker building. The name had always struck Scott as fairly ironic, the Walker building. No doubt named after the architect who designed the structure or whoever financed it. Placement of the 30-storey smoked glass and chrome monolithic structure was so central in Garden Heights, that any desirable location could be arrived at in no time on foot, but any resident who could afford to live within those exclusive walls would certainly never be seen to arrive in such a fashion. Jack himself drove a black, convertible Lexus that spent the majority of its life swapping one security patrolled underground car park in the city for another. At least that's what he drove the last time Scott saw him. Cars were replaced almost as frequently as girlfriends, so by now both of those positions had probably been refilled.

Arriving at the front door Scott found it had been left ajar, no doubt in expectation of his arrival. He entered and as there was no sign of Jack in the open plan living area, he walked across the polished, French oak floor (so he'd been informed by one of Jack's previous girlfriends) to look into the kitchen, but glancing across the balcony he saw his brother outside taking a phone call. Judging by his animated body language and stern expression, Scott decided not to interrupt and instead took a seat on one of four white sofas arranged around a spotless square black glass table in the centre of the room. He resisted the urge to put his feet up on the table and light a cigarette.

A few minutes later the sliding glass door whispered as Jack eased it open and came in from the balcony.

'Hey Scott,' he said, his deadpan expression giving no clue as to the intention of their meeting, and walked over to a decanter on a small granite table by the far wall. 'You want one of these?'

'Yeah thanks I will,' Scott replied, and Jack poured a few fingers into each of their glasses. Swallowing a mouthful from one, he topped it up again and brought the glasses over and put them down on the table Scott had avoided putting his feet up on. Jack settled into the sofa opposite with a sigh and again reached for his glass.

'So how are things with you, little brother?' Jack asked, this time taking only a sip from his glass. Not being much of a whiskey drinker, Scott also took a drink and resisted the urge to wince as the golden liquid slid down his throat leaving behind a trail of fire. His brother would no doubt take offence as this was bound to be some impeccable vintage single malt, so Scott faked an expression of impressed surprise, which appeared to please Jack, before answering.

'Pretty much the same as ever, really. Same shit, different day,' Scott said with a grin. 'I heard you on the radio last week, good show.'

'Thanks. The shows are being syndicated now so they'll go out to most of the country.'

'Your celebrity status being etched into the minds of the listening public far and wide,' Scott quipped, but his attempt at humour washed over Jack leaving no trace of an impression.

'Listen Scott,' Jack said leaning forward, 'there was an incident in the club last night.'

Scott guessed from the look on his brother's face that this was going to be something to do with the reason he'd wanted to see him today.

'OK, well it was a Friday night, I expect that's not so unusual. So what happened?'

'A guy was shot in the club,' his brother said, 'so yeah it was pretty unusual. Maybe that sort of thing happens at those seedy fucking rock bars you hang out at, but not where I work, Scott,' he said, putting his glass back down hard enough for some of its contents to slop over onto the pristine table.

'OK Jack, calm down, I get it's a big deal but what's this got to do with me?'

'Your friend was in, with that Dominic thug.'

'Who, you mean Twinkle?'

'Yeah.'

'That hardly means anything, there were probably three thousand other people there too. Why is Twinkle being there a problem?'

'The shooting happened in an area just out of the cover of the closed circuit cameras,' he said and paused, holding Scott's gaze looking for a reaction.

'I still don't get it, Jack. What are you trying to tell me, or ask me or whatever it is you're doing?'

'Everyone goes through the archway, you know the metal detector, coming into the club so there's no way to get a gun in undetected.'

'Right yeah, it's the same pretty much everywhere these days, so?'

'So someone got one in and managed to use it to good effect avoiding cover of the cameras. There's no way that could be done without help from at least one person from the club, presumably the door staff. It's no secret that Dominic is at close quarters with Paul McBlane, and has been known to get his hands dirty when it's needed. The door staff at Aura and half of the other bars and clubs in the city are employed through McBlane's security company, and nothing ever happens on one of his patches without serious consequences.'

'So you're saying it couldn't have had anything to do with Twink and Dominic?'

'No, I'm saying it very much looks like they were involved, and with McBlane's blessing.'

'But why would he be involved if it's gonna make his security company seem inept? No-one would want to use them if that's the case.'

'Some of Garden Heights more high profile venues have been sold on to outside investors recently, and the rumoured amounts involved are a long way short of what you'd expect. No names have been mentioned as the investors buying in are doing it through offshore holding companies. McBlane's made no secret in the past of wanting to be more involved in the business than just minding the door while the owners get rich.'

Scott thought he could now see where his brother was going with this but kept quiet and allowed him to continue. Jack finished the contents of his glass and sat back on the sofa, exhaling heavily through his nose.

'The guy who was shot last night was the owner's brother, Scott. The circumstances surrounding the attack and the target can't have been a coincidence. I know what you get up to, and I know you're pretty close with that Twinkle guy, so I want to know if you knew anything about it.'

'No, I still have my doubts that Twink would get mixed up in something like this, even if it is true,' Scott said, although he didn't know how much of the statement he believed himself. With the wrong company, and the right drugs, Scott had no idea how far Twinkle could be manipulated. Maybe he had been right to worry last night when he'd seen Twinkle and Dominic out drinking together. 'Whether I'm right about this or not, you'd do well to distance yourself from these people. There can be no happy ending for someone like you in all of this.'

'Alright Jack, I appreciate the heads up, but really, don't worry about me. I'll check with Twinkle next time I see him but I doubt he'd be that stupid,' Scott said, and drank the remaining whiskey from his glass, this time making no effort to mask his distaste. 'I have to go,' he said, standing.

Jack got up too, still holding Scott's gaze. This time it didn't look like suspicion in his brother's eyes, but Scott couldn't tell what it was.

'What I've told you here goes no further, Scott. Understand? If I'm even half right about this then the information alone is dangerous. I just told you my suspicions to persuade you to back off.'

Walking towards the lift, Scott pulled out his phone and

started to text Neil. He wouldn't say any of this over a phone call or a text, but he made it clear he needed to see his friend at home before they went back into the city that night.

Moving through the revolving doors from the warm interior of the lobby into the cold street outside felt like making the transition from summer straight into winter. The temperature seemed to have dropped dramatically during his short visit, but Scott wasn't sure if it was the weather or the news he'd received that had chilled him the most.

Chapter 5

The sex had been good but unfulfilling. Jack obviously knew what he was doing and was far more experienced than she was but the whole act had seemed pretty methodical to Angela. Very different from the first fumbling encounter when she'd lost her virginity, but equally as unsatisfying.

After Jack had finished they lay in bed and talked for a few minutes before he fell asleep. That's when he'd made the promise to call her. Angela had expected he would ask her to get dressed and leave, maybe offer her some cab fare that she'd be too proud to take, but he hadn't.

She lay awake a while listening to the rhythmic rise and fall of his breathing as he fell into a deeper sleep, thinking how different the night had ended up from the one she had nervously envisioned while getting ready to meet up with Scott.

Angela ran her fingertips over the white cotton sheets on Jack's bed feeling how soft and smooth the material was. She knew there was no chance of her falling asleep here and didn't think it would be such a good idea even if she could. Jack had begun to snore quietly, his breath exhaling in a soft hiss. She swung her legs slowly out of the bed and began to dress, being careful not to wake him. Angela stepped lightly into her panties and then slid on her dress and shoes and shook out her hair with both hands so it wouldn't look so obvious that she'd just climbed out of someone's bed. She picked up her bag then made her way out of the apartment.

Angela hadn't expected much more than memories from her chance encounter with Jack. She certainly hadn't expected him to call like he'd promised to, and was surprised when he did.

She hadn't told Stephanie about her intended meeting with Scott so there'd been no reason to confess that she'd been stood up. Stephanie's brutal line of questioning after she'd heard that Angela had possibly just had her first one night stand was more than she could handle anyway.

'What were you doing there in the first place?' Stephanie asked suspiciously after Angela told her where she'd met Jack.

'I just decided to go out for a few drinks and ended up there,' she lied, trying to dampen the flames of Stephanie's curiosity. Steph had had more than the occasional one night stand over the years, and was more than willing to share all of the details with Angela the next day irrespective of her reluctance to hear them.

Jack took Angela out fairly regularly over the next few weeks. He would call her on nights he wasn't working and they'd go out to an expensive restaurant; she presumed they were expensive, anyway. No prices were listed on the menu and he always insisted on taking care of the bill. They'd go for a few drinks afterwards and then back to his place, where inevitably they'd end up having sex. After Jack fell asleep Angela would get dressed and leave the apartment. It was the kind of relationship that her friend Stephanie would have killed for. There were no strings, he spoiled her and when they were together she received nothing but first class treatment wherever they went. Jack was attractive and very charming, and there were no uncomfortable silences to fill in their conversations during meals. He had no end of stories to tell and anecdotes to share that never failed to make her laugh, but none of it seemed particularly personal. She never felt that Jack was seeing other women on the nights they weren't together, and fidelity had never been discussed anyway, so she didn't really feel like she had a right to bring it up. But she felt the whole scenario could play out exactly the same with any other girl in her position; there was no depth of emotion or bond to really tie them together. On occasion when Angela would mention this, or try to discover a little more about his personal life, family or friends outside of work, Jack would withdraw a little, and the atmosphere between them would noticeably cool.

'I love spending time with you, Jack,' she'd said to him one night in a restaurant, as she took hold of his hand, 'It's just that you still feel like a stranger to me, and I want you to be so much more.'

She looked away as she said that, afraid by coming on too strong she'd scare him off and be left with nothing, but as she released his hand he leaned forward and took hold of hers again.

'I really like being with you too. Emotional closeness just isn't something I've had a lot of practice with. After my parents died I tried to bury all of my feelings. The pain of that kind of loss is just so hard to bear it was easier to pretend it didn't exist. I guess I've been locked up pretty tight ever since.'

'I'm so sorry, Jack,' She said, meeting his gaze again, 'I had no idea. I don't want to cause you any pain, but if that is how you're feeling then I just want to be there for you and help you through it.'

'OK,' he said smiling at her, 'so how do I start?'

'Well just talking like this is good,' she said with a grin. 'You could tell me about your parents, and your apartment is beautiful but there are no photos or anything personal to make it feel like a home. Maybe it just needs a woman's touch.'

After the restaurant they drove back to Jack's apartment and spent most of the night on the couch talking and sipping wine, before eventually heading to bed as the first fingers of dawn began to reach around and take hold on the city that lay below them. That was the first night that Angela slept in Jack's bed.

They awoke around lunchtime having slept for only a few hours. She showered while Jack cooked them both some eggs. The conversation while they ate was light, he even seemed a little coy at times, but smiled a lot.

They travelled down to the foyer together where she kissed him goodbye as he set off for work. Angela went and bought a coffee nearby and sat alone with her thoughts as the city geared up for another day. Afterwards she wandered and, without even realising she was going to do it, ended up at a tattoo parlour where she had her earlobe pierced for a second time, and a small silver hoop slipped through it.

* * *

A clutch of huddled figures stood around at the bar in The Highlander waiting to be served, but the majority of Christmas refugees were gathered around the tables. Scott claimed a vacant bar stool in Angela's area and waited for her to finish serving the others.

'Always nice to see a smiling face at the bar,' Angela said sarcastically, as Scott sat down and began to knead his temples with the tips of his fingers.

'Glad you appreciate the effort,' he replied back with a dismissive smile.

'I didn't think you'd make it down today with the weather being so nice outside and bearing in mind what you put away last night.'

'Thanks but I'm a big boy, I can cope. Besides, you think I just hide away indoors during daylight like some kind of vampire?'

'No dummy, I just mean when we get a day like this so close to Christmas its wall-to-wall with the credit card crew out there. You'd think the shops were giving their shiny shit away for free today there's so many of them.'

Scott couldn't help but laugh at Angela's seasonal cynicism. For someone who had such a positive attitude most of the time, the festive cheer always fell short of wrapping Angela up in its warm cocoon of merriment. Without being asked she went to fetch a beer for Scott. She'd changed into deep blue cargo pants that she wore with her scuffed black boots, a loose fitting black t-shirt with a shapeless blue and black checked shirt worn open over the top. It sometimes puzzled Scott how she could still look so feminine despite her sexless outer garments, but as she handed him the bottle of Heineken, there was no denying how good she looked.

'How long left till you finish for the day?'

'Another few hours.'

A customer came up to the bar and Angela went to serve. Scott took a drink from his bottle as his thoughts returned to his brother and the conversation they'd had. He had intended to come out and see Twinkle to discuss whatever opportunity he had hinted at the night before, but after hearing what Jack had said he wasn't sure it was now something he should do. He was out now though and Twinkle wasn't usually hard to find so he figured he may as well hear what the old man had to say.

'You staying out for the night now then?' Angela asked, as she returned from serving.

'No, I'm gonna finish this then I think I'll see if I can run into Twinkle.'

Angela looked at him earnestly for a moment but passed no judgement.

'I've just been to visit Jack,' Scott said, eager to change the subject.

'How's he doing?' she asked, smiling thinly as her hand raised and brushed against the two silver hoops in her right ear. 'It must be a couple of years now since I ran into him. Is he still doing those radio shows as well?'

'Yeah he's still got all that going on, and no doubt more

besides. The endless pursuit of wealth and happiness,' Scott said, and grinned.

'So what prompted the family reunion today then, a thick slice of Christmas guilt?' she asked.

'Yeah I guess it was something like that,' Scott said, not wanting to divulge anything Jack had said about Twinkle. 'He'd texted when my phone was off and asked if I could call in. I saw Stephanie getting out of the lift in his building.'

'Really, what was she doing there?'

'She didn't say, visiting Jack though I suppose. She's PA to the manager at Aura so they know each other.'

'She say anything about not meeting me last night?'

'Just that she got caught up with some stuff. She looked disappointed about it though.'

Angela nodded and then went to serve another customer. Scott drank the remainder of his beer.

'I'll see you later, Angela,' he said, and walked back out into the mass of shoppers.

A cursory glance around a few other bars had turned up no sign, so Scott decided to try John Henry's, one of Twinkle's favourite haunts. A conversation with Aldo, one of Twinkle's old drinking buddies, revealed he was expected there within the hour.

Deciding to wait, Scott sat down with a pint away from the bar at a corner table and lit a cigarette. The clientele in there on Sunday afternoon were the same as most other afternoons. From middle aged to old men, drinking and cursing at the world like it was the last bus which had just left the stop without them. Being a city centre bar these didn't tend to be old codgers waiting for the wife to prepare Sunday roast before staggering home to eat and then sleep it off. They mostly drank there until they passed out or were thrown out. That's why Twinkle likes the place so much, Scott thought, looking around at the faded wood veneer tables, and the faded souls drinking at them.

Misery was soaked through the place like the old beer soaked through its carpets.

One bright point in there was Joanne. Scott saw her come in breezily to start her shift while he waited at his table. Joanna was the longest serving of the bar staff. She seemed able to suck up any amount of negativity and scorn and just turn the other cheek without becoming bogged down in it like her workmates. She joked that the staff roster had its own revolving door, and that name tags were essential as she never recognised anyone on her side of the counter. She had a cheery demeanour, maybe just edged above five feet in height if she wore heels, and she often joked that she was as wide as she was tall. The regulars had accepted her as one of their own now, and made sure any tips given went directly to her and not into a jar to split with the rest of the staff. Scott picked up his glass and went to sit with her at the bar.

'Hey Joanne,' he said, taking a seat on a free stool.

'Hello Scott, and a merry Christmas to you.'

'Yeah, let's not get too carried away and just leave it at hello,' he said and grinned. 'There's never been anything merry about this place for a long time.'

Joanne laughed heartily, an infectious sound that had the same effect on the atmosphere as a defibrilator on an arrested heart.

'So what brings you into this fine establishment today then?'

'Just a few quiet drinks.'

'Quiet we can do, and drinks we can do as well, so you're at the right place,' she said, beaming.

'Twinkle should be in soon so we can all exchange gifts.'

'Ha, now that I'd pay to see.'

'You were friends with his missus weren't you?'

'Yes, I still am. Don't see her much since she moved away but we still keep in touch.'

'You think they'll ever get back together?'

'I doubt it. The only way she'd ever have him back was if he quit all the drink and, well, the other stuff as well,' she said, tapping her nose. 'It'd be the best thing he could do though. Poor old duffer has been as miserable as sin since they left, never mind what he might tell you. He worshipped her and those kids, she just couldn't take any more though. The little ones were getting to an age where she couldn't hide it from them anymore, she wouldn't have them growing up in that kind of life.'

Scott nodded and finished his pint.

'Another one of them then, love?'

'Yeah and one for yourself as well, Joanne.'

'Well, if it isn't some Christmas spirit come creeping into the place after all,' she said, and laughed again as she went to pull Scott's pint.

After paying Joanne for his beer and tipping more than enough extra for one of her own, Scott picked up his glass and went to play on the pinball table near the front of the bar. It was the latest attempt by management to attract younger blood into the place, although so far it didn't seem to have worked. He took a swig from the beer and put it down with his cigarettes on the ledge beside him.

Four games of pinball and another beer later Scott's vigil in the depressing bar paid off. Twinkle arrived alone, showing no surprise at all seeing Scott there waiting.

'Alright Scott, how'd the party go last night?'

'Was OK, how come you didn't stop by?'

'Other people to see. You know how it is,' Twinkle said, attempting a smile that never quite settled on his face and absently scratching the growth of stubble on his unshaven chin. That's one thing Scott had always noticed about Twinkle, no matter how bad things were for him or how fucked up his life got, he always made sure to get washed and shaved before going out into town, like it was the last connection he had to his relatively normal and happier past.

'Yeah man, I know how it is,' Scott said, although he wasn't sure that he did. 'Any word from Sharon and the kids?'

Twinkle looked at him with a practised scowl he'd reserve for anyone asking about his ex.

'Fuck that bitch. She had her chance.'

'OK Twink. So these people you had to see last night, they anything to do with the opportunities you told me about?' Scott asked, to get their meeting back on track.

Twinkle motioned towards the back of the bar and led the way to an unoccupied table. Scott took a seat and after ordering two beers from Joanne, Twinkle brought them over and sat down.

'Cheers,' Twinkle said, and downed about a third of his pint.

Scott sipped at his own, eager to hear what this was going to be about but waited for Twinkle to come to the point in his own time. Twinkle's eyes drifted around the room, not suspiciously as if he feared being overheard, but glassily as if his mind was elsewhere.

Eventually he refocused and turned to Scott.

'You can drive, right Scott?'

'Yeah I can, but I don't have a car,' Scott said, starting to feel apprehensive. 'This isn't some smash and grab you want me in on, is it?'

'Nothing like that, no. And it doesn't matter about a car, we'll have a van supplied.'

'Spit it out then, mate, enough with the mystery.'

'There's a shipment of tools and electrical supplies coming in to the docks at Eastgate,' Twinkle said in a hushed tone as he leant in towards Scott. 'Inside the shipment is a large amount of coke. We'll have a van with the trade name that the shipment is for on the side. We just drive in, sign for it, load it up and go.'

'And how much does it pay?'

'I'll split the pay right down the middle with you Scott. I was gonna just get someone for a couple of grand if you said no, but for me and you it's ten grand each.'

'It's a nice amount but what about identification and paperwork and all that stuff?'

'Already taken care of, the guy who wants it knows some Asian lad called Tazeem who can get any type of photo IDs or anything made up. All I need from you is a passport photo and it'll be done in a day. We walk in with the legit paperwork and proper IDs.'

'No point in me asking who all this is for then?'

'No, that's not important anyway, just that you're in or out. We make this go off without any problems and there's more work to follow. To be honest your name was mentioned in passing during my meeting about this, so if you're gaining some notoriety from those higher up then your days peddling around clubs are gonna be numbered anyway.'

Twinkle's eyes sparkled in eager anticipation as he leant in further, waiting to hear Scott's response. It was obvious that Twinkle reckoned this was his last chance to make something of himself and Scott thought he was probably right; it was a chance he knew Twinkle would do pretty much anything to grab hold of.

'It's a big sentence we'll be looking at if anything goes wrong with this, man.'

'It would be, but the details have already been worked out. Besides, how many nights have you got to trail all those bags of drugs around town to make anywhere near this type of cash? What you think you'd be looking at if you got caught with them? Not every club bouncer is just gonna pocket the lot for himself, especially in the quantities you move these days. Chances are you'd be pinned to the floor with his knee in your back until the feds got there to take you away for a lengthy spell at a barbed wire holiday camp.'

* * *

As requested, Neil arrived at the cottage about an hour after Scott returned home.

Scott rolled a joint as he filled Neil in on everything he'd heard that afternoon from his brother. By the time the joint was smoked and extinguished, so was Neil's previous good mood.

'So really there isn't anything conclusive, it could all just be that Twink was in the wrong place at the wrong time, and that people are jumping to conclusions,' Neil said, settling into a satisfied expression.

'Yeah but you have to admit, it doesn't look good, for him or for us. You know how much he gets off on the whole image thing where gangsters are concerned. As long as Twinkle has a pocket full of drugs and a pocket full of cash he's a happy bunny. He isn't trying to chase down a fortune but if he thought he was being taken into the confidence of people like that, then shit, I can't say I know for sure what he would do,' Scott said.

'Yeah but shooting someone in a packed out club?' Neil said, continuing to defend the aged drug dealer.

'Twinkle never goes there, he's always at Blitz on a Friday night. The one night he isn't where he always is, he turns up with some psycho at a club and the manager's brother gets shot. He's being led up the garden path.'

Neil looked sullen and unconvinced, he shook his head.

'Look man, I don't want to be doing this forever. Twinkle was a good help sourcing decent drugs, but if he's connected with these type of people, we're gonna get pulled in too. We either accept this and step up, or cut our losses now.'

Neil still looked less than convinced by this and Scott was losing the will to go on arguing.

'To be honest, I've been thinking about moving away from Twinkle for a while anyway, I think we could do a lot better than we are right now.'

'A lot better, how? If you're on about distance for safety, then yeah I'm with you, but if you mean doing better by moving bigger quantities than just deals around the clubs then you can forget it, Scott.'

'You hate being a mechanic, you cry on about it all the time. Wouldn't you like to be able to kick it into touch for good?' Scott asked, already feeling from Neil's resolute expression that he wasn't about to change his mind.

'Yeah I hate having to work all the hours in the garage, but I'd rather that than spending years in jail. I like the situation as it is. We go out and party at the weekends and have enough cash to not worry about day to day stuff. If we ever did get caught it would only be with a small amount and might not even do any jail. I'm not about to risk that to buy into your *grass is greener, retirement plan in the sun.*'

Scott was faced with accepting the reality he'd suspected for a long time. If he was to get away from his life and everything here and start over, he was going to need a different partner, or else do it all alone.

Chapter 6

Jack really seemed to have taken on board what Angela had said, and since the night they'd sat up talking, their relationship seemed to have found a new resonance. The regularity of their dates had decreased but Angela wasn't worried by that. She knew Jack was busy with deejay shifts and he had taken on other projects that demanded his time as well. She had tried to talk to him about his work but he always dismissed her questions. Jack said that work dominated enough of his life already, and when he was with her it should be just the two of them without any distractions. Angela accepted this, as when they were together Jack seemed to have the ability to make the rest of the world feel so far away that all that mattered was the two of them.

Angela rode the elevator up towards the top floor of Jack's building. She nodded and smiled at a couple she'd seen there before that got off at the twenty-second floor and she travelled the rest of the way alone. She had suggested meeting Jack at his apartment to save time and somewhat reluctantly, it seemed, he'd agreed. He'd told her to come at eight, but they'd had so little time together recently that Angela decided to call in an hour early and give Jack a pleasant surprise. She smiled at what she had in mind as she walked towards Jack's apartment.

Angela tried the handle and found Jack's door unlocked. That wasn't unusual. Being in one of the most secure buildings in the city Jack rarely locked the door when he was home unless he was sleeping.

She walked inside and kicked off her heels under an occasional table by the door so she could sneak up on Jack unaware. Stepping lightly across the oak floor Angela heard him talking and presumed he must be on the phone. He wasn't seated on any of the couches and after a few steps it sounded that his voice was coming from the kitchen area.

Jack's tone was harsh, but having heard him take work phone calls before she knew this wasn't out of the ordinary. Jack may have been a patient and attentive boyfriend, but he certainly wasn't someone she'd ever want to work for. Angela stopped when she heard another man's voice. She could make out some of what they were saying now. The man was apologising, almost pleading with Jack to give him another chance, but Jack's authoritative tone silenced him in mid sentence.

'I've had enough of your shit in the past. I wouldn't have given you a second chance last time if it had been down to me but I bowed out of the decision when it was asked as a personal favour. That won't happen again. Not only do I not want to see you around me anymore, I don't even want to hear of you being in the city and my net spreads wide. Pack your fucking shit and disappear, and you know you're getting off lightly with this.'

The man stammered a few syllables, as if trying to select the words that might get him out of the situation he found himself in, but then fell silent.

'Go on Andy, fuck off!' Jack spat at him.

She had never heard him like this before, the venom in his voice, an ugly bitterness. This couldn't be a side of Jack that was prevalent to his personality, surely not. Wouldn't she have picked up on signs before now?

'Oh, and Andy?'

A second later a sound of crashing glass followed by the unmistakable thud of someone falling to the floor. Angela froze. She hadn't realised she'd been backing up towards the door, but putting her hand out to steady herself she touched something on the table. A gurgling noise followed by the sound of someone spitting thickly. The tinkling of glass shards dancing across the kitchen tiles had ceased, but now some of them crunched as something moved over the top of them. Angela had crouched to retrieve her shoes and was flailing blindly behind her for the door handle when the figure crawled around the corner. Catching sight of Angela he tried to say something but his mouth succeeded only in forming a bubble from the blood and saliva that had pooled there. It burst in his efforts to speak and ran down his chin mixing with the other rivulets of flowing blood and dripped onto the polished floor beneath him. Deep lacerations ran down the left-hand side of his face with jagged fragments of glass still protruding from some of them. Angela gagged and cupped a hand over her mouth in an effort to bite back her churning stomach contents.

Laughter from the kitchen now. 'What are you waiting for? You want me to make the call and have you removed?'

'N- nn- nn- no.' The prostate figure stammered pathetically, attempting to look back over his shoulder and tried to crawl away again.

Angela felt life return to her frozen limbs and she spun towards the door. Just about to make her exit she saw what her hand had touched on the table. A picture frame. This was unusual as she'd never seen any around the apartment before. What was more unusual was that she recognised the photo. Two little boys with matching light blue rain hats and oversized grey coats. One with a miserable look about him and the other slightly bigger boy with a broad grin stretched across his face, a grin that had become so familiar to her over the last two months.

* * *

That next night Scott sat smoking a joint on the sofa after a mundane day at Zebra. Boris occupied the seat next to him, his interest switching between a news item on TV about Carston Keaton, the Mayor of Garden Heights, and chewing at his paw. A painful montage of promises to clean up the city cycled on the screen as part of the build up to the mayoral elections.

Scott reached for the remote and muted the volume. He'd thought a lot about whether the decision to go ahead on the job with Twinkle was right or not, and he still wasn't sure. What he did know was that he had committed to it, and now there was no turning back.

After confirming his inclusion, they had each sunk two more pints, before walking to a nearby photo booth where Scott had the pictures taken that Twinkle needed to hand over for the production of his I.D. card.

Scott had the feeling of being drawn into something unstoppable again, like swimming in the sea and suddenly feeling the relentless pull of a current. What Twinkle had said was right though. Even if he chose not to go in on this job he could end up arrested for dealing a week later and in jail anyway. Either way the decision was now made. He tried to relax and took a hit from the joint. He hadn't felt much like smoking it, but it gave his mind something else to focus on for a while.

His mobile phone rang, the vibration causing it to dance across the surface of the coffee table, startling him and making Boris bark in annoyance at the sudden breach of tranquillity. Putting the joint down, Scott reached for the phone and answered it.

'Yeah?'

'Scott it's me, Angela. Can you come see me?'

'Now?'

'Yes if you're not doing anything. It's Stephanie, she's been beaten up.'

Scott waited a second, not sure he'd heard her right. Angela's breathing, faster than normal, was the only sound from the phone.

'Is she OK?' Scott asked, trying to refocus his mind from his own troubles.

'I don't know, she was found in the stairwell to her apartment and taken to hospital. She's still unconscious.'

'OK, where are you now? At the hospital?'

'No, her mother and sister are with her at the hospital now so I came back home, but I don't want to be on my own. Do you mind coming over?'

'No, I don't mind. I'll call a taxi and be there soon.'

'OK, thank you Scott,' she said, and ended the call.

Scott dialled the number for Pressman Cabs, a company based in a nearby village that he used fairly regularly. After ordering, he put his phone and keys and cigarettes into his pockets and went out front to wait.

He had only taken a few inhales from a freshly lit cigarette when the car pulled up a few minutes later. Scott flicked the cigarette into a hydrangea bush and climbed into the cab.

'Hey Reg,' Scott said, recognising the driver as he got in, although it was pretty much a foregone conclusion as the company only consisted of Reg and his brother Stan driving cabs, and their sister Iris who took the calls.

'Where to tonight Scott?' Reg asked with his usual cheerful grin. Scott gave Angela's address and sat back, only half listening to Reg talk about the latest football scores that apparently hadn't gone his way on that week's betting sheet. He also tried to ignore the smell of old man sweat and menthol cigarettes that permeated both of the company cabs. Happy for Scott to just give the occasional nod when he looked in the rear-view, Reg continued in this manner for the duration of the journey.

Twenty minutes and endless football results later, the car pulled up alongside the block of flats that Angela lived in. 'Here you go, Reg,' Scott said, and handed the driver a twenty. 'Keep the change.'

'Thanks, will you be wanting a lift back home later on?'

'I don't know. I'll be sure to call though if I do.'

'Ahh OK,' Reg said with a wink and tapped a nicotine-stained forefinger against his nose, indicating the secret was safe with him. 'Enjoy yourself then.'

Not bothering to correct the driver, Scott turned and made his way through the unlocked entrance door into her block of flats. Angela had lived here for as long as Scott had known her, and after the flats where Putty had lived were torn down he had moved to a neighbouring block here as well. They were far from the luxury of the Walker building where Jack lived but at least they were a step up from the dilapidated ruins that Putty had once inhabited.

Scott climbed the stairs to the third floor and rapped the knocker on Angela's door. The metal on metal echoed coldly across the old linoleum and down the deserted stairwell. Within a few seconds the door opened and Angela motioned for him to come inside.

She led the way into a small sitting room where a table lamp gave sparse illumination of the floral print wallpaper.

'I still didn't get around to decorating yet,' she said catching Scott's eye, and attempted a smile.

They both sat down on the faded blue three-seater sofa. Angela tucked her knees underneath her chin and, despite the temperature in the room being warm, hugged them as though she were cold. Two cups of steaming coffee sat on the table in front of them. Angela must have been watching out of the window for him to arrive.

'Have you had any more news of Stephanie?' Scott asked. Angela shook her head, as she slowly rocked back and forth in the seat. Scott took off his jacket and reached for his coffee. He didn't realise she had begun crying at first as there was no noise. Only when he looked at her to ask another question did he see the tears slowly spilling down her cheeks. Closing the gap between them on the sofa Scott wrapped both of his arms around her, holding her against him, and felt her chest heave as she began to sob.

'You should have seen her face,' Angela said as she gasped for a breath. 'How could someone have done that to her?'

Scott didn't say anything, but just kept holding her until the sobs eventually began to subside. Angela pulled away from him and brushed at the wet patch her tears had made on his shirt.

'Don't worry about it,' he said, taking hold of her hand. She looked up and held his gaze. Her eyes still wet from tears sparkled, the lashes gathered together in dark clumps. She leaned in towards him and he did the same. Her tongue warm, and soft as velvet brushed against his as they began to kiss. Angela's hands felt cool as they slid underneath Scott's t-shirt and up his back. She dragged her fingernails insistently down either side hard enough to cause some pain, making Scott want her even more. Again he swore he could taste strawberries. Their kissing intensified and they began to peel away each other's clothes. He brushed a hand over her breast and she bit down on his lower lip.

Soon the carpeted floor was covered by shirts and pants. Scott sat back wearing only a pair of shorts, Angela on the carpet before him on her haunches in just a purple satin bra and panties. Unselfconsciously she reached around behind her and unfastened the bra clasp, letting it fall free to the floor beside her. She reached out to him. Scott took her hand and stood, expecting to be led into the bedroom. Angela remained on the carpet, her other hand tugged at the waistband of his shorts until they slid down to his feet. Scott had never been as aware of his own nakedness as he was at that moment. He felt her breath, warm and inviting, just before she took him into her mouth. His eyes closed and head tilted back as he sighed. She began to work up and down him; the tightness warm, and the motion insistent.

He pulled Angela to her feet. 'Which room is yours?'

'This way,' she said, and he followed.

Scott didn't know how long they had made love for. There

had been a need in her orgasms, something that ran deeper than just sex. She had clung to him, legs wrapped tight around his waist. Fingernails and teeth bit down into his flesh during the final thrusts as she cried out his name before falling back onto the bed, panting and shivering.

As Angela went to make them both coffee Scott took in the surroundings of her bedroom. He'd been to the flat a number of times before but never until now had reason to come in here. It was much like the other rooms, not decorated in any particular style, no style at all really with the discoloured old-fashioned wallpaper that clashed horribly with the busy patterns on the carpet. It was undeniably Angela though. Posters covered a lot of the wall space. Knick-knacks and photos she'd accumulated over the years were strewn over all surfaces the same as the rest of the flat, giving it a warm lived-in feel.

Pushing the bedroom door open with her bare foot, Angela came back wearing only a large checked shirt held loosely closed by two buttons. She carried two mugs of coffee, one of them documenting her return from the kitchen with a succession of drips onto the ancient carpet. She nodded her head towards the bedside cabinet, indicating for Scott to move some of the clutter and make room for the steaming cups.

'Thanks – ow,' she said, putting them down and spilling some of the contents onto her hand in the process. Leaving the room again, she returned a moment later with an unopened bottle of Jack Daniels.

'That's for the coffee?' Scott asked with a smile.

'Yep, to make them Belgian.'

'Belgian?' Scott asked, with a laugh. 'Isn't that supposed to be Cointreau and stuff you add to do that?'

'Really? I thought it was just something you said when you mixed alcohol into other drinks,' she said, grinning as she broke the seal and unscrewed the cap.

'I think I like your version better,' Scott said, and drank a mouthful from each of the mugs, leaving room for the whiskey to be poured.

After filling them back up to the brim, and giving both a quick stir with her finger, Angela resettled onto the bed and kissed Scott on the cheek.

'What was that for?' he asked.

'Just for being here, I couldn't have handled spending tonight alone.'

'This wasn't just...?'

'No Scott, it wasn't.'

'OK.'

'I think it was pretty much going to happen anyway.' She said it as a statement, but her searching eyes indicating it may have been more of a question.

Scott just smiled and nodded. Reaching over he picked up the whiskey-infused coffees and passed one, cracked handle first, to Angela.

'You want to talk about Stephanie?' Scott asked, taking a sip from his mug.

'I don't really know what to say. It's all so horrible,' Angela said and shivered.

'Have the police any idea what happened?'

'I don't know. It was in the stairwell going up to her apartment last night. The entrance was locked so the attacker had to have been buzzed in.'

'Was it rape, or just a robbery?'

'She had money in her purse and they said she had no injuries consistent with a sexual attack,' Angela said, staring mournfully down into her mug, her fingernail absently running up and down a crack in the porcelain. Scott watched her and felt a stab of guilt, unable to prevent his thoughts returning to the same fingernail being drawn down his back during sex not long before.

He didn't remember falling asleep. He did remember them

working their way through the bottle of Jack Daniels and talking for most of the night. Now he woke up with a headache and the bitter aftertaste of too much whiskey and too many cigarettes.

Angela still lay beside him, snoring softly into her pillow. Scott got up carefully so as not to disturb her, slipped on his shorts and went into the cramped kitchen to make coffee and find something for his headache. He went through the motions somewhat robotically, needing a caffeine kick to clear the fog from his consciousness and bring the morning into some kind of focus. The only window in the kitchen overlooked a shopping centre, and Scott paused for a minute, absently watching the progress of an old woman in a bright red woollen hat carrying two big bags of groceries. She was stooped over, either against the grey Monday morning drizzle or perhaps just with age. Attempting to concentrate on his task at hand, Scott then managed to drop the jar of Nescafe from the cupboard he'd discovered it in, onto the small countertop, which in the confined space resulted in a bang like a gunshot blast. Either that or the less than muffled curses which Scott had angrily erupted with as a result managed to rouse Angela from her slumber.

Discovering some Ibuprofen in a drawer, Scott popped two out of the blister pack as Angela appeared gingerly in the kitchen doorway. She was wearing only the checked shirt again, this time with no buttons fastened. Her right breast covered by the shirt, a long curl of her glossy red hair hung down over the left with her nipple visible between the strands. He looked down at her neatly trimmed pubic hair, blonde, her natural shade. Despite the hangover, Scott longed for her again. He felt conscious of his arousal pressing against the thin fabric of his boxer shorts.

'A couple of those for me too,' she said, squinting against the brightness from the kitchen window as she leant sleepily against the doorframe, seemingly unaware of his discomfort. Scott eased the last two tablets from the pack and handed them to Angela, along with the coffee he'd just made for himself.

Chapter 7

The rest of the week dragged endlessly for Scott. He'd worked on design jobs for Zebra from home but any connection he felt to the work was little to non-existent. Angela kept him informed of the lack of change in Stephanie by phone call and text message but there'd been no mention of them getting together in person. Neil had come by late on Tuesday evening to count up the weekend's takings and divide up the profits. He'd been thrilled at how well they'd done and had talked of making the parties a regular thing. Scott had deflected the exuberance and felt none himself. He knew how ridiculous it would be for a drug dealer to regularly hold open door parties at the location of his stash of cash and narcotics, but knew that explaining this to Neil would only end in an another argument. Besides, depending how things turned out with Twinkle on the job, he might be calling time on the business relationship with Neil anyway.

The agreement with Twinkle was that there would be no contact until the day of the job. Twinkle assured him he would personally check over all the details to make sure everything would run smoothly. As sure as Scott was that Twinkle wanted to avoid jail as much as he did, he would still rather have been able to check through everything himself. Twinkle's attention to detail could easily be sidetracked, as he'd seen a number of times in the past, and Scott was more than half convinced that the old man had managed to avoid jail for so long more by good luck than good judgement. However, this was Twinkle's call, and having already agreed to take part, Scott just had to grit his teeth and go along with it.

The meet was scheduled for 11:30 on Thursday at a bar Scott knew by reputation but had never been into. The Weather Balloon was on the edge of the run-down housing estate where Twinkle lived. Or the 'Eat Her' Balloon as it was sometimes referred to by the younger patrons as the 'W' had long since vanished and probably sat now pride of place on someone's mantelpiece.

Scott entered a few minutes early and ordered a pint of Coors at the bar. The interior walls were red and edged with what was probably once gold but now looked a sickly yellowish brown. The scuffed wooden floors reminded Scott of draughty school assemblies as a child. A large TV had been bolted to the wall in a corner and had been further secured with a chain. It appeared to keep the few customers at the bar placated with its endless broadcast of sports news. Scott was just about to retreat to a table with his drink to wait for Twinkle to arrive when he saw him emerge from the toilets, wiping his hands dry on his pants.

'Alright Scott?' Twinkle said and nodded to a table he'd previously been sitting at. An almost empty pint glass sat there which Twinkle drained the remaining contents from and went back to the bar for another. Scott felt edgy; he sat sipping his pint and spinning his Zippo on the table until Twinkle returned. Walking back to the table Twinkle fished in his pocket for something and, sitting down, he passed it under the table to Scott. He looked down and saw his own face looking up at him from a laminated ID card.

'My ID card,' Scott muttered in confirmation.

'Yeah. Here do this,' Twinkle said and Scott watched as he scrunched his own card in his palm. 'Makes it look more authentic, like it's been in your pocket for ages with keys and shit.'

Scott did as instructed and noted the look of pride on Twinkle's face, presumably at how high tech his life had recently become. He probably thought of himself as some kind of working class mix of James Bond and Robin Hood. Scott just hoped the euphoria wasn't causing Twinkle any oversights that they might both end up paying for.

'Everything in place for today then Twink?'

'All taken care of: paperwork, transport, route,' Twinkle said, smiling as he ticked off each point on his fingers then patted his shirt pocket causing a rustle. Scott noted the strong smell of beer on Twinkle's breath and wondered if it was only his second pint or if he'd been in since opening.

'Let's take a walk and you can tell me all about it then,' Scott said, eager to get them out of the bar and into fresh air. Twinkle looked reluctant but grudgingly gulped down the rest of his drink and stood up, slightly uneasily Scott thought, but hoped it was just his imagination.

They walked past a fast-food place and Scott ran back to get them both some lunch. He hadn't been hungry himself but thought getting some food into Twinkle would help to sober him up. Walking to the nearby park, they both ate in silence. It was a cold morning and the schools had yet to break up for the Christmas holidays, so other than the odd dog walker it was fairly deserted. The hot greasy burger tasted good to Scott despite his initial lack of enthusiasm and Twinkle was putting away a fair amount himself, which helped ease Scott's concern. Coming to an empty bench in a secluded area dense with yew trees and rhododendron bushes, Twinkle threw the carton and paper containing the remaining fries into a bush and sat down.

Twinkle took a cigarette from his pack and lit it, pulled his jacket tightly around his gaunt frame and took a deep inhale. Taking another quick look around, Twinkle slid a hand inside his jacket and removed the papers from his shirt pocket that the rustle had hinted at back in the bar. He handed them to Scott and exhaled the smoke.

Scott looked them over. There was a customs form, already filled in with what he supposed the relevant reference numbers, and the name and an address for the firm they were to collect the shipment for. On a separate sheet was a printed street map with a route marked away from the docks, onto a highway and then off again a few miles north to what looked like a collection of farm outbuildings.

'What about the van?' Scott asked after looking over the papers for a third time.

'Supermarket car park,' Twinkle said, turning his wrist to look at his watch. 'It'll be dropped off there in about an hour; I've been shown where to look. Once you've got the escape route memorised, you've to burn that sheet.'

'Escape route? You make it sound like we'll be fleeing with a dozen squad cars chasing us,' Scott said, shaking his head. Watching Twinkle carefully, Scott held his lighter below the customs forms, as if about to burn them by mistake instead of the evidence of their intended destination. Twinkle made no move to stop him. Scott knew then that Twinkle's mind wasn't remotely focused on the job and that he could only count on himself. If it came down to it he'd just have to leave Twinkle behind.

'You know what I mean though Scott,' Twinkle said with a grin as Scott set fire to the correct sheet of paper. 'Back to the pub for a few pints while we wait then?'

Having managed to keep Twinkle away from any licensed premises during the next hour, they arrived at the car park. Being so close to Christmas the place was overrun with avid shoppers looking to stock up for the holidays. The arrangement had been to park the van in as far away a spot from the supermarket as possible, to ensure there would be a free bay. Twinkle led the way through the rows of parked cars to a dirty four year old white Transit van in a remote corner of the lot. A company logo was emblazoned on the side reading: 'D. Mearns Electrical and Engineering Ltd.', matching the name on the customs forms that were now in Scott's pocket.

'What do you think then?' Twinkle asked as they approached the van. 'Pretty impressive, isn't it?'

'Well it's a van with a name on the side, so as far as that goes, yeah I'm impressed.'

'You can mock now Scott but come tonight you'll be thanking me for this shot when you've got a pocket full of cash,' Twinkle said and cackled.

Twinkle let them both into the van with a spare door key he already been given and Scott found the ignition key under the driver's seat where Twinkle said it would be. The interior, unlike the paint work outside, was spotless. All surfaces looked like they had been professionally cleaned. Scott imagined the van was stolen and would have had the plates swapped out but no trace remained of who the previous owner might have been. Buckling up first, Scott turned the key in the ignition and the van started up first time. Twinkle was saying something else about how well everything would go but by now Scott had begun to tune him out. Scott took the paperwork out again, familiarising himself with it and running through in his head any possible questions that they may be asked when collecting the shipment, until he felt confident he could handle any queries without nervously having to think up an answer on the spot. He checked the petrol gauge and wipers and adjusted the mirrors, then set off for the road towards the Eastland docks.

The day began to prematurely darken under a heavy layer of black cloud, and within the first mile of their journey fat raindrops had begun to fall. Scott had been paying particular attention to other road users along the route, especially any that had taken the same turns as them, but he was still made a little nervous by the sudden reduced visibility.

By the time they arrived at the docks the rain had become torrential and the sky even darker and more overcast. A flood of water ran down the side of the road and through the gateway into the docks. It mixed with the oil deposits from the procession of trucks that drove in and out all day, making the gathering pools of rainwater shine with a purple and green reflective hue. The adjacent car park contained around a dozen haulier trucks and numerous vans of various sizes and colours. A signpost indicated that the three storey red brick building directly ahead housed the reception area. They parked as close as possible and ran to the entrance.

The inside was overbearingly warm and humidity hung heavily in the air. A gas fire on high setting behind the counter and a thick inner door made the reception feel almost tropical, apart from the musty damp and oil smell that was released from the carpet. A fat man behind a counter, with thick round glasses and a moustache, glanced up momentarily as they walked in.

'Bitter out there today,' Twinkle said, rubbing his hands together and smiling at the uniformed official. The comment was greeted by a grunt and the man continued shuffling through the papers on his desk. Scott took out the forms from his pocket and unfolded them as he walked to the counter. Unsure of exactly what he should say, he decided to say nothing and just leaned over and placed them down with the ID card he'd been given next to some forms the man was currently frowning at on the desk.

'Two minutes,' he mumbled without looking up. Scott put his hands back into his pockets and strode around the room trying to remain calm. He had noticed from the outside that all the ground floor windows had been bricked up at some point, meaning the only light in the reception came from six fluorescent tubes, and the only thing to look at were regulation posters on the walls. One of the overhead lights flickered slightly and once Scott became aware of it, he found it increasingly difficult to focus on anything else.

'OK let's see here then,' the fat man said more to himself, and picked up the papers Scott had put down on the desk. Tapping a few buttons on his keyboard, he read what came up on the screen whilst smoothing his moustache between forefinger and thumb.

'Mmm right, you want to go to Station B for collection,' he said, gesturing with a finger that looked to Scott like something that should be in a bun with fried onions and ketchup. 'It's already been cleared. I've just authorised pickup on the computer, just take your 200C with you and show it over there.'

Scott nodded, picked up his ID card and papers the officer had indicated as being the 200C, and left in the general direction the finger had wagged in.

'See, this is fuckin' easy man,' Twinkle said, nudging Scott with a gleeful look on his face as soon as they got outside. Scott immediately shot a look over his shoulder to make sure the inside door had closed tight and that Twinkle couldn't have been overheard.

'Shut the fuck up. This isn't easy, it's fucking risky you stupid old bastard and acting like an idiot is what will get us caught. Unless someone speaks to you directly, don't say anything until we're loaded up and back in the van. Right?' The look he gave Twinkle let him know in no uncertain terms that this wasn't the time to argue. Twinkle's eyes narrowed and lips pulled tight over his teeth, but he slowly nodded his understanding and walked on in silence.

The rain was still falling heavily and they were both soaked through. Scott had given up trying to avoid walking in the puddles. He could hear squelching from his feet each time he took a step. A large signpost opposite the reception indicated roughly the same direction that the officer inside had for Station B. They walked back to the van and drove to make the collection.

The area of large warehouses was surrounded by high steel railings that had once been painted turquoise but the steady erosion of rust over the years left only patches of the original colour intact. The whole area would have thrived a decade or two ago but the demise of the shipbuilding industry along the river had seen the main factories have to retool to adapt to the changing market. Most had shut down completely with a ripple effect impacting other local businesses as a result. The docks themselves were in an obvious state of neglect due to the drop in trade and therefore lack of revenue that came through the port. A gutter high up outside Station B had cracked and the heavy rainfall that gathered on the roof flowed through the break, cascading down causing a flood just outside the entrance. Scott drove through the pooled water and parked up in a vacant bay inside.

Around the inside walls were grey metal shelves around thirty feet high. Labelled boxes sealed in plastic wrap sparsely occupied them. The centre of the floor space was devoted to pallets. Some were crowned with various sized wooden crates although most lay empty. Two yellow fork-lifts were stationed near an office cubicle on the right hand side of the warehouse. One had a bumper sticker that read: My other car's a Porsche.

'Just wait by the van,' Scott instructed, 'I'll go and sort this out.' Twinkle grunted and reached inside his jacket for cigarettes.

Through the greasy windows Scott could make out someone sitting inside the office, whistling to accompany the crackly sound of a portable radio that was struggling to maintain reception. Scott walked up to the door and tapped twice on the glass.

'Yeah,' a voice said from the other side. Scott pushed the door, greeted the man and handed him the collection forms along with his ID card. The man gave an appraising glance at the picture and then up at Scott, which was more than the first officer appeared to have done; he then entered the reference number onto a computer keyboard on his desk. Pausing for a few seconds, the man leaned in, squinting at the screen. Taking a step backwards, Scott positioned himself in the open doorway in an attempt to survey any movement in the warehouse. If this was a sting operation and the drugs had been discovered, he knew this was the time he had to be ready if there was to be any chance of escape.

'Is your transportation ready?' the man asked, without bothering to turn his head and check for any parked vehicles.

'Yeah, a van in the bay down there,' Scott said and pointed, unobserved.

'OK I'll have them brought over for you to load up,' he said, tapping a few more keys which resulted in a printed receipt spilling out onto the desk in front of him. 'Sign here,' he indicated, after ripping the receipt free from the printer. Scott duly signed the name that matched his ID, wondering if the slight tremor in his hand had been noticeable. He took a copy along with his ID card and nervously made his way back to the van.

A brief red arc shone in the gloom of the doorway as Twinkle flicked away his cigarette butt which extinguished in the water outside.

'Are we good?' Twinkle asked as Scott approached.

'Seem to be,' Scott said and heard a whine behind him as a fork lift moved into position in front of a pallet, then a hydraulic whir as the pallet was lifted. He opened the back of the van and waited as their shipment approached. Again he checked the exit for the presence of any vehicles that may have contained watching police. The fork lift came to a halt just short of the van.

'You want the whole lot hoisted in now or you want to check through it first?' the driver asked.

'Just stick it in there man. If anything's missing it's

somebody else's problem, you know what I mean?' Scott said with a grin, pleased with his improvisation.

The driver laughed and nodded; a few seconds later it was all loaded up and Scott quickly closed the rear doors. Twinkle glanced from Scott to the driver and back again as if unsure that the job was actually finished. Scott understood his feeling, as it did seem to have been too easy. He thanked the man again and motioned for Twinkle to get back in the van.

Scott's heart was hammering in his chest as he tried to slide in the ignition key and missed, the key slipping against the plastic steering column. He cursed, and looking down, tried again. This time sliding into the ignition barrel, Scott turned the key and fired up the engine. Twinkle was beaming and talking excitedly like they were already free and clear, his fingers drumming rhythmically on the dashboard. Scott checked the mirrors and craned his neck around to survey as much of the warehouse and the road outside as possible. As satisfied as he could be that there was no obvious trap about to spring, he reversed the van out of the parking bay and turned towards the doorway out of the warehouse. Moving off slowly, Scott drove through the pooled water and back along the access road for the storage stations. As they passed by some stacked metal shipping containers, an unmarked white van with its headlights on became visible up ahead. It edged slowly through the main gate and stopped just inside, blocking the only exit road out of the docks. Twinkle fell silent, as if only now becoming aware of the possible threat they still faced.

'Fuck,' he said, regaining his power of speech and anxiously looking from side to side to see any other possible police vehicles. 'Fuck.'

Scott held the rising feeling of panic at bay. 'Stay calm, it's just a van.'

'Just a van that's stopped right in our path out of here, Jesus. What the fuck are we doing? Ten grand each and we could be facing ten years in jail? Fuck me.'

Scott tried to block out Twinkle's anguished cries and swallow the growing panic within himself. He proceeded slowly towards the main gate and what he hoped would be their continued freedom. Still there was no sign of movement from the other van. The rain continued to fall and even with the wipers on high speed, visibility was poor. Scott could make out a shape in the driver's seat but couldn't be sure of any other occupants. They were within fifty yards of the gate now and having thought of nothing else, Scott flashed the vehicle's main beam twice.

The stationary van began to move slowly away from the gate. Scott edged them forward again and as they approached the other vehicle, they could see the solitary driver bent over what looked to be the illuminated screen of a mobile phone.

'Fuck, it was just some bloke sending a text message,' Twinkle said, although he still didn't sound like he could quite believe it. 'Go Scott, get the fuck out of here.'

Needing no further encouragement Scott accelerated through the gate and beyond. Overhead streetlights illuminated the wet road and reflected up in a pink glow. Scott navigated the first few turns without thinking too clearly about where he was going. He regained some composure and began checking and rechecking the mirrors to make certain they weren't being followed and tried to recall the *escape route* as Twinkle had called it. Taking the next left onto Freemont, he turned the van in the direction of the highway, and only then did the frantic jackhammer beating of his heart begin to gradually subside.

Twinkle was still shaken, spinning left and right in his seat and staring intently at every vehicle they passed by. Eyes pinned wide in a state of alarm, he muttered to himself constantly as they drove.

'Twink, calm down,' Scott said, trying to keep his voice level. 'If any feds go by, you looking like that is gonna get us pulled over, even if they don't know anything.'

Twinkle sat back, his knuckles white where his hands gripped the seat either side of his legs but he continued muttering. Doing his best to ignore the distraction, Scott took the turning onto the highway heading north.

'They'll make hundreds of thousands out of what's in there,' Twinkle said; his tension seemed to have subsided enough to allow him to speak.

'Probably, yeah.'

'It's not right man. We took all the risk and all we get is 10K each?'

'That was the agreement.'

'Fuck the agreement. I'm getting on in years, Scott,' Twinkle said, his voice sounding shaky and brittle. 'The ten grand isn't gonna last me long. What then, more of this?'

'This was your gig Twinkle. You asked me to come along. If you're getting cold feet now then take your pay and go do something else.'

'Do what? All I've ever done is be a fuckin' drug dealer. I don't want to die in jail. Scott there's hundreds of thousands worth of cocaine right in our possession, right there,' he said, looking over his shoulder. 'I know people down South who could move this, no problem. No need to get anyone up here involved. We can make the sale then vanish forever.'

For a brief second the thought grew wings and flew through Scott's mind like a bat at midnight. 'No way Twink', he said, struggling against the temptation. 'You know they'd never stop until they found us. No amount of money is worth getting killed for, and you know it would be anything but painless.' Scott fixed his gaze on the road ahead. He didn't like the new direction the day was turning in. This definitely wasn't a possible outcome he had anticipated.

'I can't do this without you Scott. With that kind of cash we could disappear and never be found.'

'Shut the fuck up Twinkle. I said no. Under no

circumstances are you gonna make me think this is a good idea. We deliver the van, get paid then go. That's it.'

Twinkle fell silent again. Resigned to a success he had dreamed of that morning, but one which now didn't seem so sweet.

Scott indicated and steered the van off the highway, continuing to check in his mirrors for anyone who could be following them. Making two complete circuits of the roundabout, Scott satisfied himself that there were no pursuers and turned onto an unlit side road that led to the location where they were to make the delivery. Twinkle's silence continued – intensified. Perhaps realising the magnitude of what he had tried to coerce Scott into doing. Whether the stupidity of his request had sunk in, or the futility in continuing to try, Scott didn't know, but he half wished Twinkle would say something to relieve the tension which now hung in the van like thick fog.

'Almost there man,' Scott said, trying to lift the mood. He didn't want anyone detecting that something was wrong when they delivered the cocaine, or they might very well insist on knowing what it was and that wasn't a situation Scott wanted to get into.

The road wound along for a couple of miles without any traffic passing by, nothing but fields on either side marking their progress from the highway. Scott could see the logic in arranging for the drop off to happen out here. There was no way anyone could follow them from the ground without easily being spotted.

The van crested a slope in the road and the collection of buildings appeared up ahead. They looked like they had probably once been used for storage for either crops or farm machinery. Built from a combination of stone and corrugated iron, they now looked unused and dilapidated. The foundations of the building constructed mostly from old stone had subsided into the earth on one side, giving it the appearance of casually leaning as if waiting lackadaisically for a particular event to unfold.

Scott turned off the road and killed the headlights. The rain had relented now into a fine drizzle. The wipers continued to pulse their rhythmic beat. Muddy pools were scattered around below them on the uneven ground. There were two cars parked behind one of the buildings, out of sight from the road. Pulling up alongside them, Scott gave Twinkle what he hoped was a reassuring look and then turned off the engine and got out.

A wooden door stood open in front of the parked cars and he could see a dim light from within. Unsure of what else he should do, Scott slowly advanced towards the doorway. A metallic bang from behind made Scott's frayed nerves sing, but a quick look showed it was just Twinkle slamming the van door.

The inside of the building smelt of wet straw and rot. Scott could just make out Dominic Parish and another equally large individual, whom he didn't recognise, illuminated by a battery powered lantern hung on the wall behind them. The bluish white glare glinted off the man's earlobe from what Scott guessed must have been a diamond stud earring. Nobody spoke until Twinkle entered the building too, then Dominic gestured for him to close the door. Scott's heart was hammering in his chest again; he tried to slow his breathing and appear as calm and confident as he could.

'It done?' Dominic asked. His voice split the silence like an axe.

'Yeah,' Scott answered, even though the question had been aimed at Twinkle.

'Any problems?' This time he focused on Scott and directed the question at him.

'No,' Scott said, hoping he sounded convincing.

'Alright then. Keys,' Dominic said and held out a hand. Scott took the door key Twinkle had first been given, added the ignition key and dropped them both into the giant outstretched palm.

'Here,' Dominic barked after pocketing both of the keys from Scott, and held out a different car key. 'That's for the blue Mazda parked outside. You drive back to town and leave it where you got the van from. Put your ID cards and papers in the glove box. Lock the doors and put the key under the seat. Twinkle, someone will contact you.' With that Dominic walked towards the door. His silent companion collected the lantern and walked past Scott to follow.

'What about our money?' Twinkle asked, his voice sounding thin and weak compared to Dominic's authoritative bellow. The previously silent character now laughed. The first noise he'd made since they arrived; tiny triangles of light danced from his ear.

'Like I say Twinkle, someone will be in touch. You really think we'd turn up here with twenty thousand not knowing if anyone dressed in blue was along for the ride? No. Everything will be inspected and then you'll be paid,' Dominic said in the patronising tone of one explaining something to a small child.

After that, they both left. The sound of the two engines starting up as Scott and Twinkle remained rooted in the darkness. They heard the car and van reverse up, then drive out onto the road and away.

'We should go,' Scott said. Twinkle didn't respond but Scott heard him follow as he made his own way back outside.

Scott opened the unlocked door and climbed into the driver's seat of the Mazda. Twinkle was a few paces behind and Scott watched him approach the car on unsteady legs. His face was pallid and older than Scott had seen it look before. The craggy lines that made up the character in his face now seemed like scars of defeat, inflicted on him over time.

The car started with one turn of the key and a few minutes later they were back on the road towards the highway, this time headed for home.

'We didn't get paid right away but everything went OK.' Scott said, attempting to put a positive slant on the outcome, and reached to turn on the car radio; anything rather than the oppressive silence. He tried a few more attempts to engage Twinkle in light conversation on the journey back but each was greeted only by mumbled acknowledgement that he'd even been heard.

'You want dropping off at home then Twink? I can take the car back on my own and go grab a cab after that.'

'No, just drop me at the Balloon.' The first words he'd uttered since they got in the car.

'You sure? It's been a long day, you not rather get a few cans and just drink them in the house?'

'The Balloon.'

Scott was a little unnerved. He knew Twinkle would be drinking like there was no tomorrow to try and escape the events of the day. Scott didn't care one way or the other if the old man woke up in a ditch. But he didn't want him saying anything stupid to some local scumbags after having a skin full that could jeopardise him as well. Reluctantly accepting there wasn't anything he could do to prevent this, he agreed.

Twinkle got out of the car outside of The Balloon, bringing Scott's day full circle. He said he'd phone once there'd been word of the next meeting. Scott nodded, shifted the car into gear and drove off.

Chapter 8

Scott woke suddenly the next morning sheathed in a cold sweat. After a few seconds he realised the combined ringing and vibrating of his mobile phone on the thin carpet beneath the bed was the cause of his alarm. It was Angela, who told him that Stephanie had woken up. She sounded tired but excited, although she said there was no new information on the attack. After promising to come up to the hospital and see her as soon as he could, Scott hung up the phone.

He hadn't had much sleep. Thoughts of Twinkle inadvertently giving them both up plagued him throughout the night, and now, despite not having had anything to drink himself, he had woken with what felt like a hangover, probably attributed to fatigue.

Scott made coffee and fed Boris while his computer was booting up. He sat down to enjoy his coffee and inhaled greedily from the first cigarette of the day, as he sifted through emails to work out which jobs needed his attention first. Despite the intake of caffeine and nicotine he couldn't keep his attention focused for long. The images and words on the screen floated around like driftwood caught in the pull of a tide.

Deciding to try and tackle his work load again later, Scott thought he would keep his promise to Angela and go up to the hospital to see her and Stephanie.

He let the dog run around out back while taking a shower, phoned for a taxi to arrive in twenty minutes from Pressman cabs and then made a sandwich while waiting for it to arrive.

Halfway through eating his hurriedly made snack Scott heard two quick blasts on a car horn from the front of the house. He threw the remainder of the sandwich to Boris, grabbed his things and left.

Climbing into the familiar sweaty menthol atmosphere of the cab, Scott saw the driver was Reg, greeted him with a quick hello and told him their destination. Reg nodded and eased the car back out onto the road.

'No call the other night, so I guess you had a good time,' Reg said, grinning at Scott through the rear view mirror.

'You got it Reg,' Scott said, and smiled hoping this would suffice. He knew by trying to deny Reg's suspicions he'd be caught up in a cat and mouse conversation for the whole trip that he really couldn't be bothered with. This way he could just sit back and give the occasional nod or grin to whatever playful interrogation the old man threw his way. More concerned with wheedling details of Scott's love life, the inquisitive driver missed the opportunity to ask the reason for his visit to the hospital.

By the time they pulled up in front of the hospital, Reg's curiosity had seemingly been satiated, and he even turned away Scott's offer of a tip.

'You keep it for your lady friend, Scott. Get her a nice bunch of flowers.'

'OK, thanks Reg,' Scott said, and climbed out of the cab.

Inadvertently taking Reg's advice, Scott stopped off in the hospital gift shop and bought flowers to hand in at Stephanie's room. The gift shop, it would appear, like the rest of the hospital was decorated sparsely with what attempted to be tasteful but inoffensive Christmas decorations. To Scott they seemed to say 'Try to smile and enjoy the season, but let's not take the piss now, people are still dying in here.' He smiled cynically while waiting in line at the checkout and wondered if Angela had shared a similar thought. Probably not, after all, until a few hours ago her friend may have been one of the ones dying. Having no idea what to get, he had selected a moderately priced bunch of varied colours, and asked for a couple of packs of cigarettes while he was at the checkout. The woman gave him the generic *thank you come again* smile and handed Scott his change.

Scott strode towards the lifts wielding the flowers like a sword. The third floor, ward nine, Angela had told him. He squeezed into the first available lift along with a blur of white coats and other visitors. Somebody pressed for his floor so Scott just waited, doing his best to protect the already partly squashed flowers he held on to.

At the third floor, he extricated himself from the lift as best he could and began reading the directions on the sign opposite when he heard his name called. Turning, he saw Angela drinking a vending machine coffee and made his way over. She was still here, keeping watch over a friend whom she had hardly been in touch with for years. Scott wondered if there was anyone in his life that would bring out such devoted conviction in him.

'How is she now?'

'Better, the Doctors say she's stable and they're just monitoring her now. She hasn't said anything about the attack though, just that someone must have jumped her from behind and that's all she knows.'

'Will they be keeping her in much longer?'

'If she continues to recover without any complications they say she should be out in three days.'

'Christmas Eve.'

'Yeah, I didn't expect you to be keeping track though,' Angela said, grinning.

'One is without transport, so one needs to keep tabs on the bus schedules,' he said in mock indignation, broadening Angela's grin into a smile.

'She's awake if you'd like to go in,' Angela said, and swept her hair back over her shoulder. Scott caught a glimpse of her right ear which now held a third silver hoop.

For a second Scott wasn't sure what she meant until her eyes drifted from his face to the flowers he was still holding.

'Right – yeah, OK.'

Angela led the way back onto the ward. Scott followed, avoiding looking through any of the windows onto the rooms they passed. Sick people made him uncomfortable. He never knew how he should act around them and found it difficult to shake the mocking guilt of his own good health.

'The new earring is nice, you just get it done?'

'Oh, yeah just recently.'

'How many more do you plan on getting?'

'I'm really hoping this will be my last one.'

Pushing open a door Angela stepped into a small room with only one bed; most of the others in the ward had been six beds to a room. The curtains were partially closed restricting the amount of light inside. Walking in, Scott was overwhelmed by the smell of antiseptic and bandages.

'You want me to open these now?' Angela asked in an upbeat tone, walking towards the window.

'No, leave them,' Stephanie said, through swollen lips. Her mouth and one bruised and swollen eye were all that was visible of her face, the rest wrapped tightly in fresh white bandages.

'Ahh, are you OK then Steph?' Scott asked. A stupid question he thought, but didn't know what else he should say. He passed the bunch of flowers from hand to hand, uneasily. Her attention shifted from Angela by the window and she turned her one uncovered eye in his direction.

'I'll just peachy.' She said stiffly.

Angela came and took the flowers from Scott and busied herself filling a vase with water from a tap over the sink and arranging them.

'Good to hear you'll be out for Christmas then,' he said, trying to adopt the same upbeat tone Angela had used when they'd first entered.

'I can't wait.'

'OK well I might go and leave you both to talk. Nice to see you, Steph,' he said and backed out of the room. Angela caught up with him halfway down the corridor.

'She's still pretty messed up by it all,' Angela said almost apologetically, as she pulled on Scott's sleeve to make him turn around.

'Yeah of course. I just stopped by to say hello, anyway. Call me later?'

She nodded and smiled.

After getting home and discovering he still couldn't focus on any work, Scott made more sandwiches, wrapped them and threw them and a Coke into a bag. Slinging the bag over his shoulder he whistled for the dog and left by the back door. The afternoon was grey but not too cold. Scott zipped up his coat as a precaution against a breeze that made the patches of wild grass nod as if in agreement.

Having watched as the sandwiches were made and then placed in the bag, Boris wasn't straying too far ahead this time. He was following his usual sniff then urinate routine, but kept trotting back to see if anything tasty was yet on offer.

Cupping a hand to shield the flame from another gust of wind, Scott lit up a cigarette, then as an afterthought decided to turn off his phone. Maybe all he needed was some uninterrupted pressure free time and some fresh air to get his head together. Thoughts of Twinkle's impending call haunted both his days and nights giving him little rest. This afternoon he would push all of that to one side. If he called then so what? Let him call back later.

Right now Scott felt directionless. He'd had the bus dream again last night, memories of it returned to him now as he walked. Although he didn't dream too often, or at least didn't remember them if he did, Scott tried to pay attention to anything he remembered the following morning. This was a recurring dream he'd had from time to time over the years. The location would often change but the main elements remained the same. He'd be riding a bus, always sat on the upstairs deck, and to begin with everything would be fine. After a while it would become clear that the bus was increasingly travelling too fast. When he would try to alert the driver, the bus would accelerate even more, tipping dangerously as it attempted to turn corners, further heightening Scott's anxiety. Sometimes the scenery passing by would be familiar: his old school bus journey, a route he'd travelled years before to an old girlfriend's house. But mostly it was just generic dream landscape, the feeling of familiarity without actually recognising the setting. Sometimes there'd be other people on the bus that he knew. They would look at him but never speak. Paige travelled with him on occasion, often sat next to one or another of his regular customers. No matter how hard he would try, Scott would never be able to get off the bus, make it slow down, or even see the face of the driver.

Trying to push it all out of his mind again, he looked up to locate Boris and found the dog had led them on their usual route and was now already stationed by the Elephant Tree waiting for Scott to catch up.

Sitting down on the fallen trunk Scott took out the sandwiches. The crinkle of cellophane and the smell of the freshly cut sandwiches unearthed memories of his mother. A day when they were children, Scott, Jack and their mother picnicking here, perhaps. Memories of his parents, his mother especially, came as fleetingly as dream fragments, like the sudden flight of a bird at the end of a long corridor, by the time he turned to look it was gone. Sometimes it got hard to distinguish memory from fantasy. When he was still a child,

Scott would often lie awake at night imagining them all still together as a family, visiting places they had never been. Happy. He knew not all returning memories could be trusted, but fictional or not he would savour whatever he could.

Taking a sandwich from the pile he tore it and tossed one half to Boris. The dog caught it in mid air and devoured it greedily, almost as if Scott might realise he had made a mistake and take it away from him. Chewing thoughtfully on his half, Scott looked up into the thicker grey clouds now gathering like dense flocks of migrating birds. The temperature had begun to drop and there was probably only around an hour of light left in the day.

So far he'd avoided looking at the face in the tree. His uncle had looked to it for wisdom and guidance, but often all Scott felt was judgement and malice. He knew this was more down to his own mood at the time, but some days it was harder to convince himself than others. He felt watched, like the eyes of a painting that would follow you around the room. Eventually he gave in and looked up at the face and was met with the unshakable feeling of making eye contact with a stranger. He shivered. From the angle he sat at, it was mostly the elephant side he could see. Scott stood and slowly walked around watching the face change. The appearance of deep lines in its apparent skin caused by the formation and growth of tree bark. The deep recess of an eye socket. The trunk, one of many large branches to have been cut off long before Scott's time here. He kept moving around. The ridge slanted away on the far side of the trunk then curved upwards into a lump that looked like the definition of a human cheekbone. Below that a slight rise before dropping away into a hollow shaped distinctly like a mouth. Minimal light now with the amalgamation of large rain clouds overhead. The more Scott moved around the tree, the more the mouth appeared to be twisted into a vicious sneer, the eye above the cheekbone pulled back into a squinted look of contempt.

Scott took a step back. The unmistakable feeling of scorn, bitterness and loathing ran through him. A sudden rumble of thunder overhead took him by surprise and he barely stifled a cry. Boris, equally alarmed, began a succession of panicked barking. Raindrops began to fall all around them as the blanket covering of clouds commenced a shedding of their load. The rainwater released a fresh green scent as it permeated the surrounding fir trees. The feeling that had previously inhabited Scott had now passed.

He halved the last sandwich with Boris and picked up his bag, cursing the weather for ruining what he'd hoped would have been a peaceful afternoon out, and started back towards the house.

Having resigned himself to a soaking, Scott plodded back with little urgency. As he climbed over the wooden stile at the bottom of the land he was reminded of his phone as it pressed insistently against his ribs from his inside jacket pocket. Scott reached for it and turned it back on. No messages.

The last Friday before Christmas, Scott had been told by Jack years before, was known in the industry as *Black Eye Friday*. The office blocks and other businesses generally broke up for the holidays at midday, their staff spilling out onto the streets and inevitably into the bars like excited children who have a whole summer of no school to look forward to. They generally tended to be the folk who would enjoy the odd weekend night out, not the kind of people accustomed to all day drinking benders. So when alcohol consumption started at twelve noon instead of eight at night, the consequences tended to be fairly predictable and often disastrous.

For Scott and Neil it had become something of a ritual for them to hit the town early and enjoy, for Scott at least, what was probably the best part of the holiday season seeing alcohol-crazed white-collar workers beat the shit out of each other, or even being thrown down a flight of stairs by overly stressed doormen, in the past had been enough to put a smile on his face. But this year because of the party they'd thrown last weekend, half the population of the bars they frequented had heard about it and subsequently all wanted invites to this week's event. Having repeated the same thing dozens of times already, that the party was a one off and no, there wasn't a repeat this weekend, Scott was quickly tiring of the whole affair. Keeping the customers placated was bad enough, but Neil was still convinced that laying on a regular venue could be the future for them, and no amount of dissuasive comments from Scott were about to change his mind.

After giving explicit instructions to Neil to continue fending off party requests and to sell as much gear as he could before they hit the club, Scott decided he would have a few drinks in a more sedate environment and meet back up inside Blitz later.

John Henry's was a depressing place most of the time, but Scott at least knew he wouldn't be plagued by the customers like he had been at every stop on their usual route. Right now a few quiet drinks and to blend into the background was what Scott felt he needed.

The bar looked pretty much exactly as he'd left it on his last visit. There were more bodies now, but he recognised many of same faces in the same seats from earlier in the week. Scott went to the bar, he didn't see Joanne so ordered a pint from the first barmaid he could flag down, and lit a cigarette while he waited.

'I'll get that for you,' a voice he didn't immediately recognise said from behind him. Scott looked over his shoulder and was surprised to see Twinkle.

'Twink,' Scott said with a thin smile. He hadn't heard anything since the job so didn't know of any possible developments either good or bad, and naturally felt a little suspicious. 'I didn't realise it was you.'

Twinkle pushed in beside him at the bar and catching the barmaid's attention got her to pull another pint to go with Scott's, then paid for both.

Picking up their drinks, they saw a table just being vacated by three old men, and went to sit down.

'There been any word yet then?' Scott asked.

'No, nothing yet but I expect the call will come through tomorrow.'

Scott stubbed out his cigarette and swallowed a mouthful from his pint. After the mood Twinkle had been in following the job, Scott had expected a more low profile approach and for him to avoid the city and stay drinking locally. Watching Twinkle over the rim of his glass though, he seemed to have recovered from the crisis of confidence he'd suffered during the job and everything that followed after.

'You stay out for long after I dropped you off last night?' Scott asked tentatively.

'Yeah, I was in there 'till closing, then on the cans back home after that. I must've fallen over trying to get upstairs or something,' he said, lifting a handful of hair away from his temple revealing an angry purple bruise the size of a tomato.

Scott took another drink from his glass and looked at the wound, allowing Twinkle time to continue with his story. This was pretty much what he'd expected to hear, but was more concerned with what might have been said in the bar rather than any injuries Twinkle had sustained through the subsequent drunkenness.

Twinkle took a drink also, and moved his hand up to reflectively run fingers over the damaged flesh, leaving his story hanging.

'Did you bump into anyone or talk to anyone while you were out then?' Scott asked, prompting him.

Twinkle snapped back from whatever drunken nostalgia he'd been reliving and his hand fell from his temple sharply onto the table. 'No Scott, I didn't talk to anyone. Jesus, is that why you're here now? To see if I've been saying shit that could put you at risk?'

'No, that's not it,' Scott said, trying to regain control of the conversation, as he glanced cautiously around. 'I didn't even know you'd be in here, I just came in for a change of scene.'

Twinkle appeared to relax and gave a shrug. 'I know I was a bit out of it then, Scott, but I didn't talk to anyone that night. After I woke up this morning at the bottom of the stairs like that, and then remembering everything from yesterday I knew it was time to at least try and make a change.'

'So you what, joined the Red Cross?' Scott asked sarcastically.

'No, fuck off. I phoned Sharon.'

Scott was more surprised by this than if Twinkle had taken on voluntary work for a charity organisation. Any time her name was mentioned Twinkle would curse at any involvement they'd ever had together and reiterate his vow never to speak to *that bitch* ever again.

'What happened then, did it go OK?'

'Yeah it did. I told her that I wanted to kick the drink and to start over, fresh, hopefully with her and the kids.'

'Just like that?'

'Well no, not right away or anything, she doubted I meant any of it which is understandable, but I kept going and must have said some stuff that hit home 'cause eventually she started to listen to me. She said I could come and see them on weekends and stuff to begin with, see how we go. Probably to make sure I'm really not gonna be drinking and taking shit at clubs, that'll be why she said weekends, but that's fair enough. I reckon I have a chance to start again now Scott, I have to do this.'

'You know where they are then?'

'Yeah I always knew. I stayed in touch every once in a while, birthdays for the kids and that.'

This surprised Scott as well. Twinkle had always claimed to maintain a zero contact policy since she had taken the kids and moved out. At least that's what he had always had his friends believe.

'That's really great Twink, it is. But what about this meeting we've got coming up and commitments that are gonna follow on from it?'

'I know it was me got you involved but I just can't go through with any more. I'm sorry Scott but that's the way it is.'

'I understand that, but it's not me you need to convince.'

'Yeah, well I'll just try and explain it the way I have to you, and if the worst comes to the worst and I have to walk away without any pay then I'll do that,' Twinkle said, and looked up from his pint meeting Scott's eye. At that moment Scott realised why he hadn't recognised Twinkle when he first spoke at the bar, what it was in his voice that had made him sound so different. It was hope.

Scott arrived at the club before Neil. He did a quick walkthrough then settled down with a Budweiser and cigarette to wait.

After a while, vibration from a pocket pulled Scott back from thoughts about his conversation with Twinkle. He'd said he was going home after drinks at John Henry's. No clubbing, maybe he would manage to turn his life around.

Scott pulled out his phone and checked the screen before answering. Withheld Number. That didn't mean anything. People would withhold their identity when phoning a drug dealer even if the call was innocent. Scott answered and said hello. The music around the club was loud and Scott could hear nothing from the phone. Again he said hello, and told whoever was on the other end to speak up but the connection was terminated.

Sliding the phone back into his pocket he caught sight of Neil sauntering into the club, tonight with a brunette on his arm making their way towards the upstairs bar. Her hips oscillated as she walked, as if the worn out carpet in the club were a Milan catwalk.

Scott pushed in beside Neil at the bar, changed his order for one bottle of Becks to two and introduced himself to the brunette.

'Hello, I'm Elizabeth Flight,' she said, extending a limp hand towards Scott. The way she said her name made it sound like it should be followed by an exclamation mark. Like you'd just heard something important, something you should store away in a deep recess of your brain. Scott wasn't used to surnames. Most people he came across gave either only a first name or a nickname. When he met someone else with the same first name as someone else he knew, he would mentally assign them a number. Micky Two or Tony Three. Scott took a moment to appraise the latest addition to Neil's long list of concubines. She had a haughty smile that was accentuated by the elevated lift of her chin, giving her the appearance of looking down on everyone despite her average height. Black leather boots and a tight fitting short black dress were undoubtedly what first made her pop up on Neil's radar. She was OK looking without ever being in danger of real beauty, but the way she carried herself made you wonder if perhaps there was something there you had missed at first glance.

The barman placed both bottles of Becks and a cocktail for Elizabeth on the bar and took the note Neil held out to him.

'Custom good then?' Scott leaned in and asked Neil.

'Yeah pretty decent. Should get everything else moved in here before long, and no, I haven't invited anyone back for a party,' he said, grinning.

* * *

Saturday morning Scott was woken again by the sound of his phone. He cursed himself for having again forgotten to switch it to silent as he reached down to pick it up. Hoping to hear Angela answer him, he pressed green and said hello without checking caller ID. He waited a few seconds as his brain emerged reluctantly from the fog of sleep, and then said hello again. Nothing. Could he hear faint breathing this time on the other end of the line? He wasn't sure, but it was too early for games so he looked at the screen then hung up. Another withheld number.

Daylight violated the bedroom through the un-curtained window. Scott vowed to fix the pole later in the day, picked up his cigarettes and went into the kitchen to make coffee.

Steam from the kettle fogged the cold kitchen window. Like a child, Scott leaned across and wrote his name on the glass, and then unconsciously wrote Angela underneath.

She had promised to call yesterday but maybe she'd just been busy at the hospital or Christmas shopping. Besides, he had a load of work to finish up at home and email through to the office, which he really should have completed yesterday, so even if she called he wouldn't be able to take time out to see her anyway.

He rubbed out the names and poured boiling water into his cup.

About six hours later Scott was putting the finishing touches to his design work when the phone rang again. He checked the caller ID before answering, and saw Jack flash up on the screen.

'Almost finished, I'll have them emailed within a half hour,' Scott said as he answered the phone.

'What? Oh, right. Listen, I want you to come and see me today.'

'It's after three now and I have at least an hour more work to finish up here, so I don't think so, Jack.'

'I thought you said you'd email them to the office in a half hour.'

'Yeah well, creative timekeeping. Can't it wait 'till tomorrow?'

'Just come to the club tonight instead. I have a meeting

before my shift this evening but I'd like to see you,' Jack said, sounding a little anxious, Scott thought, which was unlike him. He usually carried the demeanour of someone who had ice water instead of blood running through his veins.

'OK I'll try.'

'And Scott.'

'Yeah'

'By yourself and don't bring anything, understand?'

'For fuck's sake, OK,' Scott said, angrily, and hung up the phone. Jack had a knack of making him feel like a child again, of being able to get what he wanted without any obvious signs of coercion.

It was past five when he finally finished up and emailed his work to the Zebra office. He took a shower to freshen up and heard Boris's excited barking and galloping up and down the hallway, usually a sign someone was at the front door. Judging by the time it would probably be Neil to sort out that night's supply; let him wait, Scott thought, and finished his shower.

Ten minutes later, with a towel around his waist, Scott trudged to the front door and opened it. Neil was sitting of the bonnet of his Hyundai smoking a cigarette, with one foot on the bumper and one on the floor.

Scott turned and went back inside as Neil hopped up off the car and followed.

'Last club night before the holidays', Neil said brightly. 'You think we should take more stuff?'

'I dunno, maybe.'

'You have everything ready or should I bag up while you get dressed?'

'I haven't started yet, so help yourself. Listen, I have to go and see Jack at Aura later tonight. I'll come round the bars with you first but will you be OK to do Blitz on your own?'

'Don't worry about it I'll handle the bars as well. You just take the night off. Elizabeth will get a kick out of seeing me fly solo anyway,' he said, grinning.

'So you're keeping her for a while then?' Scott asked. His initial impression of Elizabeth hadn't left a pleasant taste in his mouth, but he had enough going on without poking his nose into Neil's business as well.

'Yeah. Great body, she has her own place, and she's filthy,' he said with the broad smile of someone who knows. 'All boxes ticked.'

Later as Scott made his way to Aura, large snowflakes began to fall and settle on the city streets. Any evidence of yesterday's rainfall was gone and the cold dry ground provided the perfect canvas for the snow's seasonal decoration.

Two streets later and passing cars had turned the thin covering of snow to slush on the roads, taxis whispered past over the wet tarmac, reflecting the garish neon glare of Christmas lights hanging down from above.

He turned the corner and saw the queue for admittance was already lined up down the block. Scott zipped up his jacket and headed towards the entrance. The club's name was inset into blocks of stone over the doorway. Down either side, intricate pillars designed in similar fashion gave the entranceway the appearance of having been carved into a cliff face.

As Scott stepped over the red rope and approached the door, a square shaped man in a tuxedo held out a palm towards him the size of a side of ham, and simply said 'no'. Scott looked up at the doorman and didn't recognise him from previous visits to the club. Scott knew he didn't meet the dress code for a place like this, and he certainly wasn't waiting over an hour for admittance in the burgeoning queue that had already formed anyway. Another doorman made his way down the steps as Scott was thinking up the quickest way to explain himself inside.

'Hello Scott.'

Scott didn't recognise the voice and looked in the direction of its owner. A sharp glint reflecting from his earlobe immediately caught Scott's eye and identified its owner. The same face he'd seen after the job with Twinkle.

'I'm just here to see Jack,' Scott said, wanting to offer up nothing more.

'OK, in you come.'

The doorman who'd first obstructed Scott moved to begin a pat down, but was told by the other man to let him past.

Scott walked past avoiding any eye contact. He felt a little shaken and his legs were numb from cold and the sudden shock of seeing the man again.

Inside he followed the wide carpeted corridor towards the heart of the club; the deep bass that travelled down here from the three rooms of dance music sounded muffled and disjointed, like the sound on a plane at high altitude right before your ears pop.

The doors opened out onto a huge room the shape of a goldfish bowl. The centrepiece was a large circular dance floor that was packed with clubbers and slowly revolved; flooded with atmospheric smoke and illuminated by an impressive array of spotlights and lasers constantly changing in both direction and colour in time with the music. Surrounding it were two outer levels, each elevated slightly higher than the last that were almost as busy as the dance floor. People gathered, talking and drinking in standing areas interspersed with large reflective columns, or sat at tabled areas in large upholstered armchairs and couches. Three bars evenly spaced around the outside were warmly lit and staffed by people Scott would have expected to see draped over food processors or golf clubs on cheesy TV game shows, with their bronzed skin and fixed air hostess smiles. Four podiums were situated between the tabled areas and dance floor, three containing gyrating dancers, both male and female and the last, just a bit higher again, for posterity Scott assumed, contained the deejay booth.

Scott made his way to the bar and ordered two Southern Comfort and cokes with no ice. The barman tried unsuccessfully to disguise his disdainful look at Scott's wardrobe selection; perhaps assuming him to be a VIP he repositioned his serving smile and fetched the drinks without comment.

Scott took a sip from his glass while walking up to the deejay booth. Four columns of smoke simultaneously billowed down onto the dance floor and expanded out like inverted mushroom clouds, as the throbbing bass and pulsing lights slowed down. Looking up at the deejay booth Scott could see the fixed look of concentration on his brother's face. His hands moved over buttons on the various CD players and computerised mixing equipment in front of him as the music tempo began to increase. The thunderous bassline slowly returned and the congregation of clubbers on the dance floor again began to move in time. The beat picked up speed and the bass volume crescendoed to an almost deafening level before it broke back down again and the vocals flooded out, causing cheers from all around the club for Jack's atmospheric manipulation.

Jack was accompanied by two girls Scott guessed at being barely of legal age for admittance. Seeing Scott approach, Jack leaned in to whisper to them both and patted each on the ass as they vacated the booth.

'Very smooth,' Scott said, trying not to sound too sarcastic. He didn't want to start with any pointless bickering.

Jack ignored the comment. Scott handed him the other glass which his brother accepted, placed in front of him and nodded.

'Have you made plans for Christmas then?' Scott asked, figuring he may as well start the conversation.

Jack pressed some more buttons on the equipment mixing in the next track, and didn't acknowledge he'd heard the question.

'I warned you to stay away from them Scott,' Jack said finally, leaning towards his brother over the edge of the deejay booth. His voice had taken on the same parental tone he'd used on the phone earlier, and having him now looming down towards Scott was too much for him to take.

'Back off Jack. You're not dad,' Scott snapped. 'You can give me all the advice you want, but whether I choose to follow it or not is up to me.'

Jack turned back to the mixing equipment, preparing the next track to be woven into place. Scott figured he was using this as an excuse to carefully select his next words. Jack didn't like being spoken to aggressively like Scott had just done, but he was clever enough not to retaliate in a like manner and further antagonise the situation. Scott could see Jack's analytical mind processing the various outcomes of the conversation and discarding them one by one until he had settled on a course of action that would result in things best going his way. Scott thought it best to interrupt before Jack regained momentum.

'You remember that time as kids, mum and dad took us to that fairground?' Scott asked.

'Remind me.'

'We went on different rides and stuff, but I could only go on the little kid rides cause I wasn't tall enough for the height restrictions on the good ones.'

A smile hinted at Jack's lips, which Scott took as a sign he remembered.

'Well there was that ghost house thing we went in. It was all dark corridors with stuff hanging down that would brush against your face, or guys working there putting their arms through holes in the walls and grabbing kids that walked past. A tape played with chains clanking and wailing and stuff.'

'Yeah I remember, so what?'

'Well just before the end there was the Frankenstein's

monster. A life size wax model or something, but it looked so real they had even put a cage around it. By the time we got round to it there were a bunch of kids gathered up peeking around the corner at the cage, nudging each other to go first but no-one would, they were terrified. You tried to calm them down, saying it wasn't real but they still wouldn't listen. We could see you were scared too but you walked out and stood still right up against the cage and called for everyone to run past behind you. They all ran as quick as they could and didn't look back, but I was still stood frozen at the corner.'

'I called out to you, I waited but you wouldn't come.'

'I know you did Jack, I'm not blaming you. Eventually you went through to the finish and I was still stood there on my own. I tried to go past but I just couldn't do it. I walked all the way back around the place and came out at the entrance. I saw all the kids talking excitedly to their parents about what was inside, and you were stood talking with mum and dad.'

'Jesus, Scott. You were a little kid, I'm four years older than you. You couldn't have been more than what, five at the time?'

'Yeah but that stayed with me for so long after. In my head it became like a pivotal moment in life that I'd failed at. You were the kid who went past, succeeded, but I turned back and failed.'

'You do know how ridiculous this sounds, right?'

'Maybe so, but now if I have a chance to do something, to walk past the Frankenstein cage even if I do feel scared, then I want to do it.'

'That was a dummy in a cage and any fear we felt was imagined, we were never in any danger. I don't know what you're talking about doing, but if you're scared then I would imagine there is a very real danger to go with it.'

'Either way, I'm not gonna sit around forever doing hand me down jobs from your design company and there's obviously no future in my other after hours activities.'

'If you're serious about wanting to step up to more responsibility then we can work that out,' Jack said, turning and really looking at Scott, for maybe the first time that night.

'I don't want to always be in your shadow, Jack. I appreciate the offer but I just want to make enough on my own to start over with a new life for myself.'

'That again. You can't run from yourself Scott. The one thing all your problems have in common is you.'

Scott laughed at this, it sounded like something Angela would have said. 'If there's nothing else then I'm gonna go,' Scott said, and finished the rest of his drink. 'I'll try to come down and see you at some point over Christmas. Take it easy, Jack.'

He turned to leave and saw the doorman with the diamond earring watching them from the other side of the club. 'Is the guy with the earring in here new?' Scott asked, turning back to face his brother.

'I've seen him on and off for a while,' Jack said, looking curiously at Scott. 'Why, do you know him?'

'No, he's maybe familiar but that's about it. Probably just someone else with an earring like that I'm thinking of,' Scott said, to stop any further questions.

Scott walked back across the club towards the exit. He glanced over in the direction the earring doorman had been standing at but he was already gone.

An attractive girl with long white-blonde hair, a low-cut black top and tight white shorts seemed to be fending off the advances of a young Asian man in a clean-cut suit and expensive looking jewellery. She pushed him gently out of her personal space and immediately he stepped in towards her, slid an arm around her back and leaned in for a kiss. This time she'd had enough, grabbed his arm from behind her and flung it off, put both hands against his chest and shoved as hard as she could. The man looked to have had a few drinks, which maybe impaired his balance, he stumbled back trying to stay upright and slammed hard into Scott just as he was trying to pass behind them; the man dropped his glass which shattered on the floor.

'What the fuck you doing, man?' he snarled at Scott, turning around to see what he'd collided against.

'Take it easy, you backed into me.'

'Bullshit, yeah? I was conversing with this lady here and you smashed right into me. Get me another fucking drink,' he said, pointing towards the shattered pieces of glass on the carpet.

'The bar's over there,' Scott said, pointing with his middle finger before pulling it up into a fuck you gesture.

The Asian grabbed two handfuls of Scott's jacket and tilted back his neck as if about to launch a head-butt at Scott. Before this could happen, the earring doorman grabbed him by the hair and threw a single short punch directly into the man's kidneys. The Asian gave a mangled cry and fell to his knees, the doorman preventing his fall any further by maintaining his grip on the man's hair. Another member of security came towards them and hauled off the Asian towards the exit by his collar.

'Sorry about that Miss,' said Earring to the blonde girl, whose startled look resembled a sex doll with her mouth shaped in a perfect O. 'Complimentary cocktail, just you head over there and see that barman,' he said, and pointed at the man who had served Scott earlier, who was looking over.

'I bet you're glad I was still close by,' He said, once the girl was out of earshot, looking decidedly pleased with himself as he smoothed imagined creases from his jacket.

'Nice place you have here,' Scott said, avoiding the question. 'I thought I was supposed to be the one who hung out in dives.'

'Sadiq there was a VIP, a rising star in the Garden Heights business community, a multi-millionaire already. If his altercation had been with pretty much anyone else in here you can be sure it would be them on the pavement now and not him. You're just lucky we have a special relationship.'

The tempo of the music increased and scarlet spotlights began to dance around the room. The doorman's skin and eyes shone with a malevolent red, earring sparkling furiously.

'Will you be there at the meeting?' Scott asked.

'We'll see.'

'Do you know when?'

'That's not for me to say.'

Obviously Scott wasn't going to get any information so he made to walk past the doorman towards the exit. The man reached out and held him lightly by the forearm.

'Are your habits going to be an issue like Twinkle or do you have things under control?'

Scott didn't know what he was talking about so just stood and looked at him, waiting for the question to be given further clarity.

He released Scott's arm, held his own forearm out and tapped three times in the crook of his elbow with two large forefingers. 'Your habit,' he said. 'Twinkle can be a bit excessive at times.'

'I don't have a habit,' Scott said. 'As far as I know neither does Twinkle.'

The man laughed and shook his head. 'Alright Scott,' he said, and held out a hand indicating that the conversation was over and Scott was free to leave.

Twinkle could be many things but Scott had no reason to suspect him of having a heroin addiction.

Before venturing back onto the street Scott quickly glanced around to make sure the lunatic from the club wasn't skulking in the shadows looking to avenge his bruised ego and kidneys. Reasonably satisfied that he could avoid being thrust into the public eye for a pointless fight with the Z list celebrity, he pulled out his phone to call Angela. She was pretty much the only thing that could persuade him not to just head home. After five rings it redirected to answer phone. Fuck it, Scott thought and called for a cab.

Chapter 9

S cott found the Christmas holidays a fairly depressing time and given the opportunity he tended to stay longer in bed. The whole season was geared up towards families which in his case just made him think of death. By the time he did surface and have a shower it was already past one in the afternoon. Scott turned on his mobile phone intending to try Angela again; it had been a few days without any contact at all, and considering how close they had recently become it didn't feel right.

As he scrolled down through his contact list for her number the phone began to ring, Neil flashed on the caller ID screen.

'How did the night go?' he asked, as he connected the call.

'Fucking terrible man, I need to see you today,' Neil said, his voice sounding scratchy.

'Alright, calm down. What happened?'

'No, not on the phone.'

'OK then I'll wait in, just come over when you can.'

'Someplace else. The Starbucks down beside the plaza, can you be there at two-thirty?'

'Yeah,' Scott said uneasily. Neil got spooked by things from time to time, but Scott had never heard him as nervous as this. 'I'll see you then,' he said, and hung up.

Scott arrived at Starbucks fifteen minutes early. He'd called Iris and ordered a cab for twenty minutes' time but it had turned up right away.

Stan was the driver and explained they hadn't had many calls so asked if Scott wanted him to wait. Scott said he didn't know how long this would take, but Stan told him he'd be in the car park at the corner unless another call came through.

At the counter Scott ordered a large Mocha from a cheerful woman with unusually wide gaps between her teeth and a body that was shaped like a potato.

Taking his cup he moved away from the front of the shop. He usually avoided any food or drink establishments that had the floor to ceiling glass fronts. All the people walking by made him feel like a goldfish in a bowl or an animal at the zoo.

He settled into a booth, put his feet up on the seat opposite and tried again to call Angela as he waited for Neil to arrive. There was still no answer. Scott tapped his phone against the formica table-top thoughtfully. If there had been complications with Steph it was possible that Angela had been in the hospital the whole time with her phone turned off. He phoned directory enquiries and had them connect him through to Steph's ward at the hospital.

'Hi, can I speak to Stephanie Hutton, or someone connected with her? I'm a close friend of the family,' he said when the call was connected.

'One moment please,' the voice that answered the phone said. 'No I'm sorry, Miss Hutton was discharged on Friday.'

'That can't be right, I visited on Friday and the doctors told her she would be discharged on Monday.'

'I'm sure you're right but patients often get homesick and discharge themselves early, especially at this time of the year.'

'OK, thank you.' Scott mumbled, and disconnected the call.

He took a sip from the Mocha, and decided if Stan was still there after he met with Neil he'd stop by Angela's place on the way back home.

The glass door into the coffee shop opened and Elizabeth Flight walked in with someone wearing a grey sweatshirt with the hood up and combat pants, that may or may not have been Neil.

She walked up to the counter as her companion glanced around the room and Scott recognised by the long length of dirty blonde hair that hung down from the hood that it was Neil. Scott waved him over and, as Neil walked up to the booth, Scott noticed he seemed to be favouring his right leg over the left, and when he put down the hood saw a black and purple bruise that stretched from as low down as Neil's jaw bone, covered his right eye and across the bridge of his nose.

'Jesus, what the fuck happened?'

'Apparently there's competition.'

'Competition from who? Those twins with the long hair that used to deal around our route?'

'No this is much bigger. Not competition as much as these guys have taken over.'

'Taken over in Blitz?'

'No, everywhere. The whole city,' Neil said, glancing nervously around as if his attacker may have been lurking in one of the booths, ready to strike again.

'Start from the beginning, what happened?'

'Just the same as any other night, I went round the bars, Elizabeth was with me,' he said, looking at her as she put two cups down on the table and sat on the seat beside Neil. 'I moved some stuff to the usual crowd, no strangers. We saw these two guys in a couple of places over the night. Probably wouldn't have noticed them but they weren't really dressed right for those type of bars. They looked sort of as if they'd dressed down to blend in but hadn't quite got it right.'

'I think I've seen one of them before,' Elizabeth said, in what Scott found to be an amused tone of voice, as if this was just some new game she was playing.

'Seen one where, out drinking in the bars?' Scott asked, trying to repress any ill feeling he had towards her.

'No, at least not around those bars. I don't remember. Daddy has me attend so many functions I can't possibly keep track of everyone I've seen.'

'Right so they approached you in one of the bars?' Scott asked, turning back to Neil.

'No, I caught them looking over a few times but they never said anything. I thought it was cause Elizabeth looked really hot, they were just jealous or something.'

She seemed to wallow in that, as if this whole meeting was some kind of clandestine ploy Neil had thought up to compliment her.

'So you went on to Blitz?' Scott prompted.

'Yeah, it was fine in there, we didn't even see them. After we came out I still had some bags I was selling off to people, so by the time I'd finished we were just gonna head over to Elizabeth's place. They stepped out from the alley behind the club, told me they wanted a word. I walked round thinking they were gonna try buy some shit, like maybe they were undercover feds or something. I was just gonna tell them to piss off when one of them grabbed me and threw me up against a wall. His mate said that if we, and he did say we, not me, so they know I don't work alone Scott, if we want to keep on dealing then everything has to be bought through them at their prices, and we have to pay a premium on top to keep Blitz as ours.'

'So what did you say?'

'I told him to fuck off, like who the hell did they think they were and shit.'

'So then they beat you up?'

'Yeah, fuck man it was brutal. I've been in plenty bar fights over the years but this was different. There was like, an efficiency to it. Within just a few seconds I was face down in the snow wondering what the fuck had happened. They took the rest of the drugs I had too.'

Elizabeth nodded, confirming Neil's statement.

'And the cash, how much cash did they get?' Scott asked.

'Everything, it was just rolled in my pocket along with the remaining bags. It was after the club so I figured it was job done, nothing was hidden.'

'So what happens then, do we just wait until we run into them again or what?' Scott asked, struggling to make sense of Neil's story.

'No, they said someone will be in touch.'

Back in the cab on the way to Angela's flat Scott was wondering what he could do to get out of the situation he was now in. He figured just leaving their drug business for Neil to do what he wanted with might be the best option, but that would all depend how things went with the meeting in which he and Twinkle were due to get paid.

Stan could tell something was up the way Scott got back in and slammed the door shut. Other than asking for their next destination he kept quiet, casting the odd furtive glance at Scott in the rear view mirror but otherwise kept his thoughts, and more importantly his questions to himself.

The afternoon was dark and stormy, a perfect backdrop to Scott's mood. He chewed distractedly on a fingernail as Stan continued to navigate the cab along the quiet suburban streets in silence. They pulled up outside of Angela's apartment block and Scott handed some money to Stan and told him not to wait. He was out of the cab and walking towards the entrance before the driver had time to tell him the fare.

Remembering the steaming cup of coffee waiting on the table last time he'd been there, Scott looked up and tried to locate which were the windows for Angela's flat. Across the whole block they were all small, square and identical. How many had been in the living room, was it two or maybe three? He couldn't remember. He stopped for a second and counted along her floor, a shape five windows in vanished just as he caught sight of it. Had it been someone watching him? Maybe, or perhaps a cat jumping from the window ledge in a neighbouring apartment.

The entranceway was unlocked again so he didn't bother to buzz up. There'd been no-one outside on the street and the stairway in the building was equally deserted. Scott felt an increasing sensation of isolation, like he was the last man alive on the planet. He shivered and gave three raps of the knocker on Angela's door. The hallway had been quiet beforehand and he strained to hear anything from behind the door. The silence seemed to get louder until it became almost unbearable. Scott cleared his throat just to hear a sound, and knocked again on the door, this time pressing his ear up against it. He couldn't hear anything so he tried calling her name, assuring her that it was just him and that he was worried about her, but his words did nothing more than bounce back along the corridor behind him. Slowly he made his way back downstairs, turning for one last glance over his shoulder in case the door should open.

Scott decided against calling Stan's cab back and opted to just walk for a while. It wasn't like he was in a hurry to get anywhere now anyway.

* * *

Twinkle's message arrived the next day just after 2 pm. Scott had woken early but lay in bed 'til noon. He'd wandered the house unable to settle into anything. Starting one task and then leaving it unfinished and beginning something else. The message had provided a welcome focus. It simply read 'Tonite John Henrys at 8'. Now there was something for his mind to fix upon, he wouldn't need to look for distractions from the questions about Angela that relentlessly surfaced like bubbles in water.

He ate, walked the dog, came home and showered. Scott felt

he was on the verge of something, it wasn't excitement he felt but nor was it fear. When the time was right he called a cab and left. Only then did it occur to him that it was Christmas Eve.

There was no surprise that Twinkle was in the bar as Scott arrived. The speed he was drinking from his glass suggested he was in a desperate race against sobriety, and one that he appeared to be winning.

'Slow down, the night is still young,' Scott said, putting a hand on Twinkle's shoulder.

Twinkle turned to him and grinned, there were dark wet spots on the front of his t-shirt from beer that had dripped from the glass in his haste.

'Another one of these for me and one for my young friend as well,' Twinkle said, leaning unsteadily across the bar attempting to catch Joanne's arm as she walked past. She evaded his grip and cast a concerned glance back towards Scott.

'Let's go sit at a table, man. That's Sharon's friend remember, you don't want to blow things before they get back off the ground again.'

'I know, I know,' he said, shaking his head drunkenly. The tips of some strands of his hair glistened as if they'd fallen into his glass. 'It's my last night Scott. We do that thing and then I'm off the drink and everything else for good.'

Scott took a firm grip on Twinkle's elbow and half ushered, half dragged him away from the bar.

'That's enough. We'll have a couple of drinks together if you want, but no more talk of later on, OK?'

'OK my friend, whatever you say.'

Scott went back to the bar and picked up their drinks. Twinkle had flopped down onto a bench between two tables and the current occupiers of one had taken the hint and moved. Scott pushed in beside him, putting their glasses on the table.

'You been in for long?' Scott asked.

Twinkle made an elaborate shrugging gesture, which pretty

much told Scott that he'd been drinking long enough for time to no longer be a factor.

A while later they both left John Henry's. Scott had asked only the time they needed to leave, planning on getting all further information Twinkle had been given when they were alone outside. He'd kept the conversation away from anything criminal and let Twinkle go on at length about the plans he had for himself, Sharon and the kids. By encouraging Twinkle to do most of the talking, this at least had slowed down his drinking, and when suggestions to top up with spirits arose, Scott had declined them as well.

The meeting, Twinkle now told him, was to take place in a large tower block in Orchard Rise, just outside of the main city zone. Orchard, Scott thought, that was a joke. The only thing that ever grew around there was the crime rate and the amount of dog shit on the paths.

No more snow had fallen since last night but the temperature had dropped below freezing again, and what snow remained had now frozen into solid patches that crunched as they walked on them. Twinkle was a little unsteady as he walked, but Scott kept an eye on him and stayed close enough to prevent a fall should he stumble or slip on the ice. There would have been no point waiting for a cab to take them at this time on Christmas Eve. Besides, Scott didn't want anyone knowing where they were going, and was taking an indirect route to the tower block just in case. His paranoia levels were elevated but Scott was glad of the heightened awareness.

Twinkle trudged on in silence, his breath as visible as it was pungent in the cold night air. Scott reached for his cigarettes but then put them away again, he didn't want anything to slow them down now they were so close. Just get this over with and find out what to expect next.

The block they wanted was called Raven's Nook, and was one of three ugly grey concrete columns that loomed like giant tombstones over Garden Heights. They had first been built to house the homeless after the war, but these days it seemed only the lowest rung on society's ladder were housed there.

As soon as they came into view, Scott instinctively pulled up his hood. There'd undoubtedly be high resolution surveillance cameras on top monitoring the streets all around, and Scott wanted no connection between himself and this meeting. If he'd asked, Scott would have told Twinkle it was for the cold, but either he hadn't noticed anyway or simply didn't care.

The large entranceway door shrieked as Scott pushed it open. Twinkle had told him the meeting was at a flat on the fourteenth floor; as much as he didn't want to chance getting stuck in one of the elevators here for the Christmas break, Scott also didn't feel like climbing all of those stairs. He pushed the button to summon the lift. A grinding sound followed by two metallic clangs announced it was on its way.

The stench of urine wafted over them as the metal doors shuddered open. Scott covered his face with his sleeve and stepped inside; the smell even appeared to have slightly sobered Twinkle, whose face was now drawn tight in a look of disgust like he'd just taken a bite from a raw onion.

Twinkle pressed the button, the doors closed and another slow grinding noise before it suddenly lurched upwards. Either no-one else was waiting to use the lift, or no-one else trusted them and it carried them straight to their floor.

The doors opened out onto a narrow hallway of blistered linoleum which barely covered the concrete underneath. It was dimly lit from single bulbs housed intermittently along the ceiling within opaque plastic shields in an effort to prevent breakage and possibly theft. Twinkle stumbled on ahead searching for the door number he had scribbled on the crumpled piece of paper he'd taken out of his jacket pocket. Scott followed a few steps behind.

Twinkle stopped outside a door and again squinted at the

paper he held and compared it with the number in front of him. He cleared his throat and knocked three times. The door swung inwards and Twinkle walked inside.

'You coming in or not?' a gruff voice asked, as Scott had hesitated before following.

'Yeah,' he said, went inside and closed the door after him.

Beyond the doorway was an unkempt open plan living area with yellowed newspapers strewn over the bare floor, and a smell of mould hung in the air. The room was small with a kitchen cubicle on one wall, a bathroom which looked little bigger than a phone box and one other door which Scott presumed led to the only bedroom. A sofa upholstered in a dark green fabric with a paisley design was occupied by Dominic Parish and his accomplice with the earring from the initial drop off. On a matching armchair, with patches of stuffing escaping from it like rising dough, sat a man Scott hadn't seen before, smoking a thin cigar. He was sharply dressed without straying into vanity or flamboyance. A designer suit and expensive looking shoes, not that Scott was an expert but he'd learned to recognise quality from Jack's attire over the years.

'Take a seat,' the man said, waving his hand towards two wooden stools, his tone indicating it was more of a command than a suggestion.

Scott and Twinkle sat where they'd been instructed.

'I'm Paul McBlane,' he said in answer to the question that hovered on Scott's lips. 'You now work for me.' There was a pause, presumably to allow time for the sentence to sink in.

'You boys did well on the last job, so tonight you'll get paid what was agreed, but for now we'll just relax and have a chat,' the man said, and steepled his fingers, but there was nothing relaxed about the atmosphere in the room. 'Firstly, there was no cocaine in the shipment.'

'We never touched it,' Twinkle stammered, 'delivered just

like we picked it up.' Scott felt his heart lurch but he said nothing.

McBlane's hand holding the cigar casually waved away Twinkle's anxiety. 'No, like I say you boys did great but let's be fair, I'd be pretty stupid to risk such a big investment on two new lads who hadn't worked for me before,' he said, and laughed. A short hollow sound that ended as abruptly as it had begun.

'There never was any coke in there, it was just a box of crap, wires and fucking screwdrivers or whatever. But you'll get paid just the same. It's not like I'd just say fuck the agreement now, eh?'

He tapped the ash from the end of his cigar and a coil of blue smoke drifted casually from the corner of his mouth as he watched them. Twinkle fidgeted on the stool beside Scott.

'Can I offer you boys a drink or perhaps something else, while we get comfortable?' he asked, in a lighter tone.

Dominic stood and brought some Glenmorangie in an unfamiliar teardrop shaped bottle, and a small case from out of the bedroom. He then went back and returned with only two glasses which he placed beside the bottle within reach of McBlane. The case he took back to the couch, flipped the catch and opened it.

'I hear you don't partake in those activities,' He said to Scott, and nodded over to the case Dominic had unzipped and now had his hands inside of. 'Very wise. That's why I brought this.'

He lined up the glasses on a vacant TV stand between himself and Scott and poured the Scotch.

'The vale of big meadows, eh Scott?'

Scott didn't understand what that meant and was now growing more distracted as syringes and rubber tubing were withdrawn from the case.

'Shugg,' Dominic said as he handed a syringe to Earring. At

least Scott could now put a name to the face. He held out another to Twinkle.

'Fuck it, alright it's my last one though,' Twinkle said, reaching over to take the syringe, smiling despite himself.

'Don't worry,' Dominic said as he rolled up his sleeve. 'I knocked these up just before you got here.'

Twinkle nodded and did likewise. He glanced up at Scott and then quickly looked away.

'I find if you give them what they want, and you give them what they need, then they tend to stay a lot more loyal than if you deny them,' McBlane said softly, leaning in closer towards Scott. 'Course sometimes like now the two are one and the same, which makes my job a whole lot easier.'

When McBlane finished speaking he turned to Scott and winked, then took a sip of his Scotch.

'So what is it that I want and need then?' Scott asked, trying to focus on what was being said rather than the rubber tubing Dominic was tying around the man he'd called Shugg's arm.

'Maybe that's what we're here to find out, Scott. Why don't you tell me, I know you do some work for your brother and that you peddle drugs around the streets, so why did you come and do the job for me then?'

'Money, what else?'

'Fair enough, that's what most people look for to begin with, but money can be a sliding scale, the more you have, the more you want, the more you need,' McBlane said as he sharpened the ash on the tip of his cigar into a point against the rim of the ashtray. It gave him the appearance of wielding a dagger as he gestured with his cigar holding hand.

'Not for me, I just want enough to make a fresh start and then I'm gone.'

'That's a shame. So our working relationship will only be short term. Fair enough though, I respect a man who knows what he wants. So is it something you're getting away to or from then, may I ask?'

Scott shrugged. 'Maybe a bit of both.' He didn't want McBlane knowing anything more about him than he'd obviously already found out, but the man had an easy-going almost coaxing tone to his voice which made it hard to evade his subtle questioning.

'Sometimes truths are what we run from, and sometimes they are what we seek. Sometimes maybe we don't know which the fuck it is,' McBlane said and laughed again. 'For me, I like to know the truth. To be in possession of all the facts.'

Shugg and Dominic both shot up and Dominic passed the tubing to Twinkle. Scott looked at the eager expression on his friend's face. His eyes keen and alert, his tongue flicked over his lips, a few seconds would pass and he'd do it again, looking almost reptilian. Holding one end of the tube between his teeth, Twinkle tied it tight around his arm, then bent and straightened the arm repeatedly, working a vein closer to the surface. Satisfied he'd found an injection site Twinkle squirted just a little out of the syringe pointing upwards to clear any air bubbles, he placed the tip of the needle against his old blue vein that had risen to the surface like an inquisitive dolphin, but then paused. Scott wondered if thoughts of Sharon and the kids were going to make him decide against taking it. He'd said one last time, but would it be?

'What's wrong Twinkle, getting cold feet?' McBlane said.

Twinkle's hand wobbled slightly but then he slid the needle in and pushed the plunger home. Dominic and Shugg were now slouched back onto the couch, their eyes almost closed. Conscious but in a semi-dreamlike state. Air seemed to escape from Twinkle as he leaned back against the wall like someone sitting down on an inflatable chair that has been punctured.

McBlane picked up the whiskey bottle and refilled their glasses. 'To future endeavours,' he said, and clinked his glass against Scott's.

Twinkle's breathing was coming in short rasps, like an old wooden door being opened and closed that didn't sit flush in its frame. His eyes were closed. Scott turned his attention back to McBlane.

'Is there any point in me asking when the next job will be?' he asked.

'Someone will be in touch,' McBlane answered, and grinned over the rim of his glass.

'But it'll be more of the same, like the job at the docks?'

'It may be, yes, but the operation may vary as well as your level of involvement.'

Twinkle murmured something and tried to stand up. McBlane's eyes slid coolly from Scott over in his direction.

'What's that Twinkle? You ready for another one already?'

Twinkle attempted to stand, bracing a thin arm against the wall behind him, but tipped forward and fell flat. Scott jumped off his seat and rolled Twinkle onto his back.

'What are you playing at man? Chill out we'll be on our way soon,' Scott said.

Twinkle's face looked drawn and pale; his eyes rolled upwards, unable to keep their focus on Scott. He mumbled something again that Scott couldn't understand.

'I can't hear you Twinkle, just sleep it off or something, you'll be fine.'

'The old boy isn't looking too hot, is he?' McBlane said, swilling the whiskey around in his glass.

Dominic and Shugg looked more alert now. They'd sat up on the sofa and were watching Twinkle intently, as he lay like a freshly caught fish on the deck of a boat. Even Twinkle's lips looked pale now, almost completely drained of blood. His eyes closed and his body began to go limp.

'Wake up you stupid fucker,' Scott said, realising something could be seriously wrong, and slapped Twinkle across the face.

Twinkle's eyelids flickered but wouldn't remain open.

'We have to get him to a hospital or something,' Scott said, 'he looks like he's overdosing.'

'No point in that, if he's O'D-ing then he'll be dead by the time you get there,' McBlane said in a matter-of-fact tone of voice. 'He either shakes it off or he's fucked. Either way none of us wants to get tied in with heroin or anything like that or we'll all be up on involuntary manslaughter charges.' Murmurs and nods of agreement followed from Dominic and Shugg on the couch.

Scott knew there was nothing he could do. There was no way they'd allow an ambulance to be called and Scott had no transport even if he did manage to drag him outside. Twinkle's pale face had begun to turn blue, his lips now a grey-white.

'He's almost gone,' Dominic observed casually, from the couch. 'We'll need to find a way to get the body out, we can't leave him here.'

'Fuck's sake he's still breathing,' Scott said, looking pleadingly around him, but the other eyes in the room were those of circling buzzards.

'I said almost,' Dominic said, and tutted.

'He's right,' McBlane added. 'You two see what's in here to help. Scott you sit with him in case he does pull through.'

Shugg got up and went into the bedroom, Dominic to the kitchen where he began looking through the small cupboards. Scott leaned in and put his ear over Twinkle's mouth. His breath was so shallow that at first Scott thought he was already dead.

'I've found a suitcase,' Shugg said, carrying a tattered brown case back into the room.

'There's not much of him but surely he'll not fit in there,' McBlane said.

Scott's mind was racing, struggling to comprehend the events unfolding around him. They were talking about disposing of Twinkle like he was a rusty old bike that no-one rode anymore. Scott put his ear to Twinkle's mouth again but could neither hear nor feel any breath. He pressed his fingers against Twinkle's neck to feel for a pulse like he'd seen on TV.

'I can't feel a pulse. Fuck.'

'OK, let's see that case then Shugg.' McBlane said and clapped his hands. Shugg tossed it onto the floor beside Twinkle.

McBlane moved over to the couch to supervise as Shugg began sizing Twinkle up to see if he'd fit in the case. Scott felt sick, it was like watching an amateur tailor fit him up for a suit to be buried in.

'He won't fit, bits will stick out,' McBlane said. 'Have you found anything that might help with that, Dom?'

'Nothing sharp enough but I have found this,' Dominic replied, pulling something from the bottom shelf of one of the lower cupboards.

There was a bang as it dragged against the cupboard door before Dominic straightened up holding a lump hammer.

'Alright, see what you can do with that,' McBlane instructed him, and rubbed his hands together.

'Empty his pockets and take off any jewellery first. Scott, you sit back over here and let them get on with it.'

McBlane motioned to the armchair he'd first sat in. In a daze, Scott staggered across and collapsed into it. Twinkle was dead, at least Scott thought he was. Dominic had lifted his body and Shugg slid the open suitcase under him. Twinkle's pale blue hands held up against his chest and head tucked down towards his neck as if in prayer. His arm jerked suddenly, probably a muscle reflex rather than through conscious effort. It looked like a floating branch that had been snagged by a fishing line.

'You're gonna have to fold him more,' McBlane said. 'Use the hammer.'

Scott could feel the contents of his stomach flip over and over on themselves. He turned to the side and retched, frothy yellow bile spilled out onto the newspaper covered floor, filling the room with the putrid stench of previously ingested alcohol.

'Looks like someone can't hold their drink,' McBlane said, and Dominic and Shugg laughed.

Scott was still staring at the steam rising from his evacuated stomach contents as he heard the hammer fall. The dull crack of a bone splintering under its weight. He couldn't look.

'Fucking Christ,' Scott said. 'We were just talking to him a few minutes ago, we don't even know for sure if he's dead.'

Clunk – the hammer fell again.

'He's fitting better now,' one of them said, Scott wasn't sure who. He was no longer sure of anything.

Crack – Scott's stomach contracted and another thin stream of bile spilled out from his mouth.

Clunk.

'Right, try again now,' McBlane said.

Scott turned to watch as Dominic and Shugg rearranged Twinkle's broken limbs into the case. Arms and legs folded unnaturally at joints he shouldn't have. Dominic closed the case and pressed his foot down on top as Shugg pulled the zipper around it. He picked it up carefully by the handle, making sure it would hold.

'I think he might be exceeding the weight limit for carry on,' Shugg said. 'We'll have to pay extra.' They all laughed heartily – except Scott, who began to shake.

McBlane got up this time and went into the bedroom. He came back out with a small cloth bag.

'Here's your ten thousand,' he said, and handed it to Scott, tight rolls of new bills inside. He then took out a handkerchief from his pocket and proceeded to wipe any fingerprints from the whiskey bottle.

'Give us a while to get gone before you go back out. Put your feet up, finish the Scotch, whatever. OK?'

Scott angled his chin down slightly and then back up in a nod, afraid that any more movement than that would result in further vomiting. Dominic picked up the glasses and case that had held the syringes.

'Just drink it from the bottle,' he said.

Shugg carried the case containing Twinkle's broken body outside.

'Well he's definitely getting cold feet now,' he said; the three of them laughed again.

'OK Scott, and remember,' McBlane said.

'Yeah, someone will be in touch,' Scott finished for him.

He looked at his watch as they left, 00:16.

It was Christmas Day.

Chapter 10

Two days later Angela called. Scott didn't know how long he'd stayed in the flat that night. He'd drunk the rest of the whiskey before going back down by the stairwell. He hadn't wanted anything to be the same when he left, no jagged reminders of what should have been with him but wasn't on the way back out. Scott had wandered aimlessly before eventually coming across a taxi rank where he'd taken a cab home.

'Stephanie's gone.'

Scott's brain swirled, uncomprehending.

'What?' he said.

'Scott, Steph has gone. I don't know where she is.'

'You were both gone. I tried to call and I stopped by your place.'

'No she left the hospital and stayed with me. She was really scared and wouldn't let me tell anyone she was here, not even you. This morning she went to get clothes and stuff from her place and she hasn't come back.'

'Maybe she took off on her own.'

'No, she was convinced they were still after her. She was at the window all the time watching in case anyone came here. She promised she'd be right back Scott.'

'I don't know what to say.'

'OK I'm coming to your place, Scott. I can't be here right now.'

The line went dead. Scott sat staring at the now silent phone.

He had done nothing on Christmas day, just wandered around outside in the frozen woods. Hard ground, chill winds and bare tree branches that looked like they'd been dipped in sugar. None of it had seemed real, like walking around in a desolate dream where nothing happened, but one he didn't want to wake up from. To awaken would mean a return to the realities of his existence.

He didn't know if anyone had tried to call, probably Jack would have the day before so they could exchange their obligatory *Merry Christmas* but Scott had left his phone switched off. Now when turning it back on Angela had called and it seemed he would have to deal with her turning up there. At least she was embroiled in some drama about her missing friend, not like she'd be asking a bunch of questions about him he didn't want to answer.

Scott took a shower and then changed his clothes for the first time since Twinkle's death. Before that there hadn't seemed any point. He'd just slept in his clothes when he felt tired and walked around when he didn't. Boris had known something was wrong, but had just trotted along beside him when he walked and curled up beside him when he slept. At least dogs don't ask questions, and they don't judge you, he thought. Scott did feel better after washing and changing, but then felt guilty because of it. He went to the kitchen and made stale cheese sandwiches for him and Boris after the fridge refused to offer up anything more edible.

When Angela turned up, Scott was greeted with the impression she was going to be there longer than just a few hours. She had a large hiker type backpack slung over one shoulder which appeared to be loaded up with her stuff. After he'd opened the front door Angela came in and dumped it in his bedroom before going to the kitchen to make herself a drink. She was sullen and preoccupied, telling him only that she'd contacted Stephanie's mother to see if she'd gone there but was told they had neither seen nor spoken to her since she'd left the hospital.

Scott could tell Angela blamed herself and it was a feeling he could relate to. Stephanie would probably turn up though; Twinkle may turn up as well but it was more likely to be at the bottom of a lake, or when some waste ground was dug up to lay foundations for a new building.

His impression that Angela had come to stay proved to be correct. She didn't ask and he didn't say anything, she just stayed. Not the usual Angela that he was accustomed to; she was quiet and jumped at the slightest sound and even talked about going away for a while, getting out of the city, which wasn't like her at all, but having her there still felt good, helped the hours pass by a little easier, and Boris was delighted as Angela always fussed over him. She went out and restocked his cupboards and cleaned the place probably better than it had been done in years.

When they were out walking, or even sitting in the evening watching TV, Angela would suddenly grab for her phone, thinking she'd heard it ring and that it would be news of Stephanie. The phantom rings were just in her head though, and New Year arrived without any word on either her or Twinkle.

Angela had bought ready-made Indian meals, red wine and candles from the supermarket for their New Year's Eve in together. She hadn't suggested going out anywhere and Scott wouldn't have gone anyway. He didn't want to take the chance of running into anyone from McBlane's lot or whoever had beaten Neil up either. Neil would usually have been pestering Scott to go out continually over the holidays, but after the scare he'd had before Christmas he was keeping a low profile and staying with Elizabeth at her place.

Around two in the morning Angela was in the kitchen refilling their wine glasses when Scott's phone rang and Jack flashed up on the caller ID screen.

'Happy New Year,' Scott said as he answered the call.

'Fuck that. Twinkle's really done it this time.'

Scott's blood ran cold, what did Jack know about it? Scott tried not to panic and keep his voice steady when he answered.

'What do you mean, done what?'

'Someone's been shot outside of the club and one of the doormen saw him do it.'

'What, who was it?' Scott said, struggling to decipher what was going on.

'That guy with the earring you asked about the other night. He tried to grab him but Twinkle shook him off and ran. The police are gonna be after him for sure this time Scott. He even dropped his wallet as he got away from the doorman, for fuck's sake.'

Now it made sense. Eventually someone would have realised he'd vanished and reported him missing, and with Twinkle getting close to Sharon again she might have done it even sooner. This way there's an investigation to find him but now he had a reason to not want to be found.

'Scott, you still there?'

'Yeah, OK thanks for letting me know,' he said, and hung up.

'Was that Jack?' Angela asked, evenly, carrying their refilled glasses back into the room.

'Yeah, there's been another shooting at Aura.'

'Who was shot?'

'I have no idea but the evidence seems to suggest it was Twinkle that did it.'

'Do you think it was him?'

'No, no I really don't, but the police will be looking for him anyway. We should get out of here.'

'You think they'll come here tonight?'

'I don't know but they're bound to connect me to him so I need to get the drugs out.'

Scott reached for his phone again and called Neil.

'What?' Neil said into the receiver after it rang half a dozen times, breathing heavily.

'Whatever you're doing, quit it. I need to come and see you now.'

'What time is it?'

'A little after two, are you still at Elizabeth's?'

'Yeah, why do you have to see me at two in the morning on New Year's Eve? Just wish me happy New Year over the phone like anyone else.'

'Fuck off. Where does she live?'

'At the Walker building, are you coming here now?'

'The Walker building, where Jack lives?'

'Yeah, you need the number?'

'No, I'll text you when I'm near, you can come and meet me outside.'

Scott ended the call and immediately dialled Pressman cabs. The number rang seven times before Iris answered.

'Pressman cabs, you've got no chance we're fully booked.'

'Iris it's Scott, is there any way you can fit me in? It's a bit of an emergency.'

'Hi Scott,' she said and coughed into the phone, which sounded like someone shaking a bag full of dice. Reg and Stan are both working tonight but even we've been flat out with calls. How much of an emergency is it?'

Scott looked at Angela as he tried to think up an excuse.

'It's my friend's mother, she's been taken ill,' he said, shrugging at Angela as if to say what choice did he have?

'Alright Scott I'll have one of them there as soon as I can.'

'Thanks Iris, you're the best,' Scott said, hung up and went straight into the bedroom and pulled the wardrobe away from the wall. He flipped back the carpet and levered up a loose board revealing a small lock-box underneath. Taking all the money and what remaining drugs they had from the stash, Scott stuffed it all into his pockets and watched out of the window for the arrival of their cab.

A light rain was falling outside, melting the remaining patches of lying snow into slush. The cab's tyres slurred on the wet gravel as it pulled onto the driveway. Scott and Angela grabbed their coats and left.

'Reg my man, you've saved the day,' Scott said, climbing into the overbearingly warm cab. Angela climbed in beside him and sniffed as she closed the door.

'Have to be quick, there's a bunch of people gonna be real pissed off when I don't turn up for them in a few minutes,' Reg said, looking at Scott in the rear-view, and then to Angela, 'so is your mother really sick then?'

Angela first looked at Scott and then at Reg's reflection staring back at her and said 'Ahh – well...'

'Yeah I thought so. For anyone else I wouldn't do this but Scott's a good lad,' he said, quickly accelerating off the driveway scattering chunks of gravel behind them. 'So where to?'

'Anywhere near the Walker building, Reg.'

The dark countryside flew past on either side of the cab. Scott self-consciously slid a palm over the cash and bags of drugs in his pockets, then felt Angela's hand slide reassuringly into his. The only other talking Reg did was into the cab radio telling Iris he'd be back to pick up the Stillman party as soon as he could. The fields gave way to clusters of houses and then housing estates as the car sped along the wet roads towards the city.

Paying the fare as well as a healthy tip, Scott got out and thanked Reg again and watched as the cab disappeared around the corner.

'Are we going in?' Angela asked, as Scott typed out a text message on his phone.

'No, he'll come out,' Scott said, not wanting to get close enough to the building to be recognised by a concierge.

A few minutes later, a slightly more dishevelled than usual Neil emerged through the revolving doors and catching sight of them across the street, made his way over. His limp had almost gone but the streetlights reflected off his swollen and bruised face. The colour had at least now faded to yellow and orange.

'Twinkle's in serious shit,' Scott said when Neil was close enough to hear; a pang of guilt rang through him for perpetuating the lie.

'What this time?'

'Someone else has been shot, this time just outside Aura. They reckon it was definitely him.'

'Are they dead?'

'I don't know,' Scott said, thinking about it for a second. 'Jack never said.'

'So what do you want me for?' Neil asked, and Scott was beginning to feel more than a little pissed off at the impatient tone in his voice.

'The police will be looking for him, and they'll connect us. I had to get the drugs out of my place.'

'I can't take them,' Neil said, holding up both palms as if in surrender.

'You fucking are taking them!'

'No way will Elizabeth be into that, I'm lucky to be able to even stay here while those fuckers are on the prowl for us. She won't have a bag of drugs in there as well.'

Scott thought for a minute on his next move. 'Alright then, here,' he said, counting out roughly half of the bundle of cash he had. 'That's your share of the funds. As of now we're officially liquidated.'

'Might be for the best,' Neil said, flicking through the bills. 'At least till everything calms down.'

'I need a lift back to the house.'

'Elizabeth's waiting inside. Can't you get a cab?'

'It's New Year. We had to lie to Iris just to get a cab down here. You think I'm gonna wander around the city with a pocket full of drugs looking for one now? No fucking way, you're driving,' he said, jabbing a finger at Neil's chest.

Scott turned and walked off in the direction of the car park, Angela caught up after a few steps. Neil stood moaning for a few more seconds but when Scott didn't stop or turn around, he dutifully began to follow.

'What you gonna do with them then?' Neil asked him, keeping pace alongside them now.

'Bury them down by the tree.'

'Won't they like, go mouldy or something?'

'Hopefully not, I'll put them in a biscuit tin or a box or whatever.'

A police siren invaded the stillness of the night. Scott froze momentarily and then quickly sped up again, his nerve endings felt as charred as burnt toast.

'Plenty to keep them busy tonight, man, don't worry,' Neil said in an attempt to be reassuring and slapped Scott on the shoulder. Scott shook it off and quickened his pace.

More sirens taunted the night as Neil navigated his car through some of the narrow city back streets. He'd learned the most efficient routes to avoid camera cover over the years. He'd probably make a good cab driver, Scott thought. Shortly the bustle of activity from the city was behind them and quiet suburban roads led on to silent country lanes. Neil dropped them off and left with a promise that he'd check back in with Scott in a few days.

Back in the house they both searched around for a container to put the drugs in; Angela came up with an airtight refrigerator tub which seemed like it would be fit for purpose.

Pausing only to uncork a bottle of wine for the journey and fetch the best digging implement he could find – an old rusty trowel his uncle had stowed away under the sink – they headed straight out back and off into the woods.

'Do you have somewhere in mind?' Angela asked after taking a swig from the bottle.

'May as well bury it at the usual spot, if I put it somewhere else I'm bound to forget where the hell it is.'

Although the rain had stopped the ground was still wet and slippery underfoot. Sporadic cloud cover meant keeping their feet was difficult at times when little moonlight could sneak through to aid them.

Scott started digging at the base of the Elephant Tree. No grass or other vegetation grew there so the wet earth came away easily enough as he thrust the blade of the old trowel into the ground like a dagger in a Shakespearean play. Angela sat back on the log holding the plastic container, the wine bottle placed between her feet, and she smoked a cigarette while Scott dug the hole. Boris, paying particular attention to what Scott was doing, dug as well, flinging clods of earth skyward in his frenzied efforts. Angela called to the dog to keep him out of Scott's way.

Scott placed the container of drugs into the hole, pushed the wet earth back into place and stamped it down.

Back at the house they lay naked in bed with the remainder of the wine. The still filthy dog was secured in the kitchen with a promise from Scott to wash him in the morning. They'd stripped off their wet mud-splattered clothes and showered together, soaping each other's bodies before slowly making love under the steady stream of hot water.

'We should get away from here for a while,' Angela said when they were in bed together, lazily tracing circles on his chest with the tip of a fingernail. 'There's too much shit going on.'

'You said that yesterday but where would we go?'

'You remember that opportunity dad talked about at the party?'

'Vaguely.'

'Well he knows a guy with some land up in the mountains.

He has a house there with a guest cabin too, he'd let us stay.'

'Yeah? He doesn't know me though, you sure?'

'Dad will vouch for you, and besides I'd be there as well. Just stock up on a load of groceries and stuff and he'll be more than happy to see us. He doesn't go out much and it's almost an hour's drive to what we'd consider civilisation.'

'When would you want to leave?'

'First thing in the morning is good for me. We won't get phone reception up at the house but a nearby village has coverage so I can keep checking on any developments with Steph from there. There's nothing you have to be here for is there?'

'Just the opposite,' Scott said, taking a deep breath, and letting the air slowly exhale out of him. His statement carried more meaning than Angela could have anticipated.

'OK pack your stuff in the morning, we'll head to dad's first, he'll get us a car to use for the trip.'

'That backpack you brought was for more than spending a few nights here then?'

'Well I was gonna go up there eventually anyway and I hoped you'd come with, I just hadn't found the right time to bring it up yet.'

Scott woke around four hours later to find Angela had already vacated the bed and had been replaced by a slightly damp but otherwise clean Boris.

Angela must have been up for a while, the place had been cleaned through, the dog washed and lots of food supplies had already been boxed up in the kitchen.

'I've spoken to dad and he's in the process of getting a car for us now,' Angela said, and greeted him with a kiss as he emerged sleepily from the bedroom.

'It's not gonna be stolen is it?'

'No, dummy. He's gonna get it to partly pay off a debt someone owes him.'

'That still doesn't rule out it being stolen,' Scott said

grinning, and Angela punched him playfully on the arm. 'When do we have to pick it up?'

'He's gonna get it sorted and drive it out here, we can drop him back off on our way.'

'Sounds like you have everything organised, I may as well go back to bed,' Scott said and turned in the direction of the bedroom.

'Don't you dare,' she said, 'go pack up some clothes.'

Scott spent the next hour neatly packing up things he'd need for himself and the dog, plus some of the trinkets lying around the place. He didn't know how long they'd be away so he thought a little familiarity in their new setting would make him feel a bit more at home.

'You're like a woman,' Angela said, teasing him for the methodical packing.

'Be quiet, I just like to be thorough.'

'Thoroughly like a woman then.'

A car horn sounded outside and Angela went to the window to check if it was Putty.

'Dad's here, Scott. Let's get everything in the car.'

Putty stood beside an old grey Renault that juddered and spluttered a little as it idled in neutral.

'I don't know how far we're going but are you sure this will get us there?' Scott said.

'Fuck off, it might be old but I've had it checked over and it's all in good order, which on New Year's day I might add was a pain in the ass to get done.'

'Alright dad, we appreciate it,' Angela said, and gave his hand a squeeze.

Twenty minutes later Scott was driving the car back towards town. Putty shared the back seat with Boris who seemed excited by his new surroundings and happily bounded from side to side, clambering over Putty to look out of the windows; Angela rode up front and the boot was loaded up with clothes and supplies from the house.

'You want to tell me a bit about this friend of yours then?' Scott asked.

'Yeah he's a decent guy, bit weird though. Doesn't much like people.'

'Fantastic.'

'I don't mean he doesn't like anyone at all, just he's pretty selective and prefers mostly to keep to himself. I got started selling weed with him years ago when we were younger. He was never cut out for it though. He liked to smoke but could never get on with the customers,' Putty said reflectively. 'He thought they were mostly just idiots.'

'Maybe he was right,' Scott said, grinning.

'He took off some time after we had worked together. Never heard anything much from him for years. Turns out he'd met a woman named Mary, the love of his life by all accounts; and a whirlwind romance later they got married. They'd stay in one place for a while and then move again. Never really setting down roots, never had kids.'

'So what happened then, divorce?'

'No, cancer. Totally out of the blue. She went for a routine check-up and they found a lump. Six months later she was dead. Jeff was at work when she called him on his cell phone. He reckons that one moment marked the beginning of the end of his life. To this day he won't carry one anymore; after she died he said his phone was like a talisman of doom, everything was great and then a minute later it would never be the same again.'

Scott shifted his weight in the seat, unsure what to say about this personal revelation regarding someone he wasn't even sure he wanted to meet.

'Anyway, he managed to get some cash together a while ago and apparently got a good deal on this place up in the mountains. I don't know much more about it than that. I haven't seen him for a couple of years and he won't say shit on the phone, that's if you even manage to get one in his hand.'

'He's a nice guy,' Angela said. 'He's had his troubles but dad just makes him sound worse than he really is.'

Scott knew Putty wasn't stupid, and despite his first impressions of the man he now knew there was more to his personality than laziness and cunning, but that didn't mean this would be a good move. Even if Putty had his best intentions at heart, and to have his daughter along for the ride Scott reckoned he must have, they still saw things from different angles. He suspected that Putty knew more than he was letting on. With the situation Scott had gotten himself into with McBlane, he felt he didn't have much choice other than to go along with this, albeit cautiously.

They dropped Putty off near his block of flats and said their goodbyes. Angela kissed him on the cheek and said she'd be in touch soon.

Chapter 11

Detective Mark Fallon and partner Alan Bryson arrived on the scene at 02:34 to investigate another shooting, this time just outside of Aura nightclub. Nothing concrete had so far turned up from the ongoing lines of inquiry. A lot of circumstantial, but no hard evidence to give them reason to prosecute any one individual.

There had been further assaults and disappearances around the drug scene, which in itself was no big surprise, but a lot of the victims were now dealers rather than customers. It had begun to raise eyebrows down at the station and Fallon knew he was under pressure to come up with something.

He didn't know if this was going to tie directly to the last assault at the club, but prayed for something to point towards McBlane. The *victim* this time was a low level thug called Glen Thomas, who was known for being available for any act of cruelty or violence providing the price was right. It was entirely possible the shooting was by someone he'd crossed in the past, retaliating. Open and shut case Bryson was still droning in his ear, but Fallon wasn't comfortable with writing it off so soon.

The area around the crime scene had been taped off by the police who'd arrived first, and were now trying to disperse a crowd of onlookers.

'Any of this lot see it happen?' Fallon asked one of the policemen on crowd control as he ducked under the yellow tape.

'No, we've asked everyone and other than that doorman no-one saw a thing,' he said and slung his thumb in the direction of a stocky tuxedo clad bouncer talking to a patrolman by the club's entranceway.

Fallon looked over the blood splashes in the alleyway, made a few notes and walked to the ambulance that was parked up a little further down the block.

Inside the paramedics had mostly patched up the prostate figure of Glen Thomas on the gurney. He was complaining about being in pain, and the paramedic was explaining, probably not for the first time judging by the impatience in his voice, that they could administer no more pain medication to him until he was admitted at the hospital.

'Evening, Glen,' Fallon said, stepping up into the ambulance.

'Detective Fallon, I'm honoured,' he replied, in a sarcastic grimace.

Fallon indicated to the paramedics to leave and they closed the rear doors of the ambulance after them. Thomas's surly expression took a turn towards concerned.

'Right what happened? And spare me the shit cause you know I'll find out eventually, and if you've lied – well I think we both know it's only a matter of time till our paths cross again, and I'll be anything but friendly next time.'

'Just like I told the cop before. I was coming out of the club, this guy at the corner shot me then ran off down the alley.'

'Just like that. Nothing happened between you, was he in the club earlier? Do you know him? Have you fucked him over in the past?'

'No he wasn't inside, I don't think. I don't know him but I've seen him around, was that little guy with the wrinkled up face and the greasy hair, Twinkle, people call him.'

'And that's all you have, you came out, he shot you and ran off?'

'Yeah, one of the bouncers grabbed at him as well.'

Fallon cast an appraising look at Thomas for a moment before he spoke again. 'If you're fucking with me and there's people higher up involved here then you'd better tell me now.'

Thomas looked away sullenly and said nothing. Fallon reached towards him and pressed the tip of his index finger hard against the freshly bandaged area on Thomas's leg.

'Ahh Jesus fucking Christ, get off me you fucking psycho. I don't know anything else, fuck.'

'Everything alright in there?' the paramedic asked from outside, and knocked on the rear door.

Fallon opened it and got back down out of the ambulance. He looked past the waiting paramedic and pretended not to see the concerned look on his face. The officer had finished talking with the doorman so he made his way over.

'Right and you are?' Fallon said, looking directly at the burly doorman with the glittering earlobe.

'Billy Shugg. I just gave my account of what happened to that guy there.'

'Your account? OK, well I don't want your *account* of anything, just tell me what happened.'

'The guy who was shot, well he was leaving the club and the other guy stood over there and shot him. I made a grab for him but he shook me off and ran down the alley. He dropped his wallet though, that's how you guys know who he is.'

Fallon glanced toward the alley then back at Billy Shugg who looked decidedly pleased with himself. 'So he came from this way, or this way?' he asked, pointing first up the street and then down it.

'I don't know, that way maybe.' The bouncer pointed.

'OK well, he'll be on camera then so we can verify exactly what you've said.' Fallon nodded towards the solitary surveillance camera, around 100 yards up the road perched like a bird of prey on a third storey ledge.

'I don't know, maybe he didn't come from that way.'

'If you were quick enough and fearless enough to leap down from here and catch hold of the guy in the act, then you must have been watching him beforehand, thought he looked suspicious maybe; no doubt your boss will be very pleased with your work.'

The doorman shuffled his feet. 'Yeah, I guess. I just got lucky really though, maybe the guy was already in the alley. I just grabbed at him, he dropped his wallet then ran off.'

'Yeah that seems to be the way everyone's telling it. Word for word, even.' He flipped closed the notebook he'd been writing in and went to see if his partner had had any more luck gathering information.

Bryson was stood chatting with the patrolmen who had now mostly succeeded in convincing the initial crowd to disperse. He wasn't holding his notepad and pen so Fallon figured whatever questions he'd had, had already been answered.

'You ready to go?' Fallon asked, when there was a break in the conversation.

'Yeah.'

They walked briskly back to the car to get out of the cold night air.

'You get what you wanted?' Bryson asked with a smirk.

'Not sure what you mean by what I wanted, but I got enough to know this isn't as simple as you'd like it to be.'

'Shit, so we need to keep poking into this? One scumbag shoots another scumbag, big deal. Someone will stumble over this Twinkle guy at some point and that'll be it. Just move on.'

Fallon had been partnered with Bryson for the last couple of years. Initially they'd gotten on fine, but any commitment and hunger for the work which Bryson used to have seemed to have taken a big dip during the last six months.

'I'm gonna look into this Twinkle guy anyway, it's the only lead we have so far. See if anyone who knows him can shed some light on what he was into.'

The streets had been understandably deserted and when they pulled onto the highway they found it no different. The snow had completely gone in the city, and even though the day was grey, the rain had given the world a clean fresh look, like an old car that's just been polished.

Angela unfolded a scribbled map and list of directions she'd been given by her dad and said she should be able to follow the route and get them there. After about an hour Angela told Scott to turn off at the next junction, then follow a long winding road that would lead them up to the mountains. They drove in silence for a while, the quiet beauty of the countryside drifting past them on either side of the car. Boris had settled down to sleep in the back. A suggestion of mist lurked in the distance without ever seeming to draw closer. Angela slept. Faces of curious sheep followed the progress of the car as if hypnotised. Scott remembered his uncle Bob being able to replicate the exact baaing sound of a sheep and even lure them into what appeared to be a conversation; he smiled at the memory of simpler times.

An old abandoned tractor stood rusting on a verge between two fields, an object that had served its purpose and now been discarded and forgotten about. He thought of the tattered brown suitcase; and of the contents within it.

Farmed land grew sparser and uncultivated brush and wilderness now made up most of the landscape. It would have made a nice painting, Scott thought, the kind you'd likely see on the wall in an old pub, but it would look like the colour had been sun bleached over the years leaving only greys and faint pastel shades remaining. Occasional clusters of buildings, farmsteads or possibly small villages became visible once in a while, signposts declaring their unfamiliar names would pass by the car.

Once the road had begun to climb more consistently, Scott gently shook Angela to wake her.

'What time is it?' she asked, sleepily rubbing her eyes.

'Afternoon. You want to check the route to see if I've missed a turning?'

Angela unfurled the paper again and traced down it with the tip of her finger.

'Have we passed a signpost for Black Acre Woods yet?'

'Nope.'

'It shouldn't be long now then.'

Patches of snow became more common on the higher ground. At first covering the tops of hills around them like white chocolate sauce poured generously over a dessert, and now gathered in small drifts by the sides of the road.

'So when was the last time you saw this guy?'

'Not for years now, I used to see him all the time when he and dad were working together.'

'He's fine with us turning up now though?'

'He will be, yeah, I've brought a note from dad.'

About twenty minutes later Angela, who'd been studying the route plan more intently, told Scott to slow down shortly after seeing the sign for Black Acre Woods.

'There's a turning somewhere close that's hard to spot – there,' she said, indicating a barely visible dirt track that angled through a wall of pine trees. For the first ten feet or so the lower branches had been stripped away from the trunks of the trees on each side of the track and some kind of trellis fashioned between them up above. Ivy grew up both trunks and across the trellis forming a living archway. 'Yeah this is it.'

Scott drove under the arch and took the car slowly up the track, not wanting to risk any serious damage that could easily be sustained from the deep potholes or sharp rocks that emerged from the dirt like corpse fingernails. Half a mile or so along what Angela had described as the driveway, an old wooden cabin came into view and as they drove nearer they saw the main house a little further on, behind a wall of thick eucalyptus bushes.

Scott parked up and they both got out; a squeal of wood from behind them announced that the door to the main house had been opened.

'Jeff,' Angela said turning, and smiled at the man peering suspiciously at them through a pair of thick black-rimmed glasses. He had long brown hair that cascaded wildly down either side of his face and a full beard that was peppered with grey. He wore a sweater that was so thick it looked as if it may have been sheared from a sheep, dipped in green dye and then wrapped around him. Scott noticed that he still wore a gold wedding band.

'Angela?' he asked cautiously.

'Yeah you old hippy, come and give me a hug.'

He tottered down the four wooden steps from the house and made his way towards her, smiling.

'I didn't know you were coming. Your dad never said the last time I spoke to him.'

'No it was kind of spur of the moment,' Angela said as they embraced.' I've brought a letter from him though, and some supplies.'

'Bring them in then,' he said releasing her, and nodded in the direction of the house as he began to study the note Putty had written.

'This is Scott,' she said, as she let the dog out of the car and began to take out boxes of food.

Jeff fixed Scott with an undetermined look and nodded, then motioned for him to follow them inside.

Scott picked up one of the boxes of groceries and followed Angela, Jeff and Boris into the house.

A faint musty smell like Autumn when initially entering was replaced by the warm charcoal scent of a large smouldering open fire. Bare stone walls and natural exposed wood beam ceilings, coupled with a lack of any discernable modern features or decoration gave the house a timeless quality that might be too sparse for some tastes, but Scott found endearing. A chandelier hung from the ceiling that had been fashioned from deer antlers with covering around the bulbs that looked to have been made from deer skin. The fireplace was lined with horse brasses and an old fashioned revolver hung centrally above it.

'Did you make that?' Scott asked, pointing to the chandelier.

'Yes,' Jeff said, without looking up at where Scott was pointing.

'Do you hunt?'

'No,' he said; his eyes slid over Scott and stayed there for a moment, 'the materials came from deer I found who'd been winged by hunters and fled up here to die.

Scott nodded, but said nothing further.

Jeff finished reading the note. Scott again noticed Jeff peering in his direction from between the top of the paper and his thick bushy brows.

Later that night, they sat around the kitchen table and ate a vegetable casserole that Jeff had prepared, whilst working their way through three bottles of wine. Angela did most of the talking and although Jeff seemed interested in her conversations, he offered up little back in the way of dinner table anecdotes. Most of the input he made came in the form of questions, and most of those were directed at Scott. He had an intrusive gaze and quietly confident manner that seemed to strip away the layers of protective deception Scott would usually adopt around strangers. Scott knew Jeff had at least once in his life been involved with drugs during the days he'd worked with Putty, so he was open about his own dealing and even elicited the odd smile from Jeff with some of his tales. Angela seemed happy that the initial introductions had gone well and before they realised it was already past midnight and Jeff showed them down to the guest cabin.

'It's not been used since I took the place on,' he said, turning the handle and giving the door a shove with his shoulder to force it through the swollen wooden frame.

The inside smelled of cold wet wood and stale air. Jeff started a fire in the grate which released tendrils of warmth into the room, making it feel a little more homely.

'You can leave the windows open tomorrow to get some fresh air back in here, but I'd keep them closed for now, we'll most likely have frost again tonight.

The first week went better than Scott had expected after his initial impression of Jeff. Their host was hospitable if not overly talkative. He would often vanish for a few hours, and sometimes for most of the day, without offering up any explanation as to where he'd been, but they would discover lists of chores left for them to do in his absence. There was an old red Toyota 4x4 pickup parked out behind the house that would sometimes be gone at the same time Jeff was, but mostly remained in the same spot with Jeff nowhere to be found.

'Dad said he was always something of a loner, even way back when they were younger,' Angela said, in answer to Scott's question regarding Jeff having gone missing again one day, as they stood chopping vegetables in his kitchen.

'You think he just goes off wandering in the woods all the time then?'

Angela shrugged and kept her focus on the carrots she was dicing.

'Dad said he'd quit construction work in favour of long distance trucking so he could spend more time on his own. Maybe having us around is taking its toll on him.'

'You should bring it up over dinner then. The possibility of us going back, see how he reacts.'

'OK. I was going to go into the village to get some things

this afternoon and check for any news on Steph. I'll call dad then too and see what he thinks.'

Jeff came back into the house around two that afternoon, offering no more information as to his whereabouts than on other such days. Angela got a list of things he needed and took a drive with Scott down the mountain to the village.

Other than a small pub, a church and a post-office-cum-general store, there wasn't much else to distinguish Bloody Bush as a village. The locals had grown a little more accustomed to seeing Scott and Angela as this was now their third trip, but still retained their suspicious air around them. Any questions put to them seemed more about information mining than just regular chit chat, and no background conversations took place in their presence when other locals happened to be in the vicinity.

The owner of the Post Office was called Maurice. A sixtyish-year-old with a large red nose that was pebble-dashed with broken capillaries, and a smooth bald head with a fuzz of grey hair around the side like the tide mark on a dirty bath. He had a gruff manner, distrusting eyes and a cough like kicked gravel.

Angela turned on her phone and managed to get a weak signal, so dialled home for any news on Steph. Scott busied himself retrieving items off the list from the uncluttered shelves and put them on the counter in front of Maurice.

'Still here then,' he observed with a nod, as if confirming something he'd suspected all along.

'Yeah, for now anyway.' Scott replied.

'Winters up here are bleak once the snow starts to settle in. Been clear enough so far but once the roads get covered you may have to bed in for weeks. No ploughs come along this way I can tell you. That vehicle you got there will be no more use for getting you about in than a pair of flippers.'

'Thanks for the warning,' Scott said and stretched his mouth into a smile.

'It wasn't a warning, is a fact,' he said peering at Scott through bristled brows. 'You still up there with that bearded fella?'

'Jeff, yeah we're staying in the cabin,' Scott said, and distractedly looked at his watch. Time had little relevance up here, he'd noticed. Days could slide by unnoticed like water in a brook, but the momentum would gather up and impregnate moments like this making them seem almost endless in comparison.

He tapped the face of his watch with a forefinger in a gesture to check if it was still working.

The bell at the entrance danced and jingled as the door of the shop swung open. Scott was pleased to see Angela walk in, the tension that had been building in the air began to melt and Maurice returned to reading his newspaper.

'Dad says just wait it out, that Jeff'll be fine.'

'OK then. What about Steph?'

'No word on her at all, but dad said there's a detective been asking questions about Twinkle and he's been looking for you. Did you know he'd gone missing?'

Scott felt as if the distance between them and home had just grown a lot smaller and that even up in the mountains he still hadn't gone far enough to escape his troubles.

'No. How long has he been missing for?'

'Dunno, dad didn't say. The detective has already spoken to Neil though, and he's been around all the bars asking questions there too.'

'Come on, let's pay for this lot and get back,' Scott said, and as he turned to walk back to the counter, discovered Maurice's attention had gravitated from his newspaper to their conversation.

As they brought the box of groceries into the house, they were welcomed by the mouth-watering aroma of one of Jeff's culinary creations drifting through from the kitchen.

'I'm making chilli and plenty of it, so I hope you're hungry,' Jeff announced as they carried in the supplies.

'Definitely,' Angela said, 'and dad says hi, by the way.'

Jeff nodded and kept stirring the pot on the stove, Boris sitting dutifully by his side.

'You mind watching this for a bit Angela?' he said, 'Scott you can give me a hand to chop some wood out back.'

For someone who used words like they were in finite supply, this was relatively a full conversation for Jeff, and Angela and Scott exchanged glances before Scott followed him outside.

Jeff led the way around the house to where a stack of logs lay beside an axe and chopping block. Scott took a firm grip on the handle and yanked it free from the stump it was embedded in.

Jeff sat down on an old wooden bench and pulled out a pack of cigarettes, took one out and lit it.

'I didn't realise you smoked tobacco,' Scott said, levelling the first log up on the stump to take a swing at.

'Only sometimes, everything in moderation, so they say anyway.'

'Does that go for company as well?' Scott asked, and brought the axe down, easily splitting the log in half.

Jeff chuckled as he exhaled a cloud of smoke. 'You starting to feel like you've outstayed your welcome, young Scott?'

'Well, despite being a great host, you tend not to be overly vocal, so me and Angela were thinking maybe it was time we moved on,' he said, selecting another log from the pile to be chopped.

'No, it's not time for you to go yet. We have things to discuss before that happens.'

'Does this have something to do with the letter Putty sent up for you?'

'What makes you say that then?' Jeff asked, peering quizzically at Scott through a wisp of smoke.

'You just seemed to be focusing as much on me as you were the letter when you were reading it,' he said, and brought the axe down again. A brief flash to the night Twinkle died startled him, the hammer falling onto his still warm body. Scott shook his head.

'You've got an eye for detail,' Jeff said, flicking loose ash from the cigarette. 'I'm sure that's served you well being a drug dealer.'

'I guess it has, from time to time.'

'So that's your career path then?' Jeff asked.

Scott got the impression that Jeff only asked questions he already knew the answers to, like a lawyer, and despite the feeling of being cross examined he still wanted to know where the questioning was leading, so he obliged with the answers.

'No, not a career – maybe not anything anymore.'

'Things change, you have to adapt,' Jeff said and looked wistfully out over the tops of the trees that grew down the receding slope to the side of the house.

'Is that what you're doing out here then Jeff, adapting?' Scott said. He wiped the sweat from his forehead with the back of his hand and picked up another log.

'Nope, not anymore. I'm already as adapted as I'm ever likely to get,' Jeff said, and Scott saw his beard shift as he grinned. 'So what's your next move, Scott?'

'Well, I thought I had some stuff lined up back home but now I'm not so sure. I guess maybe I thought I had what it took to go the extra mile to get what I wanted from life, but then I see people who really do go that extra mile, and I know for sure I don't want to be like them.'

Scott put down the axe for a moment and glanced at Jeff to see him peering intently back, as if Scott were a riddle he was trying to work out the solution to. Scott waited, thinking he was about to say something, but Jeff just continued to stare.

'You alright?' Scott asked, perplexed by the sudden silence.

'What are you like with confined spaces?' Jeff asked him suddenly, ignoring Scott's question.

'What like elevators and stuff? OK I suppose, why?'

Jeff stood up from the bench and walked to the outbuilding Scott had presumed to be a garage or workshop behind his parked pickup. Turning a key to release the padlock, Jeff slid back the door. They both went inside and then he closed the door after them and bolted it from the inside. The smooth concrete floor was large enough to accommodate two, possibly three parked cars, but at the moment stood empty other than some building materials scattered around, and two large wooden workbenches with clamps and vices fixed to them. Various other tools hung from brackets along the walls.

'I wouldn't exactly call this an enclosed space, Jeff.'

Jeff shook his head and walked to what looked like a manhole cover behind one of the benches in the corner of the room. He opened a drawer and took out a metal tool with which to open up the hatch. Inserting the tool into the slot he twisted it ninety degrees and then heaved the metal covering off leaving a circular black hole where it had been. Jeff reached into the darkness and clicked a switch illuminating a roughly circular tube which descended around fifteen feet, a steel ladder bolted to one side with which to climb down.

'OK, well that's more of a confined space,' Scott said.

Jeff grunted as he knelt down and swung his body around onto the ladder and began to climb down. Although he hadn't been instructed to, Scott thought it best he should follow. The room below was around ten feet square with whitewashed walls. Large electrical boxes were mounted on one wall with cables protruding from them as thick as Scott's wrist. Another wall was dominated by a sealed airtight door that Scott thought looked something between the door from a giant fridge and that of a bank vault.

'This is the reason you're up here Scott,' Jeff said, looking at him earnestly. 'Putty spoke up for you as someone I should consider but I made up my own mind while you've been here.'

Scott still had no idea what was going on, so he remained silent as Jeff unlocked the huge metal door with a key he took from his pocket, and then opened it.

The door swung inwards revealing rough limestone walls forming an oval tunnel behind it. A blue –white illumination shimmered around the walls from a light source around a corner further ahead.

'What is this place?' Scott asked, running his fingers along the surface of the slightly damp limestone on either side of him.

'Caves. Been here for hundreds of years, thousands maybe,' Jeff said, striding ahead.

Scott followed him a few steps behind, becoming conscious now of a low pitched electrical hum, like the type always superimposed aboard the ships on sci-fi shows he'd watched on TV as a kid. The light got brighter and the hum louder as he followed Jeff further down the cave as it veered to the right.

Rounding the corner Scott saw the cave open out on either side of them to a width of around thirty feet; the ceiling rose and the floor dropped away to a height of he reckoned maybe twenty feet. A plasterboard wall had been installed a little way ahead with a closed door in it, but what had really got Scott's attention were the rows of tiny cannabis plants on shelves below long fluorescent tubes.

'Jesus, did you do all this?' Scott said.

'Yeah, all my own work.' Scott could see the pride on Jeff's face at the accomplishment of what he'd built.

'Does Angela know?'

'No, no-one does. You're the first one to see it. Putty knows I'm up to something but doesn't know what, and he knows better than to ask,' Jeff said. 'This way.'

He led Scott to the door in the plasterboard wall and turned the handle. As the door opened light flooded out, so bright it was like receiving a piece of the sun as a gift that you had just removed the wrapping from. Scott held up a hand to shield his eyes until they adjusted to the brightness, Jeff had already strode inside.

Beyond the doorway stood row after row of bushy cannabis plants in formation like Roman soldiers. Thin plastic tubes ran to each of the plants from huge water containers positioned along one side of the cave. The illumination came from high intensity lights that hung down over the plants at intervals of every four or five feet.

'Fuck me, I think I just entered the Twilight Zone,' Scott said, looking around him at the complexity and precision of the equipment, 'this must have taken you forever.'

'It's been a long time coming,' Jeff said, stroking his beard as he looked thoughtfully along the rows of plants.

Scott felt his hair blow in a draft and looked up to see one of many oscillating fans attached along the cave walls behind him; interspersed below them were a number of bright red fire extinguishers. Large ducts were attached to the ceiling, Scott presumed to vent in and out fresh air.

Having apparently been happy with what he'd observed from the plants, Jeff walked further down the cave to another floor to ceiling plasterboard wall, this one smaller as the cave here tapered in, narrowing from all sides. This time, beyond the door were three small partitioned rooms: a living quarters with two armchairs and a small TV, a kitchen area complete with a small stove and cupboards overflowing with various tinned goods, a refrigerator and a sink, and a small sleeping quarters with a bunk bed and two mattresses.

'Are you expecting a nuclear war?'

'Hardly, no, but I like to be prepared. One more thing,' Jeff motioned towards a small hatch in the roof above the living quarters.

Opening the hatch revealed another corrugated tube leading

up with a ladder attached; this time the tube was longer, perhaps thirty feet.

'That's an escape hatch to the surface, just in case. It leads out into the woods a way behind the house.'

'Because you like to be prepared?'

'Exactly.'

Around the dinner table later that night Jeff explained to Angela where he and Scott had been that afternoon.

'So that's where you keep disappearing to,' she said, 'we thought you were off hiking around on the mountain foraging for strange looking mushrooms or something.'

Jeff chuckled.

'So you said that was why I was here,' Scott said, 'what do you mean by that then Jeff?'

Jeff ate another forkful of the steaming home-made chilli, considering his words carefully before answering.

'When I first took this place on I knew about a small cave on the land, that's why I wanted it. I had planned to run a small cannabis farm and just live off the proceeds, hopefully put a little away for retirement, but when I was removing some of the stone for ventilation, part of where I was digging fell through.'

'So the giant cave had always been there and no-one ever discovered it?' Scott asked.

'No. There are plenty of legends about the caves and their previous uses back through history. Old Maurice down at the Post office will happily chew your ear off all day long if you get him started about them, and Amos the landlord at the pub is just as bad, although I'd rather you didn't speak about them when you do go down to Bloody Bush, in fact not to anyone.'

'So if the cave had been discovered previously, how did it get undiscovered?' Angela asked.

'The caves, from what I can gather, were generally used for hiding. Rich landowners would apparently hide in them during times of war from invading forces; also bandits would use the caves to stow away after committing robberies, hiding away from the authorities seeking them out. When I rediscovered this one, I found the remains of three people who'd been sealed up inside.'

'Three bodies?' Angela asked.

'No, just bones and scraps of cloth. Likely they'd been there for hundreds of years.'

'So what did you do with them?'

'Chucked them away in the woods, what do I care? They were probably just muggers and thieves who the authorities tracked down and just decided to seal up the entrance and leave them inside to die. Whatever, the fact remains that it's mine now and that's what we're here about,' Jeff said, prodding the table with a forefinger.

Angela refilled their wine glasses and Scott clicked his lighter open and snapped it shut several times while waiting for Jeff to start speaking again.

'When I took the place on, like I say, I had anticipated a modest size project that I could comfortably manage on my own. Opportunity knocked when I found the big cave so now I have something bigger than planned that unfortunately I can't run single handed. I talked to Putty a while ago when I'd decided to expand out, about the possibility of either him or someone he knew moving out here to work as part of a lucrative project. You see where I'm going with this?'

'Yeah,' Scott said.

'He said you were the one I should see.'

* * *

'So you're faced with a dilemma,' Angela said, when they were back in bed together at the cabin. 'Do you want to take Jeff up on the offer?'

'I don't have many other options and it seems like a pretty great deal.'

'You gonna talk to Jeff tomorrow, tell him you'll do it?'
'I think so, yeah.'

* * *

The next eight weeks passed pretty quickly. Jeff proved to be a patient teacher but would accept no lack of effort or commitment from Scott as far as the plants or any of his other duties were concerned. Scott was pleased with the workload though, and didn't mind the increased hours as the crop came to fruition. His days for the most part were spent in the cave tending to the plants, nutrient tanks and ensuring that the equipment was all operating correctly. Jeff's mobility, especially on cold mornings during the winter, could sometimes be a problem; but as Scott's knowledge of the operation grew, and Jeff's confidence in Scott's ability along with it, he was happy to take over the reins as head gardener.

Once their first crop was harvested Scott still hadn't made any longer term plans, and until Angela pointed out to him that he was still in fact living out of his suitcase, it hadn't even occurred to him to do otherwise. Her clothes and personal effects had long since found their way into the closet and drawer space in the cabin, and she seemed completely at home there now.

Angela's walks to the village to check on news about Steph were still a regular part of her week, but as time had gone by they had become less anxious events and were now more routine. Nobody had heard anything and Angela had begun to think maybe Steph had just taken refuge with a different friend as she had previously done with her.

Angela had already left the cabin when Scott woke the next day. He hadn't had much sleep, his thoughts as ever returning to Twinkle. He'd had no news regarding the investigation to bring Twinkle in for the shooting outside Aura for a while, but Scott doubted it had just blown over.

The suitcase he'd brought had largely remained packed. Cycling through the clothes like a conveyor belt, take them off the top, put them clean back on the bottom. It sat at the foot of the wardrobe in the bedroom as he'd initially been unsure of their length of stay. But after Angela had teased him about living like a hobo, claiming he wasn't living up at the cabin but squatting there, he'd decided to take out all of his stuff and make more of an effort for it to feel like a home.

Scott began to take out his clothes, putting some into the empty chest of drawers and hanging others in the unfortunately coffin shaped old wardrobe. What remained from the roll of bills he'd brought from the divided up stash with Neil he tucked away in a drawer inside one of his socks. That would continue to do for groceries and whatever cash they may need on a day to day basis. The cloth bag containing the money from McBlane he took out and slid under the bottom of the mattress.

He took out a small ivory Buddha and placed it on top of the chest of drawers. An ornately carved wooden box Scott used for storing his toiletries he carefully removed to put alongside it, but tripped over one of his boots as he walked across the room. Scott dropped the box as he fell to brace himself for a collision against the drawers, and raised his forearm up just in time to prevent his head from taking the brunt of the impact.

Dazed, he sat on the floor with one leg sprawled out on either side of him. Scott turned his arm to see a gash of around four inches that blood was beginning to well up in. The chest of drawers barely moved due to their sturdy build, but his uncle's wooden box had been less fortunate, having come apart, scattering Scott's photos and toiletries across the floor.

He wiped the emerging blood onto his pants and struggled into a kneeling position to begin gathering up the box's contents. One side had sustained some surface damage to the intricately patterned wood and had scarred some of its paintwork onto the chest of drawers. The bottom of the box,

Scott noted, had come dislodged in the collision and picking it up he attempted to slot it back into place. Turning the box upside down, Scott noticed a folded piece of paper that was still wedged in the underside of the box, behind the panel that had broken off. Removing the paper, Scott put the box down on the floor and unfolded it.

Briefly scanning through, it appeared to be a letter sent from his mother to someone called Robert. Looking at the scattered items and photos on the floor Scott saw other similar pieces of paper that he didn't immediately recognise as his own and gathered them together. Sure enough they were more letters from his mother and judging by the dates on them, had been written over a period of many years. Scott checked them all again and organised them so the oldest were on top of the pile and began to read:

Dear Robert,

I can't tell you how much last night meant to me. I've watched you around school these last couple of years and thought you would never notice me. Boys my age seem so immature and boring I could never be interested in them the way I am in you. I know we've only been out twice now but I don't regret anything that happened last night, I've wanted it for so long and after such a wonderful night at the dance it just felt so right. I hope you still feel the same and don't regret anything you said.

Forever Yours,

Kay.

Scott read the letter through again once he'd finished it the first time. He'd never heard mention of any Robert in her past, but the letters were hidden away in one of his Uncle Bob's prized possessions. Was she talking about him? He'd had no idea there had been any history between his mother and Uncle Bob. He sat back feeling a little stunned, lit up a cigarette, put the first letter aside and began to read some more. Sure enough he saw even more of his mother's lust and desire to be with Robert confirmed in the next few letters, and some in way more detail than he would have liked. They had been in a serious relationship when they were younger. The passion that flowed from his mother's words on the pages, the intensity of the emotions she conveyed to him made her seem more real, more alive than in any of the brief memories he still held of her. Scott wondered what had happened to make the situation turn out so differently from the future that had been envisioned in his mother's letters.

Dear Robert,

I didn't believe Shelly when she told me about you and her. I knew she had always been jealous of our love, and bitter that you had chosen me over her but I didn't believe the horrible things she'd said until I followed you last night. I saw you with her, Robert. I saw the two of you together. All those things you told me were lies. Are you telling her the same, making the same promises to her that you did to me? I truly believed we would be together forever but now you have broken my heart and I can never forgive you. It's over Robert. I don't want to see you ever again.

Kay.

So he'd cheated on her. These revelations about his family seemed in such contrast to the images and memories of them he carried around inside of him. Memories of his mother were few and distant, but this vibrant and passionate young woman seemed so different from the nurturing and level headed ideal of her that resided on the parental pedestal in his mind.

Scott looked at the remaining letters in his hand, wondering what other secrets lurked on their pages, waiting to be revealed. He flirted with the idea of just destroying them, but decided that not ever knowing be worse than any home truths he might discover.

Dear Robert,

Four months have passed since we broke up and I have spent most of that time at home alone with my studies. I know you have continued to see Shelly, and now I can say I hope things work out for you, perhaps our relationship was never meant to be. I am writing this letter for more than to wish you well, though. During the time I spent at your home I struck up a friendship with your brother Thomas and we have maintained that friendship since. From the time we broke up Thomas and I have studied together on occasion and we enjoy each other's company. I write now to tell you that Thomas has asked me on a date and I think I would very much like to go. I'm not so much asking for your blessing as I am, perhaps, wanting to let you know that it will happen, and I don't want you to feel in any way betrayed or that a secret has been kept from you. I know how hurtful betrayal can be and I wish if possible to spare you from that. I hope you understand and that this causes no ill will between you and Thomas.

Kay.

It was Bob then. This must be the time when she and his dad, Thomas, first began seeing each other. Angela came into the cabin looking for him as Scott finished reading the letter.

'You just decide to trash the place?' Angela asked, looking at his things that still lay scattered across the floor. Scott had been so engrossed in reading his mother's letters he'd forgotten about clearing up.

'Got sidetracked,' he said, beginning to reread the last one again. 'Apparently my mother used to put it about with my uncle before my parents got together. I just found a bunch of old letters hidden away in Bob's wooden box.'

'Oh.' Angela said, 'is that a bad thing then?'

'Well I never knew about it; if there was nothing to be ashamed of or no reason to hide it then why the secrecy?'

'Yeah but you were really young when your parents died, maybe Bob just didn't feel it was his place to say anything. Besides isn't that your parents ended up together what's important, not something she did before that? Sometimes finding out stuff like this only cause pain, Scott. Maybe you should just leave them. '

'Maybe,' he replied, leafing through the pages. 'Anyway, according to what I've read so far, he cheated on her so she dumped him, then dad asked her on a date.

Scott kept flicking through, reading more of the letters as Angela tidied around him.

'Bob's relationship with the other woman ends, then it looks like dad is gonna propose. Then Bob gets caught up in all of his philosophy stuff. It makes sense though, when he was sitting for hours down by the tree he'd often say things about looking for meaning in suffering. I just never realised this is where it first came from. Samsara I think he called it, the circle of suffering before attaining Nirvana.'

'Do you really think you should read any more?' Angela asked. 'I mean, this is all private stuff between two people who are now both dead, nothing is gonna change what happened in the past, maybe you should just put them back.'

'I hardly have anything tangible of my mother to hold on to,' Scott said, already reading on. 'If this is gonna give me an insight into who she really was then I want to find out. Good and bad, at least I'll know more.'

Angela figured she should hang around so she made coffee for her and Scott as he continued reading.

'Shit. It looks like mum still had feelings for Bob when she was about to marry dad. She asks him not to come to the wedding and everything.... Maybe dad knew something wasn't right though cause this is where he asks mum to move overseas..... Bob and her are still seeing each other, and she's married to dad now.'

'Are you OK?' Angela asked, putting two cups of coffee down and sitting beside him on the floor.

Scott looked up from the letter and caught Angela's eye. 'I'm OK,' he said and forced a smile.

'Do you think less of your mother now because she had the affair with your uncle?'

'No – I don't know. I just need to go through the rest of the letters before I can process it all, I think.'

Angela nodded and finished tidying away the things that remained on the floor.

'OK they've emigrated now... Bob keeps sending letters...She finally writes back, fucking hell.'

'What is it?'

'She doesn't know if Bob is Jack's father.'

'Oh my god. Do you think he has any idea?'

'I don't know. Bob always seemed to have a closer bond with Jack but I assumed it was because he was older and they could do more stuff together,' Scott said, and turned to the next page.

'This is where my grandparents die. There's a fire at their home. Apparently it was ruled as arson, I never knew that. I can't believe there were so many secrets. Bob is using his share of the insurance money to move over here. Mum is telling him not to, that it could tear what's left of the family apart – Bob ignores her and comes anyway – Yeah they start seeing each other again, I can't believe it – Now it looks like mum is finally coming to her senses. She says she loves him but she doesn't know if she can continue like they are. She won't leave dad and she doesn't want to risk hurting him if he ever found out about the affair.'

Scott flipped through a couple more pages.

'This is the last one. It's dated about a year before I was born.'

Dear Robert,

This is a decision I have agonised greatly over during the last months. The risks that have been taken either accidentally or carelessly have on a number of occasions almost caused our affair to become exposed to Thomas. I have tried so very hard to battle with my conscience over my right to be happy with you, but as I have said before I have a responsibility, a duty to Thomas and to Jack. It has begun to feel recently by your carefree actions as if you actually want Thomas to discover us, so I am then forced into a separation. That makes me doubt the man you are inside, Robert, and causes me to even doubt the validity of the feelings I have for you. The man I fell in love with would never have wantonly destroyed his brother's life, even if it did mean he would be free to pursue the woman he loved. It pains me deeply to say this, but the time has come for our relationship to end. I will always cherish the memory of our time together, and no doubt we will still see each other on family occasions, but as for anything more than this, it is now over.

Please respect my wishes and write me no more,

Kay.

Scott pulled out everything Angela had replaced inside the broken box in case there were any more letters. He pushed and pressed at the box, looking for any other possible compartments where more may have been hidden, but found nothing.

'I have to go home and talk to Jack. I need to tell him what I found in the letters, but I need to hear him say that he didn't know anything about it.'

'But Jeff's leaving soon to go and sell the crop; and what about me and Boris?'

'Will you look after the dog? I'll probably just be gone a day or so, then I'll come right back. Is Jeff here now?'

'No he went out a while ago to make some phone calls and arrange the sale.'

'OK, just give him an outline of what's happened, tell him I'm sorry but I'll be back as soon as I can.' Scott said and kissed her.

Chapter 12

Scott put some things in a bag and threw it into the back of the Renault. A snow so light was falling that it looked like dandelions releasing their seeds during summer. Never seeming to touch the ground they would float around, carried by the smallest currents of air. He knew the trip would need to be quick if what Maurice had told him was right, that once the snow started to lie, the roads up to the mountain would become impassable. The winter had been relatively kind so far but heavy snow had been forecast for the coming few days.

'Drive big, or don't drive at all,' the presenter on local radio crackled out from the car speakers. 'If the south westerly catches those clouds we can expect at least six inches by tomorrow.'

The route back was easy enough to recall. Once the snaking side roads had been replaced by straighter and wider main roads Scott made a call through to Jack. His brother picked up on the second ring.

'Where've you been hiding away? You know everything that's been going on back here?'

'Just taking a break. Why's what's the deal?'

'A Detective Fallon for starters. He's been all over looking for you, poking into stuff because of that shit with Twinkle. I told you that fucker was nothing but trouble but you wouldn't stay away.'

'I've been away, Jack. A minute ago you were complaining about that, make your mind up.'

'Funny. What do you want then, why the call now?'

'I'm on my way back. I need to talk to you.'

'I'll be at the apartment this afternoon,' Jack said, and the line went dead.

Scott dropped the mobile phone into his lap. The gears grated before sliding into place as he accelerated along the slip-road and pulled the car onto the highway back towards Garden Heights. The snow was still falling but melting as soon as it landed on the wet tarmac. He hoped that would remain the case for his journey back.

Scott found a spot in the car park where Stan had waited during his last visit. He slid coins into the slot of the ticket machine and pressed the button, a printed parking ticket was ejected which Scott ripped free from the machine and took back to the car.

He didn't recognise the concierge this time as he made his way inside, so reported to him that he was an expected guest and waited while the man called up to Jack's apartment.

'Go right up sir,' he said, with a brief tilt from the waist.

Scott just caught an elevator as the doors were closing and pressed for the top floor. As the smooth ascent began, Scott's mind again cast back to the lift he and Twinkle had taken on the night of his death. He took a deep breath and let it out slowly. This wasn't the time to get sidetracked with remorse.

He was the last passenger onboard when the lift arrived at the penthouse floor. Scott walked to Jack's door to find it open. He walked inside and pushed the door until he heard the metallic click of the catch falling into place behind him.

'So what was so important to disturb you from hibernation and bring you back to the city, little brother?'

Scott whirled around. Jack was standing beside the large table in the centre of the room with his customary glass of whiskey in hand; although Scott couldn't help but notice the apartment was far from its usual standard of pristine cleanliness. On the table there was a pile of unopened mail and an ashtray with a cigar butt amid a dusting of ash. Jack's shoes had been kicked off and lay on the oak floor like dead fish washed up on the beach. Scott sensed this may not be the time to bring the letters to Jack's attention, but he was here now and patience wasn't Jack's strongest virtue.

'I found these,' Scott said, holding their mother's letters out in front of him. 'They're letters sent over the years from our mother to uncle Bob.'

Jack took a sip from his glass and then rubbed the back of his neck with his free hand.

'OK then, let's see,' he said, taking a seat on one of the couches. He put down the glass and extended his hand for Scott to bring him the letters.

Scott walked across and handed them over. He went to fix himself a drink and then sat on the opposite couch and waited for Jack to work his way through them all.

His brother made no comment as he read, simply laying down one sheet after another onto the table as he finished them, pausing only to take an occasional drink from his glass.

'OK, so what?' He said finally, relaxing back onto the couch. 'So the old lady had a thing with Bob.'

'It's a bit more than that though. He might have even been your father.'

'Unlikely, besides it's all finished with now so what difference does it make?'

'What about the fire? Did you know it was arson? He used the insurance money to follow you all over here to start things up with our mother again.'

'That doesn't prove anything.'

'No it doesn't prove anything, but then our parents dying in the car crash and him being a mechanic? He could have staged the whole thing when she finally wouldn't come back to him. Think about it Jack. His suicide years later could have been due to the guilt of what he'd done. Not being able to live with it anymore. You knew him way better than I ever did, do you think it's possible?'

'Like I say, Scott, that's all in the past. They're all dead now and you have more immediate problems to deal with.'

'Fallon, I know.'

'Yeah, Fallon. You gonna speak to him before you vanish off again, wherever you've been to?'

'I don't know, I really just came back to show you the letters. I hadn't thought much past that. It's not like I have any information that can help him anyway.'

'From what I've heard he thinks there's more to the shooting and Twinkle vanishing than meets the eye, and you're as close to it all as anyone.'

'OK, there's no point arguing with you about this right now, I'm gonna get going. I'll be back in touch in a while,' Scott said, putting down his barely touched glass of whiskey, and walked to the door. 'I really thought those letters would have mattered to you though, Jack. Finding out stuff like that about our family? Possibly even who your father is?"

'So I'll just say I haven't seen you if anyone comes asking again?' Jack asked, sidestepping Scott's last comment.

'I don't know Jack, I haven't done anything wrong. Not really wrong anyway and I don't know where Twinkle is, so tell them what you want.'

Scott turned the handle on the apartment door, left and closed it softly after him. The lights in the hallway seemed brighter than when he'd arrived moments before. Scott moved his hand over the sensor to summon the lift then rubbed his forehead, trying to work loose the tension before it could cement itself into a headache.

He squinted against the harsh glare that poured out of the empty lift as the doors opened and he walked inside. He pressed for the lobby and thought back over Jack's reactions, or rather lack of them, as he'd read through the letters. His absence of visible emotion was fairly typical of Jack when dealing with any serious issues, another one of his finely honed abilities. But to learn that your own father may not be who you thought but actually your uncle? Scott couldn't wrap his head around it, no reaction at all. Nothing.

The lift stopped periodically on other floors, letting people on board, so Scott moved to the back of the car to make room. As the doors parted onto the lobby, Scott waited as the other passengers disembarked and caught sight of Neil seated in the lobby waiting area behind an open newspaper.

Neil saw Scott as he strode over, put down the newspaper and turned to face him.

'What's with the paper, you on a stakeout?'

'Sort of yeah, Elizabeth saw you coming into the building so I came down here to wait for you leaving. Figured if you were in to see Jack you wouldn't be very long.'

'So what is it? Have you seen those guys again who turned you over?'

'No but I'm still keeping away from the bars. I have seen a detective Fallon though, asking all kinds of stuff about Twinkle but also about you.'

'Yeah Jack filled me in already.'

'Do you know where Twinkle is?'

'No.'

'Well he seems to think you're the best route to find him.'

'I've pretty much just been through all this with Jack upstairs, nice to see you man, but if there's nothing else,' he said, and after a second began walking to the exit.

'Just watch your back, Scott.'

Scott spun back around to look at Neil.

'I've been keeping a low profile, hardly been out at all, but Elizabeth remembered where she'd seen one of the guys that jumped me. It was in here, in this building. Couldn't have been anything to do with me either 'cause at that stage I hadn't even met her.'

Scott nodded, not really understanding what it meant, and left.

He walked briskly back to the car pulling up his hood against the sharp winds that whipped at him once he'd left the cover of the building. Snow was falling heavier now.

Scott got into the car, started the engine and used the wipers to clear the layer of snow from the windscreen. He knew he should start the drive back up to the mountains before the weather got worse, but wanted to pick up a few things from the house first and just take a little time out to try and think through what was going on. He knew he couldn't stay around the city too long. The fact that he'd seen Twinkle die at the hands of McBlane and then he'd vanished would make them uneasy. He couldn't risk running into any of them and he knew McBlane would have eyes everywhere.

Scott pulled out of the car park and drove past the Walker building again to turn onto the main street. Two men in a stationary dark green Volvo opposite appeared to watch him as he drove by. This is crazy, Scott thought to himself. All this stuff from Jack and Neil has just made me paranoid. I'm finally about to make some decent cash and get away from this place and now I'm jumping at shadows. I'll get back to the house, relax, maybe have a drink or two and if I feel up to it, then I'll make the drive. If not, then I'll go first thing in the morning.

He turned on the radio and pressed the preset buttons till he found a station he could tolerate. Something mellow to help slow his thoughts. No-one had followed him from the Walker building he reassured himself, took a deep breath and settled back into the seat.

The gravelled patch on the approach to the house was covered with a thin layer of unblemished snow. Scott parked up, walked to the front door and let himself in. The house was in complete darkness, but he slowly walked from room to room turning lights on to make certain he was alone.

Satisfying himself that the house was empty, and again cursing his newly developed hyper tension, Scott went into the kitchen to make some coffee. He didn't know exactly what it was he'd be looking for around the house. Just to poke around for any other things his uncle may have hidden to shed more light on what he'd learned about his family.

The kettle clicked off as a cloud of steam billowed from the spout, fogging up the kitchen window. Scott began pouring the boiling water into a cup with a teaspoon of instant coffee, and heard three loud thumps on the front door. His nerves immediately began to jangle like sleigh bells. His hand holding the kettle wobbled, spilling boiling water onto the counter, and he dropped the spoon. He put the kettle back onto its stand and trying to compose himself, strode to the door.

'Scott Lawrence?' a man in a dark grey suit asked, holding out a sheet of paper as he opened the door. 'I'm Detective Fallon, and this is a warrant to search the premises,' he said, without waiting for confirmation that he was indeed the named person on the warrant.

Fallon waited on the step while presumably another detective and three regular policemen pushed past into the hallway and began searching rooms. Fallon was around six feet tall, medium build, was clean shaven and had short brown hair cut in an unremarkable style.

'Sorry for the intrusion Scott, you want to come have a seat with me while I ask a few questions?'

'I'm sure I don't have a choice, so follow me,' Scott said, and led the way through to the living room.

'Give us a minute,' Fallon said to a uniformed officer who had begun searching through magazines and papers under the coffee table. The policeman nodded and closed the door after himself.

'Alright, what's this about then?' Scott asked, folding his arms in his lap.

'Well, I'm sure you already heard from speaking to your brother and your friend Neil that I've been asking around for the whereabouts of a certain friend of yours.'

'Twinkle, right; but I wouldn't exactly call him a friend.'

'What would you call him then, a work colleague, a business partner?' Fallon asked, and as much as Scott wanted to instantly dislike the man, he couldn't deny he had a certain affable air to him. Not the arrogant self righteousness that he'd come to expect from friends who'd been in similar situations before. He still maintained his guard though, aware this could simply be a ruse to get him to trust the detective and open up to him.

'I would just call him someone who I had the occasional drink with while out in the city.'

'OK, I'll save the round and round here with you Scott and lay my cards on the table. How's that sound?'

Scott nodded and waited for the detective to speak again. Fallon licked his lips thoughtfully and readjusted his seating position on the couch so he was more directly facing Scott.

'Twinkle is missing,' he said, and flicked open the thumb from his clenched left hand he had laid on his knee. 'He's involved in a shooting outside of a certain nightclub.' He uncurled a finger. 'There's way more to it than that, as the guy who was shot is a two bit scumbag and I doubt the bouncers would even report if they saw it happen, let alone try to catch the guy that did it. Let's face it, who's to say they wouldn't get shot in the process?' Another finger uncurled. 'You and Twinkle are close.' Another finger flicked out, and he raised his right hand, palm out, to silence Scott's protestations as soon as he began to make them. 'You know something about what's going on,' he said, extending his little finger, leaving an open palm held out towards Scott.

This time he didn't make a move to silence any rebuttals

Scott might make, but Scott wasn't making any, he just sat in silence looking back at Fallon.

'There's something else going on here Scott, I know that. And I'm pretty sure you've managed to get wrapped up in it. I have my suspicions, but the people I'm after cover their tracks really well, and that's if they even leave any tracks at all. The warrant here is just a formality. I'm not expecting to find anything regarding either Twinkle's current whereabouts or the shooting at the club, which is why we're here now instead of weeks ago. It's you I wanted to see,' he said, and looked Scott straight in the eye, digging around in his head for a reaction.

He slipped the previously outstretched palm into an inside jacket pocket, withdrew his card and offered it to Scott. 'If you're involved in any way, by choice or by accident, then I think you may end up needing my number.'

Scott took the card and slid it into a pocket without looking at it or saying anything.

'We almost done then lads?' Fallon shouted, angling his head towards the closed living room door but keeping his eyes on Scott.

A few seconds later the door was partly opened by the other detective, who put his head through the gap and nodded. Fallon stood up and looked to Scott, as if expecting him to do the same. Scott remained seated.

'Alright Scott, I'll be seeing you then,' he said, and walked back into the hallway closing the living room door after him. Scott waited until the sounds of heavy footsteps filed back outside and he heard the latch of the front door click back into place as it locked after them.

The whole episode had taken probably less than ten minutes from start to finish. Scott felt slightly shaken by the intrusion but more confused than concerned from the manner of Detective Fallon. He went back into the kitchen and re-boiled the kettle, filled the remainder of his earlier cup with water and picked the spoon off the floor. Taking a sip from the cup he slid his other hand into the pocket containing Fallon's card, his forefinger tracing a line around its edge. He withdrew the card, tore it up and dropped the pieces into the trash. It wasn't as if he'd have any need to call the man.

* * *

Scott woke early the next morning and immediately went to the window to see if the weather had been kind during the night. Anxiously pulling back the curtain, he revealed a scene that would have been more welcome on a Christmas card than on his front garden as a thick layer of snow carpeted everything in sight.

His own personal search, the previous night after that of the uniformed intrusion, for anything that once belonged to his uncle, had yielded nothing in the way of letters or any other such nuggets of information. In fact the only artefact from the past that had been revealed on his insistent poking and prising of the various objects had been dust.

Scott had bundled together a selection of clothes for both cold and warm weather the previous night, thinking of the varying atmospheric conditions of his living in the cabin and working down in the cave with Jeff. The house here had nothing left to offer Scott; for all he knew it may have been the last time he'd spend the night here.

He called to Boris out of habit before remembering he'd left the dog with Angela up in the mountains. Taking his bag, fit to burst with all of his clothes he'd crammed into it, he left by the front door and walked to the car.

Unlocking the door, Scott removed a balled up t-shirt before dropping the bag into the car. He used the t-shirt to scrub off the majority of snow from the outside of the car.

Climbing into the driver's seat, Scott silently said a prayer to whichever deity may have been listening before turning the ignition key. To his amazement the old engine turned over first time and coughed into life.

Scott took it steadily along the country lanes as snow and ice lay in patches along many stretches of the tarmac. He was sure McBlane hadn't simply forgotten about him, and Scott didn't want to chance his luck further by driving closer to the city than necessary to meet up with the highway, so he took an indirect route along deserted stretches of road past farmland, adding over an hour to his journey time.

Eventually the highway beckoned with its many wide, snow free lanes, allowing Scott to push the speed of the Renault up as high as it would go without the risk of skidding on any unseen ice. The old car reluctantly accelerated at his insistence before topping out at around 75mph.

By the time Scott took the turning off the highway for the mountains, snow dominated the landscape in every direction. The only discernable feature of the tractor he'd noticed from the first trip was a mirror poking defiantly through its thick blanket covering of snow.

As the road gained in altitude, Scott had to suitably reduce the speed with which he navigated it. A few times he'd lost traction already and struggled to bring the car back under control as the wheels spun out on the frozen surface. By the time the signpost for Black Acre Woods came into view, Scott knew he would never get the car up the dirt road to Jeff's, so changed route and drove towards Bloody Bush instead.

An incline about a mile before the village finally proved too much for the old Renault. Scott had managed to get about halfway up but had been repeatedly defeated by the amount of ice and severity of the slope. Finally giving up, he manoeuvred the car as far onto the grass verge at the side of the road as he could, took out his bag and began to walk the rest of the way up to the village.

No snow was falling but the biting wind cut through Scott's clothes, quickly chilling him. He hurried along the road towards Bloody Bush, hoping that he might strike lucky and catch Jeff in the village stocking up on supplies. There'd been no other vehicles on the road for miles, so persuading a local farmer to give him a ride for the remaining few miles didn't look to be a strong possibility.

Smoke drifted lazily from a chimney at the pub, spurring Scott on at a faster pace to get inside out of the cold. Icy water had begun bleeding through his shoes and slowly turned his feet numb.

No sign of Jeff's pickup parked outside either the pub or the post office; in fact there were no signs of any cars coming or going at all, footprints being the only violation in the covering of snow.

Scott went into the post office and shoved the door closed after him. If the tinkling bell above the door wasn't enough to alert Maurice of his presence, then the current of icy air that invaded the shop on his entry would have been.

'Shut the door,' Maurice barked at Scott, then hacked up a knot of phlegm from his chest and spat into something behind the counter.

'Has Jeff been in, or Angela?' Scott asked, and stamped his feet by the door to remove any excess snow.

'Nope, haven't seen either of them for a few days.'

'Shit. My car got stuck in the snow about a mile down the road.'

Maurice nodded and returned his attention to the crossword in the open newspaper on the counter.

'You have any words of wisdom here to help me out then, Maurice?' Scott asked as he walked to the counter and slumped against it dejectedly. He knew the 4x4 parked outside that never seemed to go anywhere belonged to Maurice, and unless it was broken he hoped to be able to wangle a lift up to Jeff's place.

He'd let Maurice come to the conclusion in his own time. Drag it out so he could fill himself with self importance, let him feel that he was saving the day.

'My brother has a farm nearby,' the old shopkeeper said, slowly rubbing his chin between finger and thumb, 'I could maybe ask if he'd tow your car up the road with his tractor, leave it in the car park outside there at the Boar.'

This was an unexpected bonus. Scott agreed and thanked Maurice, fished the car keys out of his pocket and dropped them beside the newspaper.

A minute passed before Maurice looked up again at Scott who still stood waiting.

'What, you want to buy some stamps?'

'I couldn't help but notice your truck out there Maurice. Any chance I could trouble you for a lift to Jeff's place?'

'Nobody to watch the store. What if people come wanting to buy up all my stuff?'

Scott saw his train of thought and went to grab an armload of groceries which Maurice happily rang up and put into a box for him.

'Alright, I'll take you,' Maurice said, after Scott had paid for them, eased himself out of his seat and walked to the shop door.

Scott picked up the box and followed him outside in time to see another evacuated mouthful of phlegm go sailing across the empty lot before disappearing below the level of the snow. The old man jumbled a large key ring until the correct one became apparent and unlocked the car doors.

'You not gonna lock the shop up?' Scott asked as they climbed in.

'No point,' Maurice answered, 'no-one'll be out in this weather anyway.'

The drive up towards Jeff's was as undisturbed by tyre tracks as the car park had been back in Bloody Bush. Either Jeff had gotten finished with the business quickly or more than likely he wasn't back yet.

'Thanks a lot Maurice,' Scott said, as he picked the box of groceries out of the car, 'I'll be sure not to shop at any of your competitors.'

Maurice grunted, acknowledging Scott's sarcasm, and circled his truck around for the journey back down. Scott heard the familiar raking cough through the partially open window as the truck drove off.

'You're back just in time to help me prepare tonight's dinner,' Angela said smiling, as Scott carried the groceries through to the kitchen. He put down the box and she slid her arms around his waist, pulling him towards her, and pressed her lips softly against his before whispering in his ear that she'd missed him.

'Jeff should be back anytime now,' Angela said, 'I thought that must be him when I heard the front door open.'

'Did he take all the cannabis to sell this morning?'

'Yeah first thing. Said he expected to be back sometime today. How did things go back home?'

'Jack claims he doesn't know anything about it, but he's harder to read than the Chinese alphabet,' Scott said, walking into the living room and collapsing onto one of the couches.

'You think your uncle ever did confide anything in Jack?' She asked, sliding onto the couch next to him.

'I don't know, but I doubt I'll get anything else out of him. I did see that detective though.'

'The one you heard had been looking for you, Fallon was it?' she asked, slightly alarmed.

'Yeah, he turned up at the house with a warrant when I stayed there last night.'

'Oh my god, what happened?'

'He was OK to be honest, he had a few guys and they went through the place but hardly with a fine toothed comb. They didn't stay for long. I think he was looking at me more as a source of information than a suspect for anything. Felt like a kind of arm around the shoulder approach,' Scott said, and shrugged.

'You still have to be careful though, especially now with Jeff's thing up here.'

'Yeah, I know.'

'Anyway,' Angela said, grinning as she stood up and pulled Scott to his feet, 'I've missed you way too much to sit around on a couch chatting all day.'

'Really, so what did you have in mind?'

She leant in to kiss him again and hooked a finger through one of Scott's belt loops. Giving him her best wicked grin, Angela turned and walked towards the door, her finger securely pulling him along behind.

Scott woke to the sound of Jeff's truck crunching through the snow outside the cabin on its way up to park beside the house. Angela's naked body was pressed up against him with her arm draped across his chest. The deep sound of her breathing indicating the noise outside hadn't woken her.

Scott carefully untangled himself from Angela, re-dressed in the clothes that had been hurriedly discarded across the floor and made his way to the house to see Jeff.

'Everything go OK?' he asked Jeff as he entered and walked through to the kitchen.

'Yeah it sold. The first of many,' Jeff said, patting the backpack he'd put down on the kitchen table, and gave an uncharacteristically wide grin.

'You get what you'd expected to?'

'More than. There's been some turbulence it the market, so it would seem, and it's driven the prices up.'

Jeff put an unopened bottle of vodka on the table and took two glasses down from a cupboard. 'Join me?' he asked Scott.

'Sure.'

They sat opposite each other and Jeff half filled the glasses.

'Cheers Scott, on a job well done. Putty was right about you,' he said, and clinked his glass against Scott's. 'Did you get your family stuff taken care of that was bothering you when you left yesterday?'

'No not really, but I suppose it doesn't really matter. It's all stuff from the past I'm just finding out about now. Be nice to have loose ends tied up but maybe it's not meant to be.'

'What about the other matter that had been troubling you?'

'That obvious, is it?'

'Anyone could see there was something you were eager to get away from when you first landed up here. Wasn't my business then and still isn't now, but we've spent a bit of time together and maybe the trust has grown enough between us for you to want to share.'

'I got mixed up with some people I shouldn't have and decided it would be for the best to let the dust settle without me being around.'

'Is there anyone after you?'

'The cops came round to my place for a quick search when I got back home, but there's nothing they can put on me, it was just information gathering I think, or an attempt to anyway.'

'What about anyone other than them?'

'Well, there was a guy I did a job for which turned out to be more of an initiation, so I expect as I'm not there to follow on from it he might be a little pissed.'

'Is that what your little bag of money was about then?'

'You went through my stuff?' Scott asked, and laughed a little but couldn't help but feel a twinge of betrayal.

'I have a few times since you've been here. Putty's recommendation was a good start but I wanted to find out as much as I could about you before I told you anything about the plants,' Jeff replied, unapologetically.

'Yeah that was what the money was from. I doubt McBlane

will be happy but I'm out of reach up here while I decide my next step after all of this.'

Jeff's hand brought his glass down hard onto the table with a bang, startling Scott. 'Paul McBlane?' he asked; his body had tensed and eyes become urgent.

'By your reaction I assume he's someone you're aware of, yeah Paul McBlane,' Scott said, putting his own glass carefully back down.

Jeff unscrewed the cap from the vodka, and this time filled both glasses to the brim.

'He's a nasty bastard, Scott,' Jeff said, fixing him with an unwavering stare. 'After my attempt at a drug enterprise with Putty years back, me and McBlane got something going there for a while. He hadn't long been working the doors and was dabbling with powders and pills, knocking them out to the clubbers. I'd wanted to get into the growing side of things, but needed a place to do it and funding to get started. I was a bit naive back then, maybe a bit like you are now.'

Scott let the judgement pass without comment and took a sip from his glass.

'He sorted me a house to set up in and paid for the equipment to get it going and for a while we made some decent money. I didn't want anyone else to know what I was up to so he took all of the buds to sell. After a couple of crops he wanted to expand, get a big industrial unit, said he'd take care of everything, all I had to do was grow it.'

'I gather you didn't do it then, so why not?'

'Sometimes you can see things when you look a man in the eye. And looking at him right there and then, I knew when it came down to it he'd leave me dead in a ditch sooner than split that type of money. A retirement crop, he called it. Retirement alright, he'd have had me retired permanently,' he said, and pointed two fingers against his temple like the barrel of a gun.

'So what happened when you told him no?'

'Men like McBlane don't get told no, not by anyone who stays around to tell of it later. I just got out of there. I could have stuck around and kept it on a small scale but his idea wouldn't have gone away, and sooner or later he'd have forced me into it one way or another. That's when I moved away, started work on the trucks. Never in one spot for long, suited my needs just fine. Course that's around the time I met Mary and he was the last thing on my mind after that,' Jeff said, with a genuine smile that looked somehow out of place on him, like trying on an outfit he hadn't worn for years.

Jeff's smile faded and he exhaled heavily, looking into his drink as if trying to read something way down at the bottom.

'You ever see him since?'

'No. Heard of him from time to time, he always seemed to be involved in something, but I never let on the connection we once had. To be honest though, the talks we had about it, the vision he described is more than likely where my own thoughts about doing what I have here came from. He might not be the smartest man on the planet but he had a way of looking to the future and then making it happen. He's not someone who gives up easily. If you've gotten onto his bad side he won't forget you in a hurry.'

Scott nodded. Jeff's summation of McBlane's character confirmed his own impression of the man.

'So was it after Mary died that you decided to turn back to the plants again?'

Jeff nodded slowly. 'When she was around I used to function a lot better. We'd go out, socialise, do the regular things that couples do. After she died I tried to keep going through the motions but being out amongst other people, happy people especially, I just felt removed from it all as if it were just a bad TV show I was sat at home watching alone. After a while I just stopped trying and got used to my own company again. It made me think back to the past when I would lock myself away from the world for weeks at a time tending to the plants. That kind of solitude would be too much for most people but now I was living that lifestyle anyway but with nothing to show for it,' he said. Scott noticed he'd begun twisting his wedding ring between finger and thumb. 'Avoir le cafard, the French colonialists called it, a kind of cabin fever: extreme depression, boredom, pointlessness of existence.'

Scott lit a cigarette and swallowed the last of the vodka from his glass.

'I started looking for opportunities, places where people who kept to themselves were the norm rather than standing out as different. After a while my search broadened and then I came across this place and knew this was the one I'd been looking for.'

Jeff lit a cigarette of his own and refilled both of the glasses.

'What was the job you did for McBlane then?' Jeff asked, taking a sip from his brimming glass.

'We picked up a shipment from the docks, me and another guy. We'd been told it contained a large amount of coke but apparently it had just been a test to see how we did and there were no drugs in it.'

'So what was it you picked up?'

'Just electrical stuff in boxes, nothing really.'

Jeff scratched his beard thoughtfully as he listened to Scott. His face had taken the appearance of someone trying to locate misplaced car keys.

'And the other guy who did the job, he's still working for McBlane then?'

'No, he didn't even make it through the pay off. McBlane had apparently been feeding the guy's heroin habit and he overdosed right in front of me just as we were getting paid.'

'Fucking hell, did he prepare the works himself?'

'No, one of the men did it before we got there.'

'Sounds like he was removed on purpose, I've heard of McBlane using that one before.'

'Faking an overdose to kill someone?'

'Yeah something tied him to it a long time ago and it looked like he was gonna go down. But one of his henchmen took the fall.'

Scott thought back to a conversation with Twinkle and Neil where he'd heard Dominic Parish ingratiated himself by serving a sentence to get McBlane out of a jam and wondered if this was what Jeff was referring to.

'Had your friend done anything to piss McBlane off?'

'No. Well, there was a moment in the van when we were on the way to drop off the shipment, he talked about running, taking what he thought was a huge amount of coke and selling it himself. I was the only one with him though and I've never told anyone what he said.'

'McBlane doesn't like anyone talking out of turn, ever. And if you're on the payroll then he's twice as aware that you're alive, and he listens twice as hard,' Jeff said, and watched Scott sternly as he took a drink from his glass.

'You mean he might have had the van bugged?'

'If this was an initiation to see how you both coped under pressure then it would seem like more than a possibility. No drugs in the shipment so no chance of an arrest and whatever happened to be on the recording falling into the hands of the police. McBlane might be an old world type of figure but he's never been shy of embracing technology where it could help him out.'

Scott's mind raced back to the night in the flat when Twinkle had died, or been murdered. Had they said anything to indicate they'd heard what had been said in the van? Scott's thoughts now fuelled by alcohol and anger ran fluidly into and through one another. He couldn't be sure.

'Twinkle, the guy that died. They've framed him in a shooting outside of a club now too. They took his wallet and stuff the night he died. A doorman told the police he grabbed for the attacker which is when he dropped the wallet.'

'Older heads are wiser heads, or they should be. If McBlane did hear what your friend said about ripping him off, then no way was he gonna ride off into the sunset with a pocket full of cash. And now with the disappearance and the setup?' Jeff laughed. 'The more mystery that surrounds McBlane the better, as far as he's concerned. He knows that mystery won't win any convictions in a court room, but it elevates his status above dangerous to that of iconic, mythological even amongst the people on the street. He summoned you into the circle, Scott. For whatever reason, I don't know. But now you've left, you've become a loose thread. He won't sit back with the possibility you might cause his whole world to unravel around him. Everything with him is about victory. Win or lose. Pass or fail.'

Scott knew Jeff was still talking about McBlane, but his last words could just as easily have been describing his brother, Jack. He was a fixer, he made things right, made them work, whether you wanted him to or not.

Chapter 13

Scott slept fitfully that night and awoke on a number of occasions to terrible dreams that, once awake, he couldn't quite recall. The bus dream had been in there though, of that much he was sure. But this time, sitting next to him, staring blank eyed on a journey to an unknown destination had been Jeff.

He got up and dressed quickly. The cabin was cold and Angela must already have gone up to the main house to prepare breakfast. He pulled on his boots and jacket and braced himself for the blast of icy air before opening the cabin door.

The morning was bright with little cloud cover, and it didn't appear to have snowed any more during the night. The ground was still very much frozen though and Scott wondered if his car had been towed up the hill to Bloody Bush.

He climbed the steps to Jeff's house and stamped his feet, more to warm them up than to shake off snow before entering.

Jeff and Angela were in the kitchen talking, with Boris circling eagerly around them as a pan of sausages sizzled on the hob.

'I wasn't expecting you up for a while, the way you slept last night,' Angela said, as he slid an arm around her waist and kissed her on the neck.

'Angela told me about your car trouble on the trip back yesterday. I was just about to head down to the village and see if Maurice had remembered to sort out that tow.'

'Thanks Jeff, I'll come down with you after breakfast.'

'No need,' he said with a dismissive wave of the hand, 'you keep Angela here company, I'll be back soon enough then we can plan out our next crop down in the cave.'

Angela buttered some bread while the sausages browned, then made up their sandwiches. They sat down and ate together at the kitchen table. Spirits were high, even Scott's, despite his night of fragmented sleep. The seclusion he felt up in the mountains, away from the troubles and dangers of the city, offered Scott a respite from the anxieties that had been plaguing him. By the time they were finishing up breakfast, the ghosts of dreams that had passed through into his conscious mind upon awakening had all but faded.

Jeff was the first to notice the sound. He tossed the remainder of his sandwich to Boris and walked into the living room to look out of the window. Angela and Scott stood and followed him to see what had caused his sudden alertness. A few seconds before it came into view all three could now hear the crunch of tyres on the frozen driveway, and it wasn't Scott's car or a familiar vehicle from the village that emerged around the side of the cabin, but a white van that caused Scott's heart to lurch up into his throat.

'That's the van,' he gasped, 'the one from the job we did, I'm sure of it.'

'There's a lot of white vans in the world, Scott,' Jeff said, but he never took his eyes from the window as he spoke. The concerned expression remained rigid on his face.

'There's a square on the side that's cleaner than the rest, that's where the logo was, for the company we were supposed to be from.'

'He's right,' Angela said, seizing Scott by the forearm, 'you can see where it's been peeled off.'

Jeff walked to the fireplace and took down the revolver; he opened a small wooden drawer at his writing desk and withdrew a handful of bullets before hastily inserting them into the gun.

'Scott, you take Angela, grab the bag in there too and head out the back. Down to the cave if you need to. I'll go out and see what this is about,' he said, and handed the loaded weapon to Scott.

'Jeff you can't go out there on your own, you know what they're capable of.'

'If it's a couple of McBlane's thugs then they don't know who I am but if they see you then we're all fucked, take it and go, Scott. Now.'

Angela had already begun to walk back into the kitchen. Scott trotted after her; the cold heavy revolver felt alien in his hand. He picked up the backpack which still lay where Jeff had dropped it the previous day. The front door lock snapped shut after Jeff as he walked outside. Boris began to whine and paw at the door after him.

'Wait,' Scott said, moving gingerly back towards the living room.

'Come on Scott, we have to go,' Angela pleaded.

He crept back towards the window and watched Jeff approach the van, which had come to a stop around twenty feet from the house. The morning sunlight reflected on the van's windows turning them to mirrors, preventing Scott from seeing anyone inside. Jeff stopped by the van, the driver's side window opened a few inches revealing only a rectangle of darkness beyond. Scott couldn't hear anything being said but Jeff was gesturing almost casually as if to say he didn't know the answer to a question he'd been asked. Jeff's hands now fell by his sides, and then almost immediately his arms folded across his chest. He stood like that, unmoving for around another ten seconds before finally shaking his head.

The driver's door was thrown open suddenly, rebounding against Jeff and knocking him to the ground. Behind Scott, Angela cried out and clutched his arm.

Scott stood rooted for a moment longer. The driver's door

opened again and the hulking figure of Shugg climbed out. The passenger door opened and Dominic climbed out carrying a baseball bat in one hand, and cast a searching glance in the direction of the house. Scott instinctively shrank back against the wall. There was no light on inside the house so they couldn't be seen, but it would surely be a matter of moments before McBlane's men smashed their way in. Scott could no longer see Jeff since he had been knocked down, but the last thing he saw before he turned and ran was Shugg's foot slam down toward the ground.

Angela was two steps ahead of Scott and she snatched up Jeff's keys for the lock on the workshop. Scott followed her out back, fighting the rising panic in his chest he wedged the revolver down into the back of his pants. Trying not to obey the urge he felt to go back to help Jeff, that he knew even with the gun would be useless. Angela's natural athleticism had gained her even more ground and she was already at the door to the workshop, fumbling with the keys to open the lock. Scott picked up his pace before hearing a shout that froze the blood in his veins, almost causing him to fall.

'Hey, stop that fucking bitch.'

It was McBlane, he'd come along for the ride which meant he'd have recognised Jeff immediately, leaving Jeff naively answering their questions, unaware of who else was on the other side of the glass.

Angela found the correct key and released the padlock. Scott forced all of his weight against the sliding door which creaked and screeched on its warped and rusted runner.

'Quickly Scott, please,' Angela begged, her voice betrayed a panic that he was fighting to control in himself.

'There must be grit jammed in it.'

The door runner protested another screech of grinding metal but opened far enough for them to squeeze through. Once inside Scott threw his weight against the frame again forcing it closed and thrust the inside bolt into place.

'That won't hold them for long,' he said running to the hatch in the corner.

Scott dropped to his knees and pulled open the drawer in the workbench where Jeff kept the tool to open the manhole.

'Shit, it's not here,' Scott cried, frantically pulling out the other drawers, scattering their contents across the concrete floor.

They both looked up as a heavy smash echoed around the walls of the workshop from something being brought down hard against the door outside.

'Jesus, Scott hurry,' Angela said, her voice cracking under the pressure.

Scott pulled out the last wooden drawer and saw what he'd been looking for. Snatching up the curved piece of metal he thrust it into the small hole in the manhole cover and turned it ninety degrees.

'Get in,' he cried to Angela, straining as he lifted up the thick iron cover to allow their escape. A steady hum of strong electrical current emitted from the gloom below them.

'Shit, it's dark I can't see. Where's the light?'

'There's no time. There's a ladder below, just get in.'

Angela steadied a hand on either side of the hole, lowered herself down and dropped into the darkness. A muffled cry echoed upwards that Scott hoped was only the result of shock at what sounded like her failing to grab the ladder. He swung his legs over the edge and reached out with precision into the gaping blackness and immediately snapped on the lights. Angela sat on the floor below, one leg sprawled in front of her, the other pulled up towards her chest, cradling her ankle between both hands.

'Find the key to open the door,' he said, lowering himself down and dropping the backpack to the ground below, and began closing the cover after him.

A splintering crash was heard as the workshop door gave

way just as Scott settled the cover into place. He slid across a small iron bolt, the only thing that now stood between them and their pursuers. He dropped to the floor beside Angela and helped her struggle to her feet.

'I've hurt my ankle.'

'I can see that, but once we're in the cave we should be OK. This next door will hold them off, we're nearly there.'

She pulled out the keys again, which jangled on the chain in a parody of their nervousness. A clang rang out above them as something metal was forced against the manhole to try and prise it open. Angela steadied her breathing, jabbed what she hoped was the correct key into the hole pointed at by Scott, and turned. The lock released and she hurriedly swung open the heavy door. Taking hold of the ladder behind him, Scott climbed a few rungs then swung out and kicked at the light bulb. It exploded sending shards of glass and sparks in an arc over Scott's legs and down onto the floor beneath, plunging the room into darkness.

'That should slow them down,' Scott said and dropped down, crushing splintered shards of broken glass, and followed Angela into the cave.

'It'd take them forever to get through that door,' Scott said, bent over, hands planted on his thighs, and took a couple of deep breaths.

Angela was leant up against one of the walls rubbing tenderly at her ankle.

'Do you think you can walk on it?' Scott asked.

'I'll manage,' she said, tentatively putting weight back onto it, and winced. 'As long as we don't have to run.'

'We won't be running but you may have to climb, come on, there's another way out.'

Supporting Angela's weight with an arm around her waist and the backpack slung over his shoulder, Scott helped her hobble down through the cave towards Jeff's escape hatch at the other end. Rows of cloned cannabis plants stood proudly, ready to be repotted for the second crop they were about to embark on. Scott shook his head remorsefully at what he had brought down on Jeff. He had nothing to do with Scott's troubles, and who knew what condition he might now be in.

The door to the main growing chamber had been left open after they had harvested the last crop of cannabis buds, with just a few bulbs left on to illuminate the long space. Drifts of rotting leaves yet to be cleared away lay on the floor; Scott kicked them aside for Angela to make her way through.

He opened the final door into the small living quarters and eased Angela down into a chair while he opened up the hatch to their exit.

'You think you can make it?' he asked her, pointing upwards.

'Yeah, it might take me a while but I can do it,' she said and tried to smile reassuringly.

Scott sat with Angela while she rested a moment before he began the climb up to the surface. No lights had been installed in the upward tunnel. Probably Jeff had thought he would never have needed to use it, so Scott used the sparse illumination from his phone to navigate the rungs. A single bolt was in place at the top which Scott slid back and pushed the hatch to open it outwards. Nothing, it didn't move an inch.

Shit, Scott thought to himself, surely there couldn't be a lock on the other side, what the hell would have been the point in that? He pushed again, harder this time, and felt the hatch ease up a couple of inches. Scott relaxed and breathed out. Placing his shoulder against the hatch he moved his feet a rung higher on the ladder, took a deep breath and, planting his feet firmly onto the rung, heaved upwards, this time using the strength in his back and legs to force open their escape route.

The hatch fell outwards with a heavy crack of stone on stone. The ladder Scott had pushed against felt like it had also moved a little under his exertion. Dappled sunlight fell through the branches above, penetrating cautiously into the darkness of the hatch. Scott made a thumbs up gesture in case Angela could make out the silhouette from below.

'Scott, shall I start climbing up?' Angela's voice echoed up to him.

He looked down and could just see Angela edging up the first few rungs, obviously eager to get out of what was once his workplace but now felt like a giant tomb. He poked his head above ground and after a cursory glance around, seeing nothing but the forest he shouted down for her to carefully make her way up.

Scott examined the rivets that fixed the ladder against the stone wall and saw small cracks running outwards from both of them, like lenses in broken spectacles.

Angela pushed up a rung at a time with her good foot, then supporting her weight by gripping either side of the ladder, brought her other foot up to the next rung and then pushed again. Scott climbed out completely and dropped the backpack onto the grass, allowing more light to penetrate the tube and aid Angela's ascent.

There were no landmarks at all to gauge their current location by, but judging from the gradient of the slope Scott guessed they were around 500 yards North East of the main house. He listened for sounds of anyone moving through the woods or any vehicles but heard nothing other than the wind caressing the pine branches above him.

He saw the reason the hatch had been so hard to open. Jeff had cunningly sawn through a rock and secured it to the hatch lid with steel bolts, so if anyone had ever happened to pass by, nothing would have looked untoward. Just another rock sticking out of the ground. The upturned hatch lid now lay against a pile of other boulders a few feet further down the slope.

Angela had made progress when Scott looked back over the edge, and was now almost to the surface. He reached in an arm and took hold of her, helping her up the last few feet.

'Is there any sign of them?' she asked, cautiously looking around.

'No, nothing, I haven't heard anything either. Maybe they just gave up and left,' Scott said, hoping the words sounded more convincing to Angela's ears than they had felt on his lips.

'What do we do now then?' she asked, looking up at him, still rubbing her swollen ankle.

'We make our way down to the village, hope the car is there and come back for Jeff.'

'We should phone for an ambulance. What if he's seriously hurt?'

'If an ambulance turns up for him here there'll be an investigation into what happened and they'll find everything; Jeff will be fucked, he'll get years and years for what's up here. Besides, you won't get a signal until we get further down the mountain anyway.'

'But what if the car isn't ready and we have no way to make it back up here other than on foot? A delay like that could be crucial. What if...?' Angela's words tapered off into deep sobs, her bottom lip quivering she held her face in her hands.

'You're right, we can't wait but we can't phone an ambulance, not just yet,' Scott said, trying to think of a solution. 'You take the bag and make your way down to the village as best you can. I'll head back around towards the house and see if they've gone. If I can get Jeff and his car then I'll meet you down there and we'll take him to a hospital ourselves.'

'But what if they're still there Scott and they see you?' Angela said, looking up at him still, struggling to control her sobs.

'I'll be careful, if they are there and there's nothing I can do then I'll head straight down to the village and meet you and call an ambulance for Jeff on the way.'

Reluctantly Angela agreed and Scott helped her to her feet. She shouldered the backpack and carefully began to limp over the frozen ground in the direction of the village. Scott watched her for a few seconds until he was confident she'd be able to manage, before he set off back towards the house. Stepping as lightly as he could to make no noise, Scott followed a route back that would afford him the most cover in case anyone was still back at the house.

He rounded a curve on the mountain slope and the Eastern side of the house came into view. From this angle he was unable to see if the van that McBlane had arrived in was still parked nearby, as the driveway lay on the opposite side of the property. Staying as low to the ground as he could, Scott continued towards the house but quickened his pace into a run. Back to the wall he edged along towards the rear of the property. If there was any activity near the workshop or where the van had been then this would give him the best vantage point to observe without being seen.

Scott was immensely conscious of the bulk of the revolver pressed into the small of his back. All heat from his body seemed to be drawn out by it, leaving his teeth chattering and his fingers trembling. He skirted around the wooden bench and piles of logs Jeff used for firewood and surveyed the area at the back of the house. The sliding door to the workshop stood open by about two feet but he could see nothing inside. Even straining, Scott could hear no sounds of movement either inside or out. His hand moved instinctively to the gun wedged in his waistband and he walked further around the house. Jeff's car was still parked in its usual spot. Scott hurried towards it. Ducking down behind the driver's side door he risked a quick glance over the bonnet. The van had gone. Acutely aware of a possible threat from one of them lurking in the unlit workshop for his return, Scott stayed clear of the doorway and moved down the driveway looking for Jeff.

A small pool of blood and Jeff's broken glasses marked the spot on the frosted driveway where Scott had seen him go down.

He broke into a run and as he got closer saw what appeared to be drag marks leading away and up towards the house. Scott pulled out the revolver and held it unsteadily in both hands. He used the cluster of eucalyptus bushes for cover, cocked the gun the way Jeff had insisted on showing him one afternoon, and stepped out allowing the doorway to come into view. Jeff lay unmoving on the stairs. Scott dropped the gun and ran blindly to him, forgetting about the possible danger that might lie within the house.

Blood was matted down the front of Jeff's sweater and had stained his beard red. After seeing what they had done to Twinkle that night in the flat, Scott's heart twisted in his chest as he approached his friend, already fearing the worst.

'Jeff,' Scott whispered as he knelt down beside him.

A low gurgling sound came from Jeff and one eyelid flickered open.

'Shhcott,' he lisped through swollen lips that were caked with blood, and although they hadn't moved much Scott had seen gaps where teeth used to be.

'Take it easy,' Scott said and glanced up to the living room window beside them. The front door frame was splintered and cracked down one side where the door had been kicked inwards from their forced entry. 'Are there any inside?' he asked Jeff, without looking away from the window.

'No,' Jeff answered and winced, 'all three left in the van. Angela?'

'She's OK, she's waiting for us down at the village. I told her I'd meet her there after I made sure you were OK. How bad are you hurt, do you think you can get up?'

Jeff held out a hand for Scott to take hold of and help him to his feet. Gripping the hand, and with an arm secured around Jeff's back to support him, he slowly levered him into a kneeling, and then almost standing, position. Jeff leaned heavily against the wall of the house, his breath coming in short painful bursts from the exertion. The left side of his face was badly swollen and the eye closed. The beginning of a bruise formed beneath the damaged flesh. Scott immediately thought back to Stephanie lying in the hospital bed and wondered for the first time if the events were somehow linked. Jeff's right hand clutched protectively against the left hand side of his ribcage.

'Any broken?' Scott asked. Jeff nodded confirmation. 'Anything else?'

'I don't think so. Get the keys for my car from inside, we should leave.'

Scott pushed open what was left of the ruined door and walked through to the kitchen where Jeff kept his keys. The house was in utter disarray. Drawers had their contents tipped out, anything that had been on a surface looked to have been hurled at the walls in wanton destruction. Whether they had been looking for anything Scott didn't know, but the message they'd left behind was clear, they weren't finished with him yet. Scott found the keys by sifting through the mess of broken crockery and food that lay across the kitchen floor and returned out front to where Jeff still stood slumped against the wall.

'I've got the keys,' Scott said bouncing them in the palm of his hand.

'Any sign of the dog?'

Scott faltered, he'd forgotten all about Boris during the chaos of the last hour.

'He ran out back with me and Angela but not to the workshop. He must've gone off into the woods.'

'Yeah, probably. He'll be back.'

'He might not be the only one though, let's go.'

Scott helped Jeff down the steps and picked up the gun he'd dropped earlier before they slowly walked around the house to Jeff's Toyota. He opened a rear door and did his best to manoeuvre Jeff onto the back seat. Jeff grunted at each push or pull from Scott to help him along, and was visibly pained even from the effort of breathing; finally managing to find a position that would make travelling in the car at least bearable. Scott climbed in front and started the engine.

The drive down to Bloody Bush was frustratingly drawn out. The condition of the road surface meant Scott had to take every care to avoid any pot holes that caused the pain from Jeff's ribs to flare. Even on relatively smooth patches, any gentle movement of the vehicle would register as a grimace across his face. Scott kept checking but his phone was still without signal. Even travelling on her damaged ankle, Angela should have reached the village and would be waiting for them inside The Boar, or at Maurice's store. Scott was eager to let her know that Jeff was OK and that they were on their way. By now she'd be frantic with worry.

They rounded the last curve, the end of the driveway now almost in sight. Once they reached smoother road surface Scott knew he would be able to pick up speed. The ivy clad archway lay in front of them now but something hung suspended in the centre. Scott kept going, at first unsure exactly what he was looking at. It was Jeff who first broke the silence.

'Oh no – no, they didn't.'

Scott pulled up and got out of the car. He walked slowly towards the still twitching corpse of Boris, swinging by what looked to be electrical cable that had been looped around his neck in a makeshift noose and fastened onto the wooden trellis above. Supporting the dog's weight as best he could, Scott raised him up, slackening the tightness of the cable around his neck, allowing Scott to loosen it and slip it back over the dog's head.

He carried the dead animal to the side of the road and lay him carefully down behind a tree. Scott ran a hand over his face, wiping away tears. There was nothing he could do for Boris now. He silently vowed to come back and give him a proper burial, and make them pay for what they'd done.

'They must've seen him after me and Angela managed to

escape into the cave,' Scott said, getting back into the car, and started the engine.

'They're animals.' Jeff muttered under his breath.

They drove down to the village in silence. Making a turn, Scott caught sight of his own dirt streaked reflection in the mirror. The look in his eyes was two parts rage and three parts hatred. He tried to rationalise that it was just a dog, that Twinkle had already been killed by the bastards, but Twinkle had been an idiot. He hadn't deserved to die, of course not, but at least he'd had a say in it. They'd killed Boris just for the hell of it, a passing thought as they drove off. How'd you like that Scott, how's that sit with you? He gripped the steering wheel so tightly his knuckles were as white as the snow at the side of the road.

Scott pulled into a parking space outside of the Post Office and checked his phone. He had a signal. A call to Angela's phone went straight to voice mail. If she was here in the village then surely her phone would be turned on and she would be able to receive calls. He ran over to the Black Boar and spotted his own car at the far corner of the parking lot; Maurice had come through for him. The few staff inside were preparing for what would pass for the lunch rush in a place this remote. Scott asked around but no-one had seen Angela. There had been three men in from the city earlier, he was told by a bored barmaid with a nose stud and a southern accent, but Angela hadn't been in there for over a week. Scott crossed back over to the Post Office and went in to speak to Maurice.

'Your friends catch up with you then?' Maurice asked him, glancing up from the newspaper he had spread out in front of him.

Scott stopped in his approach to the counter. 'You told those guys we were up at Jeff's?'

'You're welcome,' Maurice said, and grinned like he'd just done Scott another favour. 'Said they happened by and noticed your car parked,' he said, jerking his thumb in the direction of the pub. 'Lucky I managed to get it towed last night or they wouldn't have seen it here this morning.'

Scott knew Maurice thought he'd done him a good turn, but keeping the bitterness out of his voice when he asked if Angela had been by took more effort than he felt he could muster.

'Yeah, she was in not long ago, asking about you actually.' Maurice looked up directly at Scott. 'She seemed kind of jittery, not at all like she normally is. Put it down to her sore foot myself.'

'So where is she now?' Scott asked, impatience bubbling up in him like acid indigestion.

'Like I said she was jittery, wouldn't stay in one spot for more than a minute, I offered her a chair but she said no. In and out she was, the damn store freezing with her letting all my warm air out. Anyway, I saw your friends pass by in that van and she never came back in so I suppose she just got a ride with them.'

Scott felt as if the remaining strings that were holding him up had just been cut. He slumped against a shelf, knocking some cans of soup to the floor where they rolled tiredly across the linoleum.

'Steady on,' Maurice said, standing up straight, but the sudden exertion brought on a coughing fit and he sat back down and attempted to catch his breath. 'They weren't your friends were they?' he asked, after spitting into his container behind the counter.

'No. They weren't my friends.'

Maurice nodded solemnly, although unaware of the severity of the situation.

Scott walked back out to the car. The tinkling bell on the shop door danced as it snapped closed behind him.

Scott didn't know what their next step should be. He'd

regaled what he'd heard from Maurice but as he was driving a lot faster now, Jeff was struggling to force out more than an odd word every now and then, most of his attention focused on breathing as the car lurched and dipped along the winding country lanes.

One thing Scott did know was that Angela's dad must be told. And he had to do it in person.

Chapter 14

Scott knocked on the door to Putty's flat and Keep opened it wide once he'd recognised Scott's voice. A glance past him both up and down the corridor showed that his presence without Angela was unexpected.

Scott made his way into the flat, hoping there would be no occupants other than himself, Keep and Putty. When he entered the living room he discovered at least something was going his way.

'Where's Angela?' Putty asked, a pungent joint smouldering between his fingers.

'Something really bad has happened,' Scott said sitting down on the old couch, resting his forearms on his knees and leaning towards Putty.

Keep came back into the room and stood silently in the doorway.

'What? What's happened Scott, where's Angela?' he asked, more insistently, his voice taking on a frantic edge, with worry that only a parent can understand.

Scott covered the main points as quickly as he could. He sketched an outline of Jeff's operation, the previous involvement with McBlane and the incident after the van turned up that morning and Jeff's assault.

Once Scott reached the end with Angela being taken away in the van, Putty rose out of his chair and walked to the wall behind him. In a single movement his right fist plunged straight through the plaster as deep as his wrist. Scott could understand her father's anger. He'd felt like punching things himself, he still did. But keeping control of his emotions was the only thing Scott could think of right now, that might see them get through this with Angela back home safely.

Putty took hold of a broken chunk of plaster and tore it away from the hole he'd made in the wall. He tore away another piece, the hole he'd made now widening, revealing some kind of partition which became more visible as further handfuls were torn free. Through the cloud of plaster dust that hung around him Putty reached inside the hole and pulled out a shotgun and a pistol wrapped in sealed plastic bags; bullets and shotgun shells lay in the bottom like dust bunnies under a bed.

Both Scott and Keep watched as he tore open the plastic and began inspecting the weapons.

'Where do we find them?' Putty asked flatly without looking up.

'I don't know where they'll be, but once they decide what it is they want surely they'll be in touch. You can't go wandering the streets carrying them. You won't be any use to Angela from the inside of a cell. It's shit, but for now we just have to wait,' Scott said. His frustration had been equal to that now shown by Putty and until the words had come from his mouth, Scott had been at a loss as to their next move. But now he'd said them, it felt right. Something Jack had said about some business deal he was about to push through years ago came back to him. Consider and then act, don't react. A worthy opponent will calculate his move to entice a response from you. Make your own play. The tactical way Jack spoke about such things always seemed as if he were discussing a game of chess. No matter how important the stakes were, he maintained a calm detachment that had annoyed Scott back then, seeming cold and almost robotic in his thinking. But right now he'd take cold and robotic in a second if it meant getting Angela away from McBlane and back safe with him. He realised in the absence of them having a play to make, they should just wait.

'Where's Jeff now, what does he think?' Putty asked, looking up from the guns. His expression betrayed agitation and fear, rather than the hate and vengeance that had driven him a few moments earlier.

'He's still in the car downstairs. He really needs to get checked over at the hospital, his ribs are in a bad way and fuck knows what else might be wrong internally.'

'Right, for now we'll wait here,' he said, looking at Scott. 'Keep, you take Jeff to the hospital and make sure he gets fixed up, then bring him back here. Keep your phone switched on. If we hear anything I'll call you.'

Keep nodded, took the car keys from Scott and left the flat.

* * *

It was around five hours later that Keep arrived back. He helped Jeff up the stairs and into the flat. Scott had made something to eat and dozed in their absence but Putty had only paced the floor and repeatedly cleaned both of the guns.

'He'll be OK the doctor said,' Keep informed them, as he helped lower Jeff down onto the couch.

'We waited for an X-ray. The doctor advised it with the injury being around the lower ribs, but it came back clear. No internal damage so they strapped them up and gave me a bunch of pain killers. Still no call then, I take it?' Jeff asked, and looked from Putty to Scott and back again.

Scott shook his head.

'I'll give them till morning and there's been no call by then I'm gonna go looking,' Putty said; a resolution showed on his face and Scott knew it was pointless to try and change his mind. He just hoped the call would come before then and that Angela was unharmed.

Keep brought some blankets in for them in case anyone felt they could sleep. Jeff took one and said after the painkillers he'd been given, he'd more than likely be sleeping soon.

'Did the doctor ask how you got the damage?' Scott asked him.

'I told him I'd done it falling down the stairs but he looked anything but convinced.'

'Yeah he kept looking at me like I was the one that done it,' Keep said, shaking his head. 'Fucking racist.'

'The doctor was Chinese,' Jeff said, and winced as he chuckled.

'Don't matter, they're just as bad.'

Putty smiled and patted his friend on the shoulder.

Scott checked that his phone had both a strong signal and battery power and placed it on the coffee table in front of him. Within the hour Jeff was sleeping and Putty and Keep had pulled both of the armchairs together and were talking conspiratorially in the corner of the room. The events of the day hadn't dampened their appetite though and joints were steadily rolled and smoked between them. Scott turned down all offers extended his way. He wanted to keep a clear head for whatever was to come next.

At 5am the next morning the silence in the flat was shattered by a sudden ring as Scott's phone came to life. Startled out of sleep he lurched forward and snatched it up. Everyone else was awake now and listening. The incoming number had been withheld; Scott connected the call.

'Yeah?'

'Scott, I hope I didn't wake you,' McBlane's voice rang out jovially on the other end, 'but I have a friend of yours here and she'd like to say hi.'

A muffled sound as the phone was handed over and then Angela spoke.

'Scott?'

'Are you OK, have they hurt you?' he asked, trying to keep his voice level. Putty was over beside Scott now and knelt down so he could listen in better on the call.

'I'm fine. Apart from the nausea from looking at their disgusting fucking faces all this....' The phone was snatched away from Angela before McBlane spoke again.

'Right, now you know she's OK I'll see you and Jeff at his house this afternoon. Don't try and do anything stupid, Angela won't be with us, but once our business is concluded I'll make a call and she'll be released in the same condition we picked her up in. Understand?'

'Yeah, I understand.'

'Oh, and I'll be keeping the bag she was carrying as a token of your gratitude that she gets to walk away unharmed.'

With that the line went dead, with McBlane's laughter still ringing in Scott's ears. He placed the phone back down on the table and relayed what had been said for the benefit of Jeff and Keep and in case Putty had missed anything.

'Angela sounded OK?' Keep asked.

'Yeah, she's keeping her spirits up. They'll probably be glad to see the back of her,' Putty said, and forced a smile that looked as natural as a horse on ice.

Within the hour Scott and Jeff were in the car and driving back up into the mountains. Putty had taken some persuasion that the best thing he could do was wait by the phone. He'd taken even more persuasion to keep the shotgun with him.

'Just in case,' he'd said, attempting to thrust the weapon, wrapped loosely back in the plastic bag into the car with Scott.

'If they don't release Angela then maybe you'll need it. But McBlane said on the phone she won't be up there anyway. If I take that along and they see it it's gonna fuck everything up and put Angela in even more danger.'

Reluctantly Putty agreed and went back up to the flat with Keep.

Jeff, having managed to sit upright in the front seat, armed with the painkillers he'd got from the hospital and his old revolver tucked inside his coat, seemed fresher but remained tight lipped about the afternoon ahead of them. His face was still swollen and bruising crept out from under his beard, now an angry purple and black. The hospital had cleaned him up and he looked better for it but his sweater still displayed medals of blood earned from their encounter the day before.

The weather had taken a turn for the better and as the altitude rose the closer they got to the mountains, there had still been no sign of frost on the ground.

Scott slowed as they approached the turn up towards the house. He steered the car under the archway, swallowing against the lump he could feel rising in his throat, and cautiously drove the half mile to the house.

The white van was already parked up around back when they got there. Dominic and Shugg were sat smoking cigarettes on the bench beside the firewood and McBlane came out from the back door of the house. He was dressed in another impeccably tailored suit, and couldn't have looked more out of place surrounded by the rugged wilderness. Despite this he was calm and self assured, as if he'd just stepped out of a plush city centre office for a lunch meeting.

'Scott, Jeff,' McBlane greeted them and glanced at his watch. 'Thank you for being so punctual. This won't take much of your time and my associates and I will be on our way.'

Scott took out a cigarette and lit it. Fighting the revulsion he now felt for these men. It was beyond fear now. He just wanted this meeting over, for Angela to be freed and to never see any of them again.

'The reason we came up here for you yesterday Scott, was simply to show you the error of your ways and bring you back into the fold. What happened with Twinkle was unfortunate but you were the one I wanted to work with.'

'You killed him didn't you? You had something in the van recording what we said on that job, when you heard him talk about ripping you off you had him killed.'

'You understand that I can't tolerate any insubordination from anyone working for me. Twinkle was a blunt object that could have been employed for certain duties from time to time. Perhaps even earned himself a tidy sum to go with it, but when I heard what he said in the van I knew he could never be trusted. If he'd been caught on an actual job he would have given every one of us up. If he was prepared to risk taking me on, then he would have given your name without a second thought.'

'Twinkle panicked, that's all it was. He got past it. You could have just not hired him again and left it at that.'

'No. He got past it because of what you said. That reinforced the strength of character I'd been led to believe you had in you Scott. And besides, when someone talks out of turn like that a message has to be sent. It was regrettable,' he said, with counterfeit sympathy, 'but unavoidable.'

'Anyway, that's all in the past. We came up yesterday to give you a little reminder that you're one of us and that it was time you came back to work. A tracking device planted on your car when you parked in the city the day before was all it took. Of course your having to abandon the car when you got stuck in the snow caused a bit of a problem. We waited for a while not knowing what to do next until that old guy came along and towed it to the village. That was handy but there was nothing else we could do by then. It was dark and I knew you wouldn't return that night so we came back the next morning. Your car was in the same spot and no-one in the pub knew anything. We were just gonna sit and wait it out again until I had a word with the fella in the shop. He's chatty isn't he? I'd heard folk in remote places like this were unlikely to talk to strangers, thought maybe we'd have to twist his arm or something but once he heard we were old friends his lips loosened up no end.

Must be quite fond of you Scott. He gave this place up right away, so up we came. Seeing old Jeff here was quite a surprise I must admit. I've thought about you over the years,' he said looking at Jeff, 'but I never expected our paths would cross again. Strange how things turn out. Two birds, one stone and all that.' McBlane chuckled at his own impromptu joke.

'But things have worked out for the best and now we all get to work together,' McBlane said, and a smile spread across his face as easy as a politician's lie. He waited for the obvious question to be asked but neither one of them spoke. Unperturbed, he continued.

'When you and the young lady made off down that hole like Alice in fucking Wonderland I was quite surprised, but once I saw that big door down there and with old Jeff being here as well the pieces all came together quite nicely. You've taken the plan we'd made years ago and made it happen here. Well good for you Jeff but now that I am aware of the situation I think I quite fancy being a partner.'

'You can have the place,' Jeff said bitterly. 'It's yours, once Angela is safe.'

'Angela is fine, I'm not a monster,' he said holding his arms apart in a gesture of innocence, 'and she'll stay that way as long as there are no problems. But you seem to have misunderstood my intentions for our future. I don't want to work underground like some kind of fucking goblin doing whatever it is you do down there. You two will stay here and grow the plants. I will take care of the sales and the money will be divided up. It might not be an even split but you'll get a fair wage.'

'If you think me and Scott are gonna stay up here growing cannabis plants so you can get rich you must be mad. I said you can have the place so take it. Get those two meat-heads to do the work,' Jeff said, pointing at Shugg and Dominic.

'They are many things but I don't suspect they're particularly green fingered. You *will* both stay and you *will* grow

217

the plants. I've already decided. And once you accept this I'll make a call and Angela will walk, then we can all have a look behind that big door down there so I can see exactly what kind of setup you've managed to assemble for yourselves. Of course if you were to agree and then somehow vanish into the night, I would come after you but more importantly I'd come after Angela. She's a pretty little thing isn't she? I thought that the first time I saw her. Dominic and Shugg there, well they were rather looking forward to spending some quality time with her last night. They have quite an appetite for young ladies. Of course I didn't let that happen. It would have been the wrong thing to do, but if ever our little arrangement here comes to a premature end, then you can guarantee that spending a night with those two will be the least of her worries. I'll let them have her every way they want and when their appetite for her soft pink flesh has been satiated I'll let the dogs finish off what's left,' McBlane said, any shred of humanity now gone. His eyes, ink black wells, soulless as they stared, challenging either Scott or Jeff to question the arrangement he had laid out before them. 'Just ask Stephanie what happens when you go against an agreement you make with me. Oh that's right,' he said with a snap of his fingers, 'you can't now can you?'

Even without the revelation about Steph, Scott knew they were trapped. To go up against him now was useless, he held all the cards. If they agreed and then tried to vanish then McBlane would do everything in his power to find them. Twinkle was killed for even flirting with the idea of crossing McBlane and God knew what Stephanie had done and how she'd ended up. He looked at Jeff and saw his own feeling of hopelessness reflected back at him.

'OK,' Scott said, 'now make the call and let her go.'

McBlane beckoned with two fingers and Shugg brought over what looked like a large mobile phone from decades earlier with an aerial like a silencer on a pistol.

'Satellite phone,' he explained, 'for when I have business in locations without reception.' He smiled at his own resourcefulness and began punching numbers.

'Yeah, it's agreed. She's free to go,' he said when the call connected, and then immediately hung up.

'How do we know she'll be OK?' Jeff asked, looking at McBlane with obvious distrust.

'We're partners now, we really need to start trusting each other,' McBlane answered dismissively. 'Right lets go take a look at what's behind the magic door.'

Reluctantly, Jeff led the way through the shattered workshop door and struggled down into the hatch. McBlane and Scott followed after, then Dominic and Shugg at the rear. It took a minute for Jeff to manoeuvre himself down the ladder and when he reached the bottom he popped another of the pain killers into his mouth and chewed it up. Scott handed the keys to Jeff who unlocked the door into the cave.

'Fucking hell,' McBlane exclaimed as he walked inside, 'I knew you must have had a good thing down here judging from the amount of money that was in the bag but I didn't expect anything on this scale.'

Shugg and Dominic walked past Scott and followed McBlane around the corner, equally in awe.

'This is an absolute gold mine,' McBlane said, more to himself than to any of them.

Jeff walked past Scott. A pained expression on his face that Scott wasn't sure was more down to his labour of love being pillaged by gangsters than the discomfort from his injuries. McBlane had stopped to admire the rows of clones that were to fill up the main chamber, running his fingertips gently across the surface of their small leaves. The glee on his face illuminated a cool blue by the light from the fluorescent tubes.

'We're gonna make so much money from this we'll be able to buy a fucking island,' he said, almost musically, and laughed.

Scott's hopes were crushed. He could see no way out for them now. He looked over at Jeff whose face was blank, almost uncomprehending. Jeff reached a hand slowly inside his jacket and Scott knew he was about to pull out the gun and shoot one of them. With that old revolver and no glasses he'd be lucky to do more than wound and would undoubtedly get himself killed right after. Instinctively, Scott pulled a fire extinguisher free from the wall beside him, held it aloft then brought it down as hard as he could onto the back of Shugg's head. The large man crumpled face first into the plants he'd been so engrossed with. Dominic spun around and started towards Scott until he saw the unsteady hand of Jeff holding the revolver.

'Oh this is just terrific,' McBlane said jovially, 'and what exactly is your next move going to be, eh?'

Scott hadn't a clue and a look at Jeff indicated his actions hadn't been premeditated either.

'Give me the phone,' Scott said putting as much authority into his words as he could, trying to make them sound like a command rather than a request.

'Why's that then, are you hungry? Are you phoning for a pizza? Make mine a pepperoni, extra cheese,' McBlane joked, but there was no humour on Dominic's face. He had inched closer and had his gaze fixed firmly on the gun in Jeff's hand.

Scott saw the distraction offered up by McBlane was deliberate to allow Dominic to gain the upper hand on Jeff. He took a step backwards. Dominic inched forward again, unblinking.

'Toss the phone now Paul or one of you is gonna get shot,' Scott said again. Jeff turned and lined up the barrel of the gun directly at Dominic's face. He flinched back instinctively, as if only now aware of the potential threat.

McBlane didn't speak but reached slowly into the bulging inside pocket of his suit jacket and withdrew the phone. He tossed it casually towards Scott and it landed roughly half way between them, pieces of the black plastic housing scattering across the stone floor as it impacted on the ground.

'Whoops,' McBlane said.

Dominic stood poised, like a coiled snake about to strike. Jeff swung the gun between one and the other, as if unsure where the most immediate threat lay.

'Kick it towards me,' Scott said to Dominic, pointing at the shattered phone.

Dominic stepped forwards a few paces and crouched by the phone. Jeff had the gun trained on him but his hand was still shaking. Dominic looked up and quickly threw the phone as hard as he could at Jeff. As Jeff stumbled back to avoid it colliding with his head, Dominic was up and charging straight at him. Jeff swung the gun back around as Dominic collided with him. Both of them fell to the floor and a muffled shot rang out, echoing back and forward off the walls of the cave. Scott ran to help Jeff. He planted a kick into Dominic's ribcage and was delighted with the resulting grunt of pain. Jeff scrambled back out from under his much larger adversary, bracing himself against the wall and clutching his ribs, as he struggled to his feet.

Dominic rolled onto his back, revealing a large bloody stain on his left thigh that was blooming rapidly. Before they had time to gain control of the situation again another shot rang out, a ricochet whined off the wall behind Jeff. Scott spun around to see McBlane crouched with a small pistol in his hand. One leg of his suit pants was ruffled up, revealing an empty ankle holster. McBlane took aim and fired again.

'Jeff, get out,' Scott shouted, and he too started to run for the door of the cave.

Jeff began to run as best he could, stumbled, but regained his footing and continued. Another shot cracked, this time followed by a succession of zinging ricochets as the bullet bounced along the narrower exit passage.

McBlane was shouting something behind them but Scott didn't wait to hear what. He and Jeff got through the doorway and he began to close it after them as another bullet impacted onto the steel plate just beside Scott's head.

'Jesus,' he cried, and pulled the door shut.

Jeff was already at the ladder pulling himself up. Once he had climbed off, Scott followed, taking the rungs two at a time.

'I'm sorry Scott. I don't know what came over me. Just the thought of them coming in here and taking everything like that, imprisoning us to work for McBlane. I lost my head.' Jeff said with an anguished expression.

'It's OK Jeff but we have to make this work to our advantage. We can't go back now.'

'Right, you have to get to the exit hatch and try to secure it,' Jeff said. 'I'll cut the power into the cave. It'll slow them down, but they'll still find the hatch before long.'

Scott nodded and took off in a run. Through the woods, pine branches snapped back and whipped at his face as he zigzagged between the trees. Blood began to well up in the cuts and trickle down his cheek. There was no way to check his bearings, the trees and everything else looked the same no matter which way he turned. He rounded the curve in the mountainside he had remembered but then was at a loss as to which direction to take. Starting down the slope, Scott looked from left to right but still no sign of the hatch. He continued along and now began to gain altitude before seeing the familiar few boulders and the gaping exit hole just above.

He dropped to his knees beside the hatch and tentatively looked over the edge. By the light that penetrated the shaft he could make out no figure climbing the ladder. He went to the hatch lid with the boulder fused to it, checking for any method of sealing it tight from the outside but there was nothing. Scott looked around at the other boulders scattered nearby and considered the possibility of piling them all around and on top of the hatch, but dismissed the idea. With the very real threat of being buried alive underground one of them would surely find the strength to push them off, if not McBlane then once Shugg awoke then he certainly would.

Scott carried the boulder lid back up to the hatch, placed it beside the hole and looked in again. He still could see no-one but thought he heard a noise from below, they must be close to discovering the hatch now, he was running out of time. His hand was braced near the top of the ladder when his fingers brushed against the rivets that fixed the ladder to the wall. That's right, he thought, the ladder was in three sections and when he had climbed up last time he'd noticed the top rivets had been less than secure. Scott began to twist one and after a moment it began to reluctantly turn. He mustered as much strength into his fingers as he could, ignoring the pain that shot up his forearms from the effort. Switching hands he kept turning, finally the rivet was out and Scott's numb fingers dropped it down the shaft. A loud clank issued from the darkness as the bolt collided with one of the steel rungs as it fell. He heard a muttering of voices from below. They'd heard it fall, and they were close.

Scott's fingers began on the last rivet, more noises from below and then a voice.

'There's light up here, Paul, over here.' It sounded like Shugg. He had regained consciousness and was able to help in their escape.

The remaining rivet still refused to turn. Scott reached out and picked up the biggest stone he could hold in one hand and swung it down onto the remaining rivet. Stone crumbled from around the side of its head. Urgent shouts and sounds of movement below and what sounded like someone starting to climb. Scott scrambled with the rivet and now it began to turn. He risked peeking over the edge and immediately wished he hadn't as a bullet whizzed past his head. Scott ducked back, his arm still draped over the side of the hatch, working to loosen the last rivet. Another bullet crack and then a whine as it collided with the stone, inches from his hand. The sound of heavy feet ascending the ladder below but the rivet was turning more freely. The feet had stopped and there was silence. Scott's heart was beating like a jackhammer as he furiously twisted at the rivet. Then another shot. He didn't remember hearing this one, only becoming aware of it by the searing hot flash and the resulting spray of blood that rained out from his hand.

Scott cried out and fell onto his back, clutching the bloody hand to his chest. A raucous whoop came from the hatch, this time sounding much closer. Scott rolled over and reached his good arm into the hole but the rivet wouldn't turn.

'Shoot him again.' McBlane's voice rang out, but from further away. It must be Shugg climbing the ladder with the gun.

'I'm nearly out,' he said, in defiance. His voice dangerously close now, he must be on the final section of ladder.

In a state of panic, Scott reached out and grabbed at the rock he'd used earlier. Swinging his arm he brought it down against the rivet as hard as he could. Manic laughter from Shugg as he climbed the remaining few steps. Scott brought down the rock in another swing. It cracked against the head of the rivet and the surrounding rock crumbled again. The ladder lurched lazily to the left then stopped. Shugg had adjusted his grip to avoid falling, but the two descending clangs of metal on metal indicated that he had probably dropped the gun. He swung again and more stone crumbled. Shugg's hand reached out and took hold of the edge of the hatch. A slow screech of metal as the ladder again tilted but this time it didn't stop. The remaining rivet gave up the last of its purchase and with a cacophony of clangs and bangs the ladder fell into the darkness. Scott heard a startled yell from below as McBlane and possibly Dominic no doubt threw themselves out of its path. A last screech and a bang like a hammer being thrown against a dustbin, before quiet returned.

Scott turned back to the hatch and saw that Shugg still determinedly clung to the edge, trying to gain purchase with his feet and scramble out. He might have dropped the gun but Scott wasn't about to take any chances. He picked up a stone and brought it down onto the fingers of his right hand. Scott thought he could almost hear the splintering of bone, but the man through his guttural cries of pain, still clung on. Scott moved closer and swung the rock again. Shugg took the full impact onto the knuckles of his left hand and the fingers immediately went limp. Scott saw the brief look of panic before Shugg fell back into the shaft, his head cracked against the stone and nodded forward, limp like the head of a child's well worn toy. Sunlight briefly winked off his earring before he fell into the darkness below. His shoulder caught against a jagged outcrop of rock and his whole body pitched sideways out of Scott's line of sight. A second later he heard a muffled thud as presumably the body came to rest.

Dangerously risking a glance over the side of the hatch Scott looked down, needing to see the conclusion of his actions. The ladder had fallen almost the full length of the shaft before becoming wedged between either wall, and hung there suspended above the ground. Shugg's body had taken impact damage from the coarse stone during the fall but the unnatural angle that it now dangled over the suspended ladder told Scott that abrasions and broken fingers were the least of the man's worries. One leg hung down limply from his perch on the ladder, one arm trapped underneath him, but his back was bent at such an unnatural angle that he couldn't have still been alive. Transfixed with what he was seeing, Scott didn't at first realise McBlane had climbed up to the wedged ladder and now reached around with the gun pointing at him again. He pulled back just as the shot was fired and felt pain erupt from his shoulder.

Cursing his stupidity Scott rolled onto his side and looked at the wound. Pulling back his shirt revealed that the bullet had merely grazed the flesh and done no significant damage. McBlane, still refusing to admit defeat, laughed triumphantly from within the shaft.

Scott steeled himself with new determination and hoisted the hatch lid onto its side and walked it into position before dropping it with a resounding clang to seal up the hatch. He could hear nothing more from inside but was convinced that McBlane must now be screaming every obscenity that came to mind as once again he was engulfed by complete darkness. Scott gathered up every rock he could find in the immediate vicinity and piled them as best he could with his one good hand on top of the hatch, then collapsed back onto the ground breathing heavily from the exertion.

His shirt clung damply against his skin, soaked through with a mixture of sweat and blood. He felt light headed from the pain in his hand and was still reluctant to look too closely at the damage that had been caused by the bullet.

Scott gathered himself and, grimacing, got unsteadily to his feet. He had to get back to Jeff and make sure there was no way they could get back out through the main door from the cave. He staggered in a half run back through the woods, no longer feeling pain from the branches that clawed at him as he brushed them aside.

Scott quickened his pace as the house came into view, and saw Jeff disappearing back into the workshop pushing what looked to be a wheelbarrow. As he approached the door, Scott heard Jeff issue a loud grunt followed by the noise of stone falling heavily to the floor.

Walking into the workshop Scott saw Jeff flipping a large rock from out of the wheelbarrow and into the pit below where it landed with a solid thud. He hadn't noticed Scott approach and was at first startled at his sudden presence.

'The hatch?' Jeff asked.

'It's sealed and the top ladder segment is gone too. They're stuck in there.'

Jeff breathed an audible sigh of relief.

'I've been piling rocks into the pit in case they find a way to force the door open.'

Scott looked below and saw Jeff had indeed been busy in his absence. A layer of various sized rocks had begun to gather already almost covering the floor of the pit.

'I'm gonna keep going with this, you get back to the city and make sure Angela is OK.'

'You sure you'll be alright out here?'

'I'll be OK as long as I can keep those bastards sealed up down there, go on, get going. And here,' he said as an afterthought, and shook out some painkillers into his palm and gave them to Scott, 'for that.' He nodded toward Scott's bloody hand.

Scott went back to the main house, opened the cupboard that Jeff kept the first aid box in and took it down. He looked at the wound on his hand clearly now, and gritting his teeth ran cold water over it from the tap at the kitchen sink. The flesh between his forefinger and thumb had been obliterated and he couldn't bend either of them, but the bullet appeared to have passed right through without hitting any bone. His hands shaking, Scott took the cap from a bottle of antiseptic and poured it generously over the wound. He suppressed a cry as the liquid bit cruelly into the ragged flesh on his hand. Pulling out a roll of bandages Scott wound them as tightly as he could around his hand, finally pinning it in place. It was far from a perfect job, but hopefully it would suffice until he could get it looked at professionally. He cleaned the flesh wound on his shoulder then fetched a shirt from Jeff's wardrobe to put on in place of his own bloodstained and torn one.

Scott took a cold beer from Jeff's fridge and drank it while sitting at the kitchen table to calm his nerves and chewed up a few of the painkillers he'd been given by Jeff. Once his head had fogged over and a cool almost novocaine numbness had washed through him, he set off in the car back to the city.

Chapter 15

Scott waited until he had Jeff's 4 x 4 back onto the highway before he risked making a call. He had managed to settle his hand into a numbed stupor but any sudden movement would cause bolts of pain to surge up his arm. Once the road was straight and clear he held the wheel steady between his knees and used his good hand to dial Putty's number.

'Yeah?' Putty said, connecting the call after just one ring.

'It's Scott, is she back yet?'

'No she called and said she was OK but that was over an hour ago and still she's not here.'

'OK well sit tight, everything looks like it's gonna work out. I'll give you more details once I'm back,' Scott said, attempting to reassure.

'All right Scott, but I'm getting restless.' Scott heard the slide click of shotgun shells being loaded, further underlining what Putty had just said.

He hung up the call but just as he had dropped the phone in his lap it started ringing again. Jack's name flashed on the caller ID.

'Jack,' Scott said, connecting the call.

'Hey little brother,' Jack said, his voice sounded different but Scott couldn't tell what it was, 'I hear you've been having some problems.'

Scott waited for seconds that felt like minutes for his brother to elaborate on what he'd said.

'What is it Jack? Do you have something to tell me?'

'You're probably back en route to the city, come see me and then we'll talk,' he said, and then a click as the line went dead.

Scott dialled Jack's number, the car veered drunkenly towards the central reservation on the highway as he tried to manipulate the steering with his knees while punching buttons on the phone. Scott dropped the phone and instinctively reached out for the wheel with both hands. A lightning flash of pain shot from his left hand up to his temple, causing him to grind his teeth. Scott gave an anguished cry and steadied the car with his one good arm. He reached for the phone and dialled for Jack. The automated voice mail picked up, Jack's phone had been turned off. He pressed his foot harder against the accelerator until it was flat to the floor. The lights above the highway flickered on signalling the oncoming night.

* * *

Angela was scared but had been able to maintain the stubborn resistance she'd put up since being dragged into the van. Her initial kicking and flailing had been quelled pretty quickly by a number of punches to the torso from one of her captors. The one who identified himself as McBlane had assured her she would be hurt no further providing she behaved.

He'd told her that if Scott played along with the role intended for him, she'd be released within a day or two. Angela wasn't about to accept anything these men said, but further struggles would guarantee an immediate violent response so she conserved her strength, watched and listened.

The largest of the three men drove the van and, after maybe a few hours, Angela began to recognise buildings in Garden Heights from where she still lay on the floor of the van. She still didn't know their destination and was abruptly told to shut up on the three occasions she'd asked.

The men had remained mostly quiet. McBlane took two calls during their journey but in both had done very little speaking. Just interjected yes and no answers at intervals to questions she supposed he'd been asked.

When sudden darkness enveloped the van, Angela had to fight down the immediate panic that arose in her. The vehicle angled suddenly downwards then proceeded to take a number of tight turns, descending further. Angela guessed their location must be one of any number of underground car parks throughout the city.

After a few more minutes the large driver manoeuvred the van into a spot and got out. McBlane reached down and removed a pistol from an ankle holster and held it directly in front of her.

'We will exit the vehicle and move quickly to an elevator. You will not struggle. You will not scream or in fact make any noise at all. You will do only as instructed. Do you understand?'

Angela nodded, her focus on the weapon rather than the face of her captor as he spoke.

The back doors were opened. McBlane held her firmly by the upper arm and directed her out. He slid the pistol into his left hand pocket where his hand no doubt still grasped it ready to withdraw quickly if needed.

Angela glanced around the lot for any possible chance of escape. There were numerous cars parked but no-one around. She was ushered towards an elevator that the large man had gone ahead and summoned. Once inside McBlane withdrew a small gold key from his pocket and inserted it into a hole at the bottom of the face plate.

'One of the perks of owning a penthouse apartment,' he said to her, grinning, 'you don't have to be bothered by the neighbours.'

Angela recognised the elevator interior now. This was the Walker building. She'd seen Jack use a key like that on occasion when they'd returned back after dates. It took the elevator right to the penthouse level, bypassing anyone waiting on other floors. So McBlane owned one of the other seven.

The elevator reached the thirtieth floor in seconds and the doors slid silently open onto the familiar freshly-scented hallway.

Once out of the lift Angela looked quickly to the left, the direction she used to walk towards Jack's apartment, hoping either he or someone else may be there to at least witness her abduction. The hallway was vacant, she was dragged in the other direction and around a corner. She'd seen no-one since entering the building and no-one knew she was there.

McBlane opened a door identical to the one at Jack's apartment and she was thrust inside. The interior was very different. There was little furniture dotted around and the walls were bare plaster. Whatever flooring was in the apartment had been covered over by thick sheets of opaque plastic that crackled as they walked across it.

'I like what you've done to the place,' Angela said sarcastically, trying to hold back any fear from her voice.

'I'm remodelling. No point in having nice things laying around if you may end up making a mess,' McBlane said coldly, looking directly at her.

Despite herself, Angela shuddered as the calculated directness of his words hit home. She didn't want to be the reason for the plastic sheeting on the floor.

'Put her in the bedroom and lock it. She won't be a problem in there and we have things to discuss.'

The other man, was it Dominic she'd heard him called? took Angela to the main bedroom and locked her inside. The room contained a bed and nothing else. No objects of any kind that could be used as a makeshift weapon. No phone or any means of contacting anyone to let them know her location. Her cell phone and the bag of money she'd been carrying when she and

Scott had fled from the house had been the first things to go when she'd been snatched into the van. She returned to the bedroom door and silently turned the handle but it didn't budge. For now she was a prisoner. She lay down on the bed and waited.

Angela started awake, the bedroom still shrouded in darkness. The voices in the other room were no longer talking in hushed tones. She got up and silently moved to the door. She'd woken a number of times during the night; twice at the sound of the larger thug opening the bedroom door to check on her. His prolonged gaze as he loomed in the doorway communicated perhaps more than a passing interest in Angela.

As she tried to decipher the conversation the door was unlocked. She jumped back just in time as it swung open and the other thug told her to follow. Angela backed away fearfully, but he reached forwards and grabbed her by the arm and pulled her out.

'Sit,' McBlane commanded, and pointed to a seat. He had a phone in his hand and began punching numbers.

Angela sat where instructed and waited. None of the three were at least visibly holding any weapons so she figured there was probably no immediate danger. Another man she hadn't seen so far was standing by the front door and didn't appear to be paying her any attention. He was shorter than the others but what he lacked in height was more than made up for in build.

'Scott, I hope I didn't wake you,' McBlane spoke gleefully into the phone.

Angela tried to mask her excitement as a flame of hope ignited in her belly. McBlane said something else and then thrust the phone at her.

Scott spoke quickly, his voice layered with concern. Angela tried to reassure him, although afterwards she had no memory of what she'd said.

McBlane took for phone away and again began to talk into

it. Angela looked around the room; the faces of the other three men watched her, like ghouls seeming to feed upon her misery.

After a few moments McBlane hung up the call. He signalled to the two men from the van and they walked to the door.

'Your unfortunate ordeal should soon be over now,' McBlane said checking his watch, 'you'll remain here with my associate and once I have concluded a few things with Scott, you will be released,' McBlane said, with the majestic air of one bestowing a great gift upon a less fortunate soul.

Angela didn't gratify his statement with a response and only stared back, challengingly. After a few seconds McBlane turned and walked out. The other man approached from his post by the door and motioned for her to return to the bedroom. Angela defiantly took a cigarette from a pack on a table as she walked past, and lit it before returning to her prison.

Over the following hours Angela watched the glow of dawn reach over the horizon; the light was orange and hopeful. The city breathed into life as another day rolled out below her. There were no nearby buildings that came close to the height she was at, and no-one below would be able to see her so trying to signal would be useless. Angela had to remain patient and hope Scott would be able to give McBlane what it was he wanted to secure her release.

The door opened once when the sun had begun to ascend in the sky, and her latest captor walked in and dropped a store bought sandwich and a can of Coke onto the bed. She was allowed a toilet break he'd said, but the door would remain open, so she'd declined.

Angela finished the sandwich but ignored the soda. Her already full bladder wouldn't appreciate the added pressure, but no way was she going to let the creep watch her pee, so for now she'd tolerate the pain and the thirst.

Angela must have dozed again and was woken by the sound

of a phone ringing in the other room. She sat up on the bed but could hear nothing of what was being said. A moment later the lock was released.

Angela stood up and tried to mentally prepare herself for what might follow. Had Scott been able to give McBlane what he wanted or was this the end of the line?

'Outside,' the man barked.

'Why, what are you going to do?' she asked, cursing the audible tremor she could hear in her voice.

'That's it, you're free to go.'

'So I just walk out?'

'Yeah.'

'What if I go to the police?'

The man laughed a mirthless and cruel sound. 'You won't.'

He walked towards the front door, opened it and turned around to wait for her.

Tentatively, Angela made her way towards the exit, and then into the hallway beyond.

'Have a nice day,' the man said, and closed the door after her.

Chapter 16

Scott parked up near Jack's building and slid a handful of coins into the meter. The city nightlife had begun to get underway. Two couples walked past talking and laughing amongst themselves, voices elevated with alcohol. A man and woman walked slowly along hand in hand on the path opposite. A current of air carried the suggestion of fast food.

Scott walked quickly to the glass doors and saw Eddie on duty as he passed through. Eddie started to smile but it left as quickly as a startled bird when his eyes fell upon Scott's left hand. Blood had soaked through the bandage during his trip back to the city, and with the look of fatigue that undoubtedly shrouded Scott, Eddie's concerned expression was more than warranted. Scott held his right hand up as questions began to form on Eddie's lips.

'I'm off to get it looked at, I just need a quick word with Jack first.'

Eddie nodded dumbly and said nothing. Scott made towards the elevators before Eddie called out to stop him.

'I forgot, he left a couple of hours ago. He left a message for you that he was going to your place. He was with that girlfriend he had a while back, the pretty one.'

'Who?' Scott asked, surprised. Why would Jack have chosen to hook up with an old girlfriend at a time like this?

'I can't remember her name.'

'Well what did she look like? What colour hair did she have?'

'Been all kinds of colours,' Eddie said, smiling, 'it was red when I saw her today though.'

'Angela?' Scott asked, incredulous.

'Yeah, that's it, Angela. Do you know her?'

But Scott had already taken off and was running back towards the car. He jumped in, started the engine, pulled out of the parking lot so fast that the rear end whipped around and smashed into the front wing of a silver Mercedes, causing its alarm to sound and all passers-by to stop and stare.

He drove off as quickly as he could, ignoring the shouts from witnesses to the damage. Scott took the quickest route he could to get back to the cottage, stopping for nothing. He jumped red lights, twice ran up onto the kerb to pass a stationary vehicle and almost ran down a motorcycle rider as he pulled out from a junction without looking.

Everything Scott had learned swirled around in his head but he couldn't keep the thoughts still long enough to be able to fit them together. The pain in his hand throbbed. A constant reminder of his limitations as it rose up through the fading medication, but Scott couldn't chance taking more. His fogged over consciousness could be more debilitating now than the pain itself.

He concentrated on the road.

Jack's Lexus was parked in front of the cottage with no-one inside. He no doubt still had a set of keys to have let himself into the cottage. Scott tried the front door and true to form Jack had left it unlocked.

'Jack?' Scott said cautiously as he entered the hallway.

A light was on in the living room and background noise of a TV. All other rooms remained silent and in darkness.

'You took your time,' Jack said absently as Scott entered the room.

He looked around quickly but no-one else was there.

'Where's Angela?'

'Angela is fine,' Jack said, noticing the stained red bandage wrapped now loosely around Scott's hand, 'what about McBlane, did he come back with you?'

'No.' Scott didn't know what answer to give. Didn't know what connection there was between McBlane and his brother.

'Is he dead?' Jack asked, seemingly bemused.

'No. At least, I don't think so. Not yet.'

Jack let out a hearty laugh that under the circumstances couldn't have seemed more inappropriate. 'Go on there Scott. It looks like even I may have underestimated your potential. What about the two that were with him, are they....?'

'The same, yeah,' Scott interrupted.

Jack smiled, and motioned for Scott to take a seat. A now familiar teardrop-shaped bottle of Glenmorangie sat on the table in front of Jack, and two glasses. One had a small amount of scotch in which Jack drank before filling both.

'To new beginnings,' he said, and held out his glass towards Scott.

Scott did likewise, reminding himself what Jack had taught him in the past about not making a play until you have one. He had no idea what was happening but one thing he did know was that Jack had answers he needed. A lot of them.

'So you're working for McBlane?'

'Not for – no. Working with – yes.'

'What did you mean about even you had underestimated me, Jack?' Scott asked cautiously, taking a sip of the scotch.

'It was me who wanted you brought in, in the first place. McBlane thought you were just another low level drug dealer like the million others out there. I told him you had a lot more potential than that. I bowed in his favour in a staffing matter a while back, so now it was time for him to do the same. Twinkle was just a way to bring you to us.'

'But those conversations we had, you kept trying to warn me away from them.'

'I knew if I tried to get you involved you'd have run a mile. The best way to get you interested in something is to tell you not to do it, always has been. You've got a stubborn streak that's wider than you are. The only reason you kept on so long with the design work I put your way was because I didn't pay you enough to be able to quit.'

'So what exactly is your relationship with McBlane, Jack? And how long has it been going on?'

Jack shook his head. 'Don't look at me like I'm something stuck to the bottom of your shoe, Scott. I didn't start up with him intentionally. I just had the misfortune of being the older brother, and the even greater misfortune of coming across some information that I had no choice but to act on.'

'What information? What are you talking about?'

'About Bob. Those letters you found confirmed a lot of what I already knew. We'd had conversations in which he'd cryptically hinted at things. It left me with all kinds of questions but he would never answer any when asked directly. I was out walking one day when I saw him down there at that damn tree. Meditating he called it, but it was just an excuse to sit and feel sorry for himself. He was crying and talking softly. I had to creep up really close to be able to hear what he said. I don't know whether this was something he did often or if that was the first time but he was confessing to all of it, over and over. Saying how sorry he was for what he'd done.'

'He killed mum and dad?'

'Yeah, he killed our parents like he killed his years before. Tried to make both instances look like an accident, you were right when you joined those dots Scott. The police investigation into the house fire cited arson but he was never named as a suspect. He was crazy over the way he felt about mum. He killed them so he could move over here and be close to her again, but once he was here it wasn't enough. Their affair took off again but the last time she told him it was over he must have seen something in her face, must have known she'd never leave dad again. Not while he was alive anyway. So he did something to the car. Mum and dad had been fighting and dad was due to set off for another weekend work trip away. Mum gave it her best shot and they reconciled. Decided the weekend away, just the two of them, might be just what they needed to get the marriage back on track. It was a last minute decision. Mum arranged for the neighbours to take us for the couple of days they'd be away and they set off together. Later that night they were dead.'

'Jack, what the fuck? So you heard him confess all this? Why didn't you go straight to the police?'

'And then what? There was no proof one way or the other. Just me apparently overhearing an old man talking to the fucking trees? So either they arrest him and then we're homeless, or they don't and guess what? We're probably homeless anyway, or he kills us in our sleep. I did the only thing I could do. I sat on it and waited. I'd come across people while hanging around the clubs, mean people who would do things for the right kind of cash. I planned to get enough together to have him taken out.'

'What are you talking about, like a hit man?'

'That makes it sound a bit dramatic but yeah, that was the idea. That's where McBlane came into things. I paid what I could up front and arranged to pay the rest over the next few months.'

'I can't believe this.'

'Well believe it, Scott. Bob killed our parents. What was I supposed to do, forgive and forget?'

'But it was suicide though.'

'No it was just made to look like suicide. I watched him Scott, he pleaded for his life which is more than mum and dad had the opportunity to do.'

'You were there when he died?'

'Yeah, I had to see it. I thought that was gonna be the end.

That we'd be able to start over with all of it behind us and I'd pay off the rest of the money I owed to McBlane.'

'So what happened?'

'After Bob died I set up Zebra. With the control I had across the board now, McBlane suggested I repay some of my debt by laundering drug money he was making through his security company. I was reluctant at first but it was pretty easy. I'd set up fake jobs, fake printers, fake clients, take in bundles of money, bounce them between accounts before finally moving them offshore. Before long the debt was repaid and we were making a huge amount of cash. We began talking about what could be done with these stockpiles that were building up. We both had ambitions in the club industry anyway, but the owners of the major venues had gotten so fat and lazy from the constant revenue streams generated that they'd never have been willing to sell. Again we just put our heads together to come up with a solution. Problems with entertainment. No big name deejays willing to work the club. Problems with security. Drugs found on the premises. Acts of violence. Even problems getting supplies of alcohol. These were all things that could be achieved with a word in the right ear and the right thickness of envelope. Even a club of pristine reputation can nose dive quickly when these factors combine in a short space of time. Before long we were picking up places at rock bottom prices and immediately getting them back on track. The beauty was that nobody knew it was us doing it, right from the inside. Right now we own maybe a third of all major venues in Garden Heights and expanding all the time.'

'Sounds like you've done really well for yourself Jack. So why did you want me?'

'McBlane had a hunger, which at the start was great because he'd do whatever I told him to make things happen. But after a while, no matter how successful we were the hunger didn't dampen. It only ever seemed to intensify, like an itch that couldn't be scratched. I knew no matter how big we got, no matter how many clubs we ended up running, eventually he would turn on me. A simple and effective way to double the size of his portfolio. I thought by having you involved in the business, even on a low down rung to begin with I could watch your progress and see how you handled yourself. With me pulling the strings you could have climbed quickly and learned a lot. Then eventually when the time was right I could reveal my part in it all and together we could have overthrown McBlane.'

'You're fucking crazy,' Scott said, incredulous.

'Why, because I'm ambitious?'

'No because you talk about killing people as if they are just losing their jobs. These are people's lives that are ending for your ambition. How many others have died as a result of all of this? Do you know, or even care?'

'Blood is thicker than water, Scott. Me and you together, there's nothing that could stop us.'

'So why Angela, then. Where does she fit into all of this?'

'That is unfortunate. Angela and I had a relationship for a while. Things were great between us but all of a sudden she stopped taking my calls. Refused to see me altogether. I don't know what went wrong but there was so much going on at that time I decided to just let it go. Girlfriends have always been something of a temporary thing in my life anyway, you know that. I got on with work, saw other women, but I just couldn't put her out of my head. Eventually it got to the stage where I had decided to try and win her back, but that was when I found out the two of you had been spending time together.'

'So you backed off on account of me? How very noble.'

'You're my brother Scott, what else could I do? I just hoped it wouldn't get serious between you and that maybe Angela and I could reconcile further down the road.'

'You know that won't happen though, surely? Angela could never be interested in someone like you.'

'That's the unfortunate part. I see how serious you both are for one another and even if Angela did have feelings for me still, I cannot let the cycle of suffering go on.'

'The fucking what?'

'Samsara, that's what Bob called it, right?'

'You've lost me.'

'History is repeating itself, Scott. The cycle of suffering goes on. Look at dad and Bob, they were great when they were kids. Then they end up falling for the same woman. They tried all ways to combat the problem but ultimately it ruined all of their lives, theirs and mum's.' We can't make the same mistakes as our predecessors.'

Scott looked at his brother but the figure sat in front of him was utterly unrecognisable from the person he'd looked up to whilst growing up. The light had completely gone from Jack's eyes, leaving behind only a cold black stare and a shell of the man he'd once been.

'You know what we need to do Scott.'

'Jack, you've lost it. Just calm down. I'll take Angela and go away. You never need to see us again. You can get on with your life here, it's all yours now.'

'It isn't just her, it's us. I built it for us. We were left with nothing because of a love like acid that ate its way through our entire family.' Jack sat back in the chair and sighed. Visibly tired and frustrated from his brother's inability to comprehend his reasoning. Scott noticed a glint of metal for the first time beside Jack's leg.

'Come on little brother, time to take a walk,' Jack said, but didn't move to get out of his seat.

Scott's eyes drifted to what was wedged between his brother's leg and the side of the chair. Jack tracked their progress; when he saw that Scott understood he smiled and nodded. Scott stood and walked slowly to the door. Jack rose behind him and followed, holding the gun.

'So where is she then, Jack?' Scott asked, but he thought he already knew the answer to his question.

'She's at the only place that would be fitting to bring this whole thing to an end.'

Scott kept walking and left by the back door. He didn't say anything now, just listening to the sound of his brother's feet a few steps behind. He's unused to travelling over ground like this these days Scott thought, and a few times heard Jack stumble, but when he turned the gun was always still trained on him.

Scott felt tired. His mind was no longer spinning, which considering all he'd learned in the last hour was a surprise. It just wasn't doing much of anything. A reluctant acceptance seemed to have settled over him and he wondered if maybe this was how Jack had felt years before when he'd tried to process what he'd learned from their uncle.

A chill breeze blew across the night. Scott shivered.

'Why don't you just forget about her Jack? I'll do the same, she can go free and we can still do everything you planned.'

Jack laughed behind him, a mirthless sound from a man who had been on the wrong end of life's ironies too many times.

'How can I forget about her? That would be like telling a compass to forget about North. Fate is set now Scott. I knew when I saw her today, when I looked her right in the eye, that she was the woman I should have been spending the rest of my life with. Don't you think that must have been the way Bob felt, all those years ago? We'll get through this. We can get past it in a way they never could. In the sleep of death, what dreams may come?'

Scott didn't understand but his thoughts immediately sprang to his own dreams, the bus dream. Could Jack have been the unseen driver all this time?

The silver birch stood just up ahead now. If Jack had left her at The Elephant Tree then he was almost out of time and still had no plan. He looked back over his shoulder but Jack was maintaining a safe distance and had the gun drawn and raised.

'Don't think about doing anything stupid Scott. It's almost over now.'

They walked further down the track and he saw her. Angela had been bound by her wrists and ankles. Ropes looped back around the tree allowing her minimal movement. Her wrists were raw where the rope had bitten into them with the effort of struggling against her bindings. Now she lay back limply against the tree, defeated.

Scott started towards her but a shot rang out behind him stopping him dead in his tracks.

'Don't do it Scott. Move away.'

He turned as his brother was lowering the pistol from the warning shot he'd fired into the air. Angela was alert now, eyes pinned wide with fear.

'What the hell are you doing Jack?' she asked, pleadingly. 'Is this because I'm dating your brother? I knew Scott way before you and when you and I started going out I had no idea you were even brothers, until right at the end. I recognised the photo in your apartment of you both as kids. Scott carries the same one in his wallet.'

'It's more than that Angela. But I don't expect you to understand. It just matters that Scott does,' Jack said, raising the gun and pointing it at Angela.

'No Jack, fuck. There has to be another way out of this, you can't let any more people die.'

'I'm sorry Scott, but in time you'll realise it was the only way.'

'I won't let you kill her Jack,' he said, walking to stand between his brother and the woman he loved.

'Don't test me. That would be a mistake,' Jack said evenly, his sight focused intently on the target in front of him; the target that was now his brother.

'I'm not testing you, there's just no other play I can make

Jack. This is all I have left,' Scott said and closed his eyes, as his brother cocked the pistol.

The roar of a shot rang out.

* * *

Despite his best efforts, the trail, if you could even call it that, was cold and Detective Fallon was under increasing pressure to move on and prioritise other cases. Bryson made his thoughts pretty clear about what he described as Fallon's *obsessive persecution of Paul McBlane*. But there were too·many coincidences that just kept piling up for Fallon to let it go.

Unfortunately no-one was talking. The only other chance he'd had to speak to Stephanie Hutton had been when she'd awoken in hospital following her attack, which had only compounded Fallon's suspicions that she knew a lot more than she was letting on. Speaking to her then got nowhere. It was clear how scared and confused she was, so he'd planned on seeing her again before she was discharged, giving her further chance to rest and recover. But then she'd gone and checked herself out early and fallen off the map.

Fallon had been to the hospital to see Glen Thomas as well and applied more pressure there. But whatever he could threaten Thomas with wasn't enough to make him give up what he undoubtedly knew.

Twinkle still hadn't turned up to shed any light on the incident surrounding him. All efforts to find him had so far proved fruitless, and without anything else to go on, Fallon was finding it difficult to justify this as his priority case, especially without the backing of his partner.

In a last ditch effort he'd decided to go back one more time and shake Neil Bennett down to see if anything worthwhile came out. They had pinpointed him as staying in the Walker building with a girlfriend, so that's where Fallon was heading.

His shift had officially ended and Bryson had been off sick anyway, but Fallon was determined so he went alone.

Flashing his ID in reception was enough to allow him to travel up to the apartment without anyone being alerted to his presence. The softly softly approach had gotten him no-where questioning this guy in the past so this time Fallon decided to go in hard.

'Open up it's the police,' he commanded, and pounded on the door five times with the heel of his fist.

The hurried sounds of the latch being withdrawn on the other side indicated that at least someone was home. The door swung inwards revealing a female with pale skin and large frightened doe-eyes, wearing a white robe.

'What do you want?' she stammered, obviously not used to dealing with an intimidating police presence.

'Neil Bennett, I need to speak to him now.'

She stepped away from the door, allowing Fallon inside.

The apartment was tastefully decorated; the only thing that seemed not in keeping with the surroundings was the man he'd come to question, who was sprawled out along an expensive looking couch.

'Get up,' Fallon barked at him.

'What the fuck is this about? I told you everything I know already.'

'No you haven't, I know you're lying and unless you give me something then both of you are being placed under arrest for obstruction of justice and taken to the station,' Fallon lied.

'Jesus Christ Neil, tell him what he wants to know,' the now panicked Elizabeth said from behind Fallon.

'I don't know anything. I don't know where Twinkle is, I don't know where Scott is, there's nothing I can tell you.'

Fallon decided to play out the bluff. He took out his handcuffs, turned and walked towards Elizabeth.

'Mother fucker you better give him something right now,' she shouted frantically, visibly shaking.

'Alright alright, there's drugs. A stash of drugs up at Scott's place,' Neil stammered.

'Go on,' Fallon said, turning back towards him.

'It's a box, buried. With our drugs in.'

'Not ours,' Elizabeth pleaded.

'No, mine and Scott's.'

'Is there anything else in the box? Any papers or other pieces of information that could reveal the location of Scott or Twinkle?'

'I don't know man, I wasn't there when he buried it.'

'Right, you'll show me where it is.'

'Now?'

'No, not if you don't want to, we can all go down to the station first and do that later if you'd prefer,' he said, raising the handcuffs again.

'Alright, fucking hell,' Neil said, before Elizabeth could protest again.

Fallon drove as quickly as he could back out to Scott's place in the country. A sullen Neil sat in the backseat not talking. He was no doubt regretting what he'd revealed under duress but knew it was too late to take it back now.

They pulled up onto the gravel approach to the property which was already occupied by two other cars: an old red Toyota 4x4 and a brand new black Lexus parked up with no-one inside.

Who else is here?'

'I have no idea,' Neil said, and sounded perplexed so Fallon didn't push it.

They got out of the car and walked to the house. Fallon turned the handle without knocking first and discovered the door was open. He cautiously made his way inside and went room to room looking for occupants. Nothing, the house was empty although a television murmured in the living room and two glasses stood on the table.

'Where are they buried then?' Fallon asked, unsure whether

he should wait here for the owners of the vehicles to return or follow up on the lead immediately.

'Out back in the woods.'

'You know the exact location?'

'Yeah I know where they'll be.'

* * *

Scott instinctively moved his hands to his chest searching for any pain or wetness from blood loss, then heard a thud like a sack of mail being dropped to the floor. He spun around. Angela remained bound to the tree, upright, eyes wide, uncomprehending.

Scott looked back around and saw his brother's crumpled body on the ground. He didn't understand.

'Scott, are you alright?'

Scott looked up and saw the voice belonged to Detective Fallon who stood with his service revolver drawn, beside the silver birch.

'Yes,' Scott said, and ran to Angela and immediately began working loose the ropes that bound her to the tree. As soon as one wrist was freed she reached out and, taking a handful of Scott's shirt, pulled him towards her. The sudden intensity of her kiss surprised him but he returned it with equal enthusiasm, sliding both arms around her back and holding her tightly against him.

When all ropes had been untied Scott's attention returned to what was happening behind them. Neil hovered uncertainly behind Detective Fallon who was crouched over his brother's body. His fingers probed Jack's neck searching for a pulse. He looked up at Scott and shook his head.

Fallon had withdrawn a police radio and was now reporting events into it. He ordered an air ambulance and gave co-ordinates to their location.

'Detective Fallon,' Scott said, 'I'm a little more pleased to see you now than I was last time. But I am wondering how the hell you found us.'

'Back to the house first and I'll explain.'

Neil, Fallon, Scott and Angela walked back towards the house. Despite her ordeal Angela had refused to wait and be taken by ambulance, insisting she was fine to walk with the rest of them.

When they reached the stile at the bottom of the land revolving blue lights could already be seen up by the house. A group of officers rushed past them acknowledging Detective Fallon, no doubt to the location he'd given over the radio. A helicopter also hovered overhead, searching for a suitable spot to land.

'Is there any sign of McBlane?' an older man in plain clothes that Scott took to be a superior officer asked Fallon, when they got back to the cottage.

'No sign sir, officers are searching the area but so far no indication he's been here.'

They went inside and sat in the living room. Angela refused any attention from the paramedic but did accept the offer of a phone call which she quickly made to her dad, thankfully in time, before he'd taken any rash measures of his own.

The next couple of hours consisted of questions and statements and again further questions. It became apparent that Fallon had been on to a lot of what had gone on regarding the violence and other criminal activity around the clubs for quite a while, but had so far been unable to produce enough evidence with which to bring charges. Jack had kept himself isolated so that no connection had previously been made with his involvement, which of course had now changed.

'So how did you turn up when you did?' Angela asked, as Fallon was rereading notes he'd taken from them.

'You can thank Neil for that I suppose. We'd been unable

to turn up any further lines of enquiry and Scott had dropped off the radar again, so I went back and shook Neil down for anything else he might know. His girlfriend was less than happy at the intrusion into her swanky apartment and insisted he gave us whatever he knew.'

Neil looked distraught at his betrayal, despite it having probably saved their lives.

'He told us about the box of drugs you'd buried and after nothing had been turned up here during your previous search I thought there may have been more than just drugs buried down there. Information on Twinkle's current location perhaps.'

Scott kept straight faced. Everything was over now and so far he looked to have been able to avoid any charges being levelled at either him or Neil, and if Jeff could be kept out of the picture completely, then that was even better.

'When we pulled up out front and saw both of the cars I suspected something was up, but it wasn't until we heard the gunshot on our way through the woods that I realised exactly what. I immediately called for backup and proceeded to the location intending to wait for their arrival. When I saw Jack with the gun drawn I knew I couldn't wait and under the circumstances did the only thing I could. Unfortunately the shot I fired to incapacitate your brother proved to be fatal. It was very dark down there and I couldn't risk simply putting one in an arm or leg and hoping that he'd drop the gun.'

'So what happens now?' Scott asked warily.

'You mean regarding the drug possession and alleged dealing that you and Neil were involved with? Well I'm told the amount recovered down by the tree isn't exactly huge, and considering your co-operation to bring the matter to a close, especially the information regarding your brother's involvement, it's highly unlikely either of you will face prosecution.'

Angela reached across and squeezed Scott's hand.

'It looks as if McBlane may have seen this coming though and decided to flee with a couple of his closest associates. Warrants were issued and searches have been carried out at all of their known residences in the last hour. So far none of them have turned up. But someone like that won't stay hidden forever. He'll turn up again one day.'

Once all of the questions had been answered they were at last allowed to go. The paramedics checked Angela over and cleaned and redressed the wound on Scott's hand, telling him he would still need to have it assessed at hospital. The police hadn't finished at the cottage so Scott and Angela decided to go and spend the night at her place, dropping Neil off outside the Walker Building on the way.

'What do we do about Jeff and everything that happened up in the mountains?' she asked, once they were alone in the car.

'I don't know about you but I'd be happy to see the back of the city again for a while. I say we head back up there for a while and live the simpler life.'

Angela grinned and leaned over to kiss him on the cheek. 'Do you think you and Jeff will start growing again in the caves?'

'I have no idea, maybe one day I guess. But with the amount of tinned food that was stored in the living quarter cupboards, McBlane may be able to stay alive down there for months.'

'Oh my God, really?'

'Yeah there's water and ventilation. It may be cold and it'll definitely be dark since Jeff cut the power, but I'd leave it a good while before I decided to venture back down again.'